The Temp

EMILY BENET

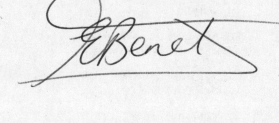

Harper*Impulse* an imprint of
HarperCollins*Publishers* Ltd
77–85 Fulham Palace Road
Hammersmith, London W6 8JB

www.harpercollins.co.uk

A Paperback Original 2014

First published in Great Britain in ebook format by Harper*Impulse* 2014

Cover images © Shutterstock.com

Emily Benet asserts the moral right
to be identified as the author of this work

A catalogue record for this book is
available from the British Library

ISBN: 9780008115784

This novel is entirely a work of fiction.
The names, characters and incidents portrayed in it are
the work of the author's imagination. Any resemblance to
actual persons, living or dead, events or localities is
entirely coincidental.

Automatically produced by Atomik ePublisher from Easypress

For my husband, Juan Diego, who warned me this would happen!

Chapter 1

There comes a point in your life when you can't go on being scared. For me that point comes most often after my third glass of free wine. I say 'free' because I do most of my drinking at posh gallery openings. I stand in the middle of the space, look around at all the glamorous individuals muttering appreciatively and I pretend I'm in my natural environment. I pretend I'm an art collector and select pieces for my many rooms in my many mansions, and then I get the bus home.

If Londoners complain that booze is too expensive, it's because they're not making the effort to track down the free stuff. There must be a show opening every evening of the week in this city and as long as you can stomach a bit of pretentious chatter then you can succeed in having an entertaining and cheap night out.

My partner in crime tonight is my best friend Farrell. He works in a bookshop and is as broke as I am. Pretending to appreciate a bit of random art is a small sacrifice to pay for a few complementary beverages. We'd volunteer our comments if it meant getting free nibbles, but unfortunately the art industry runs on a liquid diet only, and no one particularly wants our comments.

A lot of strange things make it into art galleries. Personally I don't know what went wrong with creating something you might actually want to put in your living room. I like landscapes but a

1

landscape in the world of conceptual art could be anything from a peanut on a stick to a video of a talking meringue.

The show is called *Life & Death of a Ghost* and is made up of five paintings and a stuffed chicken. The artist, who goes by the name of 'Ghost', has only used two colours: grey and green. According to the explanation displayed at the entrance, the greener the subject the 'deader' it is. The chicken is a grey lump. This means the chicken is alive. Yet it is stuffed.

I stand in front of the artist's self-portrait and try to summon some emotion. I know it's a self-portrait because I've seen a picture of the artist and can identify the bald head and thick handlebar moustache. Although I suppose the giveaway is the little label beneath it that says, 'self-portrait'.

'I expect you'd like to share your thoughts,' a voice whispers at my neck.

I turn to find the artist himself, leaning forwards, his hands clasped behind his back.

'Everyone else does,' he adds.

There's nothing worse than being put on the spot in an art gallery. People expect so much more than 'I like the pretty colours'. Not that I do like the colours, which remind me of the sludgy vegetable remains at the bottom of my fridge.

'Actually I was just wondering whether that chicken is organic,' Farrell says in his cheerful Irish lilt.

The laughter in his green eyes makes me want to giggle into my glass.

Ghost looks suspicious. 'Let me guess... RSPCA?'

'Oh, no! Just a curious fan.'

'To die for art, what greater aspiration can poultry have? I've set it free, haven't I?' He turns to me. 'And you, Madam, what are your thoughts?'

I blink away an image of a squawking, sacrificial chicken running for its life.

'I'm still trying to get my head around the concept...'

'It's going to blow you away,' Farrell says, and takes a quick gulp of wine to hide the fact that he can't keep a straight face.

Ghost just stands there smiling strangely, one hand propped up under his chin.

'Of course there is the possibility that you lack a certain artistic sensibility,' he says. 'You know our first five years of life can determine so much about how we perceive art...How we perceive life...I'll try to help you if I can,' he continues, with an affected sigh. 'But either you have it or you don't, and my feeling is that you're more than a little disconnected.'

I swallow the urge to defend myself and point at a picture in the corner labelled 'Old Man'.

'That man...' I say, trying to keep calm. 'He's turning grey, but grey means life. Shouldn't he be turning green because he's dying?'

'Go on.'

'And then there's your self-portrait... why is it green? That would suggest you're dead.'

He opens up his arms and nods, as if I've answered my own question.

'But I don't get it. You're not dead.'

'Technically I am,' he says, with a wink.

To argue pointlessly or to nod and get back to enjoying this free wine?

'O-kay...' I say, nodding. 'I think I've got it...'

'You see now?'

'Yes... yes, I really think I have.'

Farrell grins as he raises his glass. 'Congratulations, Ghost, you have a new fan.'

Normally I always go along with it. But then normally the artist is either too aloof to talk to us or too lovely to offend.

I'm having second thoughts now.

I don't like Ghost's smug smile one bit or his suggestion that I might be lacking in artistic sensibilities. If anyone is lacking anything here, it's him and it's a talent for painting. *I* could do this in my sleep. Maybe I should. Maybe I should just find a skip, grab some broken plywood, paint over it with a fat paint brush with my eyes closed, come back before closing time, swap it with one of his, and then see if anyone notices the difference.

'Actually I don't get it. If you were dead we wouldn't be having this conversation, would we?'

Ghost looks irritated. 'We are all dead, if you think about it.'

'Surely I'm alive if I'm thinking about it.'

Farrell gently squeezes my arm. He's so close I can smell his familiar woody aftershave.

'Amber... you'll get it in a minute,' he says.

'I'm not sure I will this time, Farrell.'

'You will. It's going to blow your mind, remember... like this *wine*.'

I know exactly what he's trying to get at, but just because we haven't paid for the wine shouldn't mean we can't have an honest opinion.

'Thinking doesn't mean you are alive. On the contrary, it means you are quite dead. You are only alive when you dream,' Ghost says, flapping a hand in front of him like some haughty Spanish flamenco dancer. His nails are painted green and black. I want to point out that they contradict his painting. 'We are just temporary wisps of energy,' he continues with a sigh. 'Flickering on and off like a...' He struggles to finish. 'I pity you,' he says instead. 'You'll never be an artist.'

'I'm not trying to be an artist.'

'In that case you're even more dead than I thought!'

With that he turns with theatrical aplomb and bangs into a woman behind him, knocking her glass of red wine from her hand and causing splashes of ruby to mimic a Jackson Pollock masterpiece over a group of legs. The room parts like the Red Sea before Moses and there's a chorus of devastated gasps.

'Don't panic, everyone, there are free refills!' I say, a bit louder than I meant to.

'For god's sake, Amber!' Farrell hisses and grabs my wrist, pulling me through the throng to a safe corner. Behind us I hear someone shrieking.

'Oh just leave it!' Ghost cries. 'I did it on purpose, look how the wine mirrors the death in the eyes of the chicken!'

'I thought the chicken was alive and you were dead!' a man says.

'You're all going to be dead in a minute if I don't get this red wine stain off my skirt!' a woman screeches.

'I could be an artist if I wanted to be,' I grumble, my cheeks burning.

'Shss... leave it.'

My best friend hates confrontation. I've seen him go to great lengths not to upset people. Particularly his ex-girlfriend, God rest her soul, if she were dead and had a soul. To me, she will always be Evil Eva.

'He just said you might be damaged, that's all.'

'*He's* damaged! Look at his art!'

A few heads turn and some disapproving scowls are aimed in my direction.

'Come on, compared to the shite we're usually looking at, I don't think it's that bad,' Farrell whispers. 'And so what if green symbolises death? I mean, isn't mould on bread a sign it's sort of dead?'

'Lower your voice, Farrell, or someone will pinch your idea! Next week it'll be in *Time Out... Death of the Bread* comes to London!'

'Seriously Amber...'

'You could write a poem about it...'

He frowns. I think I've touched a nerve. His writing is a touchy subject.

'Sorry, I can't help it. I've spent the entire day typing out labels and I'm fed up.'

It's only my second day temping at the catering firm and I'm already looking forward to my last. I must have written out the word 'goujons' at least five hundred times and I still don't know what it means or care enough to look it up. I would ask Vicky, who's in charge of keeping me occupied, if she wasn't so obviously upset that I've had to come in to help her with her workload in the first place.

'It's all so pointless...'

'What is?'

'What I'm doing... all these mind-numbing jobs that no one else wants to do. How long am I going to carry on like this? I want to have an exciting life, Farrell. I want to have fun, not just fun, obviously, I want to do something meaningful too...' I let out a sigh. 'I keep thinking, we've got one life, one little life... am I really going to spend it typing out labels and making photocopies?"

' Of course not,' he says, looking solemn, 'you'll answer phones too and make cups of tea.'

'Great. A lifetime spent boiling the kettle... Where did I go so wrong?'

'You haven't gone wrong. You just need to find your passion.'

It's easy for him to say. He's always wanted to be a writer. He's been working on the same book for most of his life. The first time I saw him, he was in the university cafeteria scribbling into a leather-bound notebook as if he was possessed. He was wearing a floppy brown jumper with a *Free Palestine* badge on it. His thick brown hair was sticking up all over the place, changing direction each time he ran a hand through it. Lips drawn forwards, forehead furrowed, at one point he snapped out of his fictional world and seemed surprised to find himself where he was.

I didn't speak to him then. I didn't meet him properly until a month later, when he approached our yoga class.

It wasn't much of a class really. It was the first sunny day in weeks and we were warming up by lying outside on the grass. Most of us had just rolled up our leggings or folded up our t-shirts. Not Eva, though. *She* had stripped right down to her bra, which was probably why Farrell got so nervous and forgot to tell us his name and that he'd been sent from the Drama Society. 'We're doing a play,' he blurted out. 'We're looking for help from anyone who doesn't mind a bit of painting.' I sat up, vaguely interested. 'What sort of play?' I was doing a degree in Tourism with French but I hadn't ruled out any of the other professions, including acting. 'Think *Charlie and the Chocolate Factory* meets *Heart of Darkness*,' he said. I held his gaze for a moment, squinting in the sun. I didn't know what he was talking about, but suddenly I fancied the idea of being involved in the theatre. 'Alright,' I said. A week later I was painting a six-foot candy-floss tree in bubble-gum pink.

Is it enough to have talent or do you need to be a bit insane like Ghost?

I mean no one in their right mind would think it a good idea to pickle a shark or sculpt a head out of frozen blood, but when someone does it, everyone's in awe.

Do you even need talent? Plenty of people are making their mark without it. Maybe you just need to believe you can do it. It's as the saying goes: *If you think you can, you can. And if you think you can't, you're right.*

As I take a sip from my third glass of free wine, I feel my confidence grow. I don't know what I'll do yet, but I know I'm capable of doing something. Something more than I'm doing now.

'What are you thinking?' Farrell says.

'I'm wondering what really grabs people's attention.'

'Environmental disasters?'

'Something I can do myself.'

'You *are* doing it yourself. Have you ordered a new recycling box yet?'

'Not X factor... I can't sing... what about doing a flash-mob dance?'

Farrell's eyes widen in alarm. He knows what I'm like when I start brainstorming, that if I land on an idea I think is good, I won't give up on it easily. Like the time I bought those second-hand recorders and convinced him we'd make a ton of money if we went busking in Euston station. We only got halfway through

When the Saints Go Marching In before a scowling florist told us he'd pay us a pound if we shut up. Farrell isn't always a willing partner in crime and yet he's terrible at saying no.

'Those videos get so many hits. Did you see the one Dee sent me of the guy proposing to his girlfriend in Disneyland? The one where even Donald Duck starts break-dancing.'

'But why would we do that?'

'Because then we get noticed...'

'Yeah, for dancing badly.'

'Speak for yourself.'

He's right, though. Dancing with a few friends at a club is fun, but I'm not up to performing for the millions.

'What else gets lots of hits?' I say.

'Those videos of suspiciously "hilarious" accidents where you wonder why on earth someone would be filming in the first place.' I narrow my eyes at him pensively and he holds up his hands. 'Don't look at me. I'm not volunteering to fall off a ladder for the amusement of the masses.'

But that's not what I'm thinking. I think I've just had a flash of inspiration. 'Kittens of course!' I say. 'How many emails and Facebook posts do you see about cute kittens every week? People love those things! What we need is a really cute kitten.'

I believe in brainstorming out loud. Somewhere in my mind there must be a gem of an idea waiting to be found. I need that great idea and I need it now. The thought of typing out 'goujons' for the rest of my life sends a jolt of panic through me every time it runs through my mind.

Farrell is looking baffled.

'I don't get it. What has flash-mob dancing or a cute kitten got to do with you finding your passion?' he says. 'That's what this is all about, isn't it?'

Across the room I see Ghost has recovered his composure and is now surrounded by a group of adoring fans lapping up his nonsensical jibber. Addictions, divorces and suicides aside, it does seem that celebrities have all the fun.

'I want to make my mark in the world,' I say, 'which means doing something different from what I'm doing now... the question is, what?'

Chapter 2

It's my fifth day working for Flamingo Catering and I'm taking a break from writing 'goujons' to cold-call businesses and ask if they require our catering services. So far everyone has politely declined an offer of a brochure in the post. Now I'm on the phone to someone who sounds very old, possibly deaf, and judging by the echo might be stuck in a tunnel somewhere.

'I've got a Welsh slate roof, what do I need a canopy for?'

'Not canopy, CA -NA -PE.'

'I can't hear you if you whisper!'

'WHAT ABOUT SANDWICHES?'

I can sense Vicky in the far corner shifting in her seat. She wants to butt in with a whole list of products. If she'd bothered to equip me with a few menus I'd be doing a better job, but it's obvious Vicky feels threatened by my presence and desperately wants me to fail. The big boss, Jan, is on a walking holiday in Scotland, so not around to remedy the situation.

'What sort of sandwiches?'

I stop myself saying Nutella and opt for 'SALMON?'

'Good God,' he gasps, 'I can't stand salmon.'

I glance at Vicky and catch her glaring at me with her eyes narrowed. There's a subtle shake of her head as she turns back to her computer. The tip of my pencil snaps off and I notice the angry

10

tornado I've been doodling, which has billowed off my notepaper onto the desk. I might look the part in my black pencil skirt and crisp white shirt, but I'm feeling quite hopeless.

'We can send you a brochure,' I say.

'Whatever for?'

I need to end this promptly. 'Oh, never mind. THANK YOU VERY MUCH.'

'Why are you thanking me? Have I bought something?'

I can hear his voice calling out as I lower the handset.

'Hello? Did I give you my credit card details? Hello?'

Click.

The bell rings and I look up to see a man peering through the small glass window in the door. I wave him in but he doesn't seem to understand. When he realises it's not locked, he rolls his eyes and pushes the door open.

I'm taken aback at just how good looking he is. Up until now the only men we've had come into the catering office have been red-faced lorry drivers with thick necks and blurry green tattoos. This man's tall and athletic and his face is glowing as if he's just come back from a holiday in the sun. Dressed casually in a brown leather jacket and purposefully knackered jeans he gives the impression of someone comfortable in his own skin.

He pushes a hand through his silky chestnut hair as he approaches my desk. I'm just getting over the disastrous phone call and now my cheeks are on fire again. His smile is disarming, his teeth to die for.

'Hello, there. I'm Elliot.' His accent brings to mind country houses, cricket and cucumber sandwiches served on fine china. 'I think I spoke to you yesterday about popping in.'

Vicky clears her throat, startling him slightly.

'Oh I didn't see you there...'

She stands up and holds out her hand.

'You spoke to *me*, Victoria Willis, pleased to meet you...'

I should carry on ringing up random businesses, but with Elliot

11

in the tiny office I feel self-conscious. I don't want him to hear my telephone blunders. Instead I open up the label template and begin to type out 'goujons' because judging from my previous four days at the firm they are the most popular thing we do and we're bound to need labels eventually.

The bonus of copying and pasting a single word over and over is that it makes eavesdropping very easy. With a bit of luck I'll have to take this gorgeous man's details.

'It's for an opening of a contemporary art exhibition,' he says.

I glance up, my eyebrows raised. This is my chance to break into the conversation!

'Fascinating,' Vicky says, and the word sounds silly coming out of her mouth, as if she's trying to mimic Elliot's accent. 'Where is it?'

'Mayfair...'

Vicky's eyes light up. She's already calculating the potential profit to be made on a thousand goujons. I wrack my brain, trying to remember what galleries I've been to in Mayfair. Ghost showcased his masterpieces there only last week. 'It's quite a small space, really, so I don't know quite where you'd put everything.'

'Oh I'm sure we can sort something out,' Vicky gushes. 'Our main concern is that you are happy with the food and you get what you really want.'

I cringe. She sounds so desperate.

Elliot rubs a hand over his chin. 'Alright. In that case I'll be needing a list.'

Vicky hesitates. 'A list of?'

'The food we do!' I blurt out.

Elliot smiles at me and it feels like a standing ovation. I think I've just fallen in love.

'Of course, of course,' Vicky mutters, pulling out plasticised menus, which slip and slide over each other and fall onto the floor. She bends down to collect them just as the doorbell rings and she must have hit her head as she stands up because I hear a sharp bang.

'Oh God, are you alright?' Elliot says.

'Yes I'm fine, I'm fine...'

'Are you sure? That was quite a bump.'

'Yes, I'm fine. Who is it Amber?'

I pull open the door to find the short, Polish chef brandishing a piece of paper in his hand that looks as though it has been dipped into the soup of the day. He looks furious.

'I have two emails from Vicky. The first one says the client loves garlic more than his own mother...'

'Wow! Does it actually say that? Let me see.'

I can't imagine Vicky writing something so frivolous.

'No, you idiot! I'm fucking paraphrasing!'

'Alright, take it easy,' I put a finger on my lips and throw a meaningful look behind me to alert him to the presence of a client. He ignores it.

'The second email says he's allergic to garlic!'

'Oops.'

'I have made garlic soup, I have made garlic bread, I have made garlic mushrooms... do you see where I'm going with this?'

'Do I have to guess the next thing?'

He grits his teeth and his fingers curl into a fist, causing the paper to fold and crumple. I step back as Vicky appears by my side. The colour has seeped out of her cheeks.

'Andrzej, I'm sure we discussed this...'

It's clear from her voice that she knows they haven't discussed anything and she's in big trouble. He knows it, too, and it doesn't make him any happier knowing it isn't his fault. He's going to have to de-garlic the kitchen and start all over again. I know what we're all having for lunch today. Thank God Elliot turned up before we're all stinking.

'The van is coming in two hours to collect,' he says. 'I can't do it.'

'We have to do it!' Vicky cries. 'We can't lose Mr Humphreys! He's a very important client!'

'*We* have to do it?' Andrzej smirks. 'I didn't know you were offering your services.'

I'm very aware that Elliot has been left alone and can probably overhear this fiery little discussion.

'Shall I, um, help Elliot with his order?'

Just saying his name makes me feel like I'm on intimate terms with him and I feel a prickle of heat at my neck.

'Andrzej, you can't possibly want me in the kitchen!' Vicky says, all flustered. 'You've got Tony and Eric, and that Russian chap with the unpronounceable name.'

'No! If you checked the diary you would see they are all out on duty! I have been left with one 15-year-old work-experience schoolboy, who wouldn't be able to tell the difference between a cucumber and his own...'

'I'm so sorry to bother you...'

Vicky and I spin around at the sound of Elliot's voice. He's standing there, looking a little baffled.

'I don't have all that much time. Would it be better if I came another day?'

Vicky pushes me gently forward. 'I'm so sorry. Amber would love to help you. I'm afraid I have to absent myself for a moment, if you don't mind.'

'Not at all,' he says, and he looks at me with so much hope I know I'll never ever admit that I don't know what a goujon is.

I smile with a confidence I don't feel and head back inside the office.

'So,' I say, wanting to steer the conversation as far away from food as possible. 'Tell me about your exhibition...'

He grins as he sits down on the squeaky plastic chair. It's shiny from lack of use, because everyone, everyone *except* Elliot, takes care of their catering requirements over the phone.

'Do you have to ask that by law or do you really want to know?'

I laugh, surprised. The atmosphere feels different now that Vicky has left. The salesperson and client have been replaced with a girl and a boy checking each other out.

14

'I genuinely want to know. I spend half my life in galleries, actually.'

'Then we already have a lot in common.'

I feel myself blushing and fiddle with my silver butterfly ring, turning it back and forth.

'What did you see last?' he asks.

'Oh, this conceptual artist... he's called Ghost. Have you heard of him?'

'Life and Death?'

'Yes!'

I can't believe it wasn't a waste of time after all!

'Did you go to the private view?'

'Yes! Did you?'

'We must have crossed each other.'

But I would've noticed him, I'm sure of it.

'Strange,' he says, frowning, but with a smile playing on his lips. 'I'm sure I would have remembered you if we had.'

I swallow. My heart is beating fast. 'I left quite early.'

'That makes sense,' he says. 'Are you an artist?'

Before I can answer he reaches for my hands. I look down, horrified. My nails are disgusting at the moment, with streaks of old pink nail polish and hints of glue residue from my last, indulgent set of acrylics.

'Artist's hands,' he says.

'Oh, they're terrible,' I say, snatching them back.

'I've been brought up in the industry; I can spot an artist from a mile away. My mother is Rosemary Harman, she's a portrait painter... that's her maiden name.'

This is the point where I should come clean. But I don't. I don't want to disappoint him by saying I'm not an artist. I don't want to confess that this is all I am, a temp hopping from one short contract to the next, without a plan, without a dream spurring me on.

'Look,' Elliot says, digging into his jacket pocket. He retrieves a business card and gives it to me. It's thick and creamy, with gold, embossed letters: Elliot Frinton-Smith. Not a name I'm likely to forget in a hurry.

'Why don't you come along to the show? It's next Thursday at the Earnest Taylor.'

'I'd love to,' I gush, before pathetically trying to rein myself back, 'if I'm not busy.'

'Of course. Just make sure you say hello if you come. I'd hate to miss you a second time.'

NOTHING will stop me going. Not a tube strike and not the Apocalypse. I will be there because this is the man I've been waiting for.

He gets up and it suddenly dawns on me why we are here, apart from it being destiny.

'What about the goujons?'

'Oh shit.' He looks at his watch. 'Can you email me some details?'

'Of course.'

'I hope we can sort something out in time... but as long as there's wine, we'll be fine.'

'That's my motto.'

He laughs and I feel giddy with excitement. The feeling lingers until I realise, with a pang of horror, that he doesn't even know my name. But by that point it's too late. He's already gone.

I rub his card between my fingers. It's not a disaster. All I need to do is email him. I'll wow him with my efficiency by sending him some menus right this minute.

His show is only one week away. That means less than a week to decide exactly what sort of artist I am and come up with a plan of action. I need to set my sights lower than Picasso, higher than Ghost. Somewhere in the middle. Lower middle. Bottom middle. Lower bottom?

As I search for inspiration online I find my mind wandering to other dilemmas. For instance, what exactly am I supposed to wear? And will I lose my artistic charm if I get my nails done?

Chapter 3

I leap out of bed on Saturday with the energy that comes from having a mission to accomplish. Today is my first day as an artist.

I announce the news to my housemate, who is in the kitchen eating leftovers from his lentil dinner. I moved in with Egbert over a year ago, not because he looked as though he might be a barrel of laughs (he really didn't) but because of the cheap rent. Like raw oysters and mouldy cheese, he's very much an acquired taste.

Egg, as I call him, has recently become a vegan. He has become a vegan even though he loves sausages, he loves steak, he loves bacon and he loves cheese. Egg has become a vegan because he's saving up to buy a house and to do this he has set himself a weekly budget of £3.50. It would help if he worked more than three days a week, but he feels any more would take over his life.

He's a researcher at the British Museum and complements his diet of pulses with an unhealthy ration of academic books. His scraggy red beard is probably now hiding gaunt cheeks as well as the pockmarks from the terrible acne he suffered as a teenager.

'What sort of artist are you going to be?' he asks.

'I'm not sure yet.' I pour myself a cup of coffee. 'I suppose I need to explore my childhood.'

'Why? Did something bad happen to you as a child?'

Egg doesn't get humour, or people. His only regular social

activity is a bi-monthly meeting with his historical reenactment group. There are four of them; three men and one woman, and they haven't got around to reenacting anything yet as they have to first debate the pros and cons of each era. At the moment they're gathering facts on Ancient Egypt. One of the obvious cons is the traditional clothing, which is a little scanty for the intemperate British weather.

'Not that I can remember...' My childhood was ordinary; fish fingers and trips to the park. 'What about you?'

There must be some reason Egg is like he is.

'I've just published my memoirs. You can read them if you like.'

'Really?'

'On the Kindle. They're 99p at the moment.'

'Wow, that's exciting. What's the book called?'

'*It's An Egg Life* ... you gave me the idea actually; no one else calls me Egg.'

I suppress an urge to laugh, which makes me choke on my coffee and Egbert has to slap me on the back.

'Went the wrong way,' I say, recovering my breath.

'I suppose that's the subject of my book.'

It just shows that everyone is trying to make their mark. Even the quiet, odd individuals like Egg, who on the surface seem oblivious to the outside world. Today it's my turn and I'm hoping Farrell will help me.

Farrell only lives a couple of streets away from me. It's unusual in this huge city to be able to walk to a friend's house. On average, everyone is 45 minutes away. I was the first to move into the area. I joke that Farrell followed me here but the truth is he would've settled for anywhere that wasn't Clapham.

Clapham belongs to Jenny. Jenny with the angelic smile and soft little voice, so soft I had to ask her to repeat everything she said. She was loving, too. A serial cheater, in fact. Farrell found out through photos on Facebook, which is bad enough, but the worst thing is he didn't even get the pleasure of dumping her because she dumped him first by changing her status to 'single'.

Usually it's Farrell who comes to my house, simply because out of our housemates, mine is the less annoying. Farrell lives with a sports physiotherapist called Danny. While other people do air guitar, he does air football, pretending he's dribbling the ball everywhere he goes.

'Amber, I'm in the library,' Farrell whispers. 'I'm doing research for my novel.'

'On a Saturday? Isn't it full of snotty toddlers?

'Hang on...'

I wait for him to step outside, where he can talk properly.

'What are you up to, then?'

I can tell from his tone that there's a good chance I can persuade him to join me.

'I'm exploring the subject of childhood. Think magic pens, pipe cleaners and pasta twists stuck on with Copydex. Are you in?'

I've bought it all. Glue, tissue paper, hundreds and thousands, pots of glitter.

'I'm sure some of the toddlers here will be keen. Shall I pass you over to them?'

'I'm serious, Farrell! People will love it! It'll take them back to a carefree time when they were innocent and happy and the world was a wonderful, colourful place.'

'What people? You're not seriously still thinking about doing some crazy exhibition, are you?'

'I absolutely am.'

I did text him my plan to become an artist yesterday. He should have known it wasn't a joke.

He groans.

'So are you in?' I pick at the dry skin on my lip and wait impatiently for his answer.

'I don't know why I'm in, but, alright... I'll see you in half an hour.'

So far, so good.

Farrell arrives exactly half an hour later. Being on time is his special power. He says he can't help it. Even if he leaves late, he arrives on time. He's solid. I should nominate him on that dating website mysinglefriend.com and write a rave review. But I'm worried he'll end up with an Evil Eva again, or a Cheating Jenny. It's a sad fact of life that good guys attract psychopaths.

I spread big sheets of wrapping paper over the wooden floor of the living room. The local pound shop didn't have canvases, so we'll have to make do. Farrell perches on the arm of the sofa with his default expression of quiet amusement. I toss him a purple glitter pen and it pings off his finger and rolls under the bookshelf.

'So, remind me, why are we doing this?'

I think of Elliot and feel a bit embarrassed. 'Because I need to prove to someone I'm more than just a temp.'

'What?'

I twiddle with the end of my stubby ponytail. 'You're going to think it's stupid. But yesterday this guy mistook me for an artist.'

'Which artist?'

'Not a particular artist. Just an artist in general.'

'And you denied it? Oh no, you didn't deny it... so now you've got to actually become an artist...'

I follow his gaze down to the materials piling out of the PoundLand carrier bags. My cynical half knows I'm being ridiculous. I can't just become an artist from one minute to the next because a handsome man mistook me for one.

'Can't you just avoid him?' Farrell says.

'I don't want to avoid him. He's gorgeous.'

He rubs his chin. 'Right... and you think a big fat lie is a good way to start things off with him, do you?'

'It's a white lie.'

'No at best it's a grey lie... charcoal grey...'

He's focusing on the negative because he hasn't seen where I'm going with all this yet. This is not a spur of the moment thing. I put quite a lot of thought into it yesterday. I lean over our battered leather armchair and retrieve my pièce de resistance. It's a huge blank cork board, which is crying out be used for something more imaginative than post-it notes. I felt a genuine frisson of excitement when I saw it in the charity shop's window knocked down to £2. The damage to the border gives it that extra edge, literally, because it's sort of split in two. I'm thinking we can hammer a nail into it and then spray-paint it some whacky colour.

'A cork board?' he says. 'That's your big plan?'

I run my fingers mock sexily along the edge of it.

'I think it's really stimulating! Don't you? It's about as stimulating as your outfit.'

I look down at my Saturday-morning get-up, which consists of a shapeless multi-coloured jumper two sizes too big for me and some old red leggings bobbling with age. My fashion sense doesn't kick in unless I've got to leave the house. 'Sorry, did you spend ages choosing it?' he says, with a laugh.

'Yes, hours... in fact I laid it out before I went to bed.'

'You should wear it on your first date with this guy, it might distract him from asking you loads of questions about your non-existent artistic career.'

I feel a bit self-conscious now, although it's not like Farrell hasn't seen me looking a lot worse. We were best friends at university, for God's sake. He has held my hair while I've puked up vodka and chips on the side of the road. He's seen my face blighted by the worst hangover known to student.

'They are my work clothes,' I say. 'We are working. This is our workshop. We'll work on our individual pieces and then layer them on the cork board.'

In my mind I'd pictured a wonderful, textured mosaic all pinned onto the cork board. I'm not feeling so confident now.

'So where did you meet him?' Farrell asks.

I sit down cross-legged on the floor and try out a magic pen. 'He came in to order canapés for some art exhibition he's organising.

He invited me, actually. Do you think he invites everyone?'

'No, he probably just invited you because you said you were an artist.'

'Exactly! Now do you see why I have to become one?'

He laughs. 'You've got a lot to do.'

He moves onto the floor and starts doodling a dinosaur on the corner of the wrapping paper. It's lumpy and round and looks more like a hippopotamus.

'Sorry. I shouldn't have dragged you out of the library...' I say, with a sigh.

He looks up, surprised. 'I wouldn't have come if I didn't want to. Anyway, I'd done what I needed to do.'

'This is stupid, isn't it?' I say flatly.

'It's only stupid if you're genuinely trying to become an artist because some guy mistook you for one...'

'I am.'

'But seriously...'

'He's my future husband.'

He shakes his head in mock disapproval. 'And you're already lying to him.'

'I couldn't help it. He's sort of intimidating.'

'He sounds lovely.'

'He is lovely.'

He holds up a packet of pasta twists. 'Come on Amber, get the glue.'

Feeling reluctant now, I sit down beside him and accept the pasta. The mission that got me out of bed this morning was not to recreate a day in my childhood. My mission was all about taking big steps as a grown-up. In record time, I was going to create enough pieces for my début exhibition. In my head I had already witnessed my momentous entry into the bizarre but potentially lucrative world of conceptual art. I was going to hand out my business card at the show on Thursday and tell people to come along, just like Elliot had told me.

I squeeze a blob of glue onto the paper and then squash a pasta twirl into it.

What could a face made of pasta symbolise? That we are all just a source of food? Or, perhaps, that we are all fundamentally Italian? Definitely controversial.

Farrell is giving his dinosaur a glittery pink tail. At least *he's* enjoying himself. I reach over to turn on the stereo, which has never made it off the floor despite many great intentions to buy a sideboard. A lively, acoustic guitar melody flows through the speakers, lending our workshop a cheery atmosphere. The only other sound is the whisper of paper as we move across it on our knees and the squelching suck as I squeeze the tube of glue.

A memory of being little comes back to me. I'm sitting at my play table with my dad beside me. The chair is so tiny for him that his knees bend high up above my head. I'm making a mother's day card. I can recall the soft, comforting sound of his voice as he asked me about my drawing.

My parents were always positive. They told me that I could be whatever I wanted to be. I just wish they had been more specific. My real problem has always been lack of focus. I've never had my heart set on one dream, but rather I've always flitted from one thing to the next like a moth that's come across a line of fairy lights. That's why two years after finishing a degree in tourism, I'm now working in a catering firm even though I have zero interest in food.

The door creaks open and Egbert peers in nursing a cup of coffee. We're both surprised to see him as he rarely appears when I have company. He sees what we're doing and as he takes another tentative step towards us he breaks into a smile.

'Ah, I see where you got your inspiration from...'

He's looking straight at my circle of pasta. Anyone can see it's far from inspired. It looks like a plate of congealed food; more glue than pasta.

'Where?'

'The Pasta Rasta.'

Farrell lets out an unattractive snort. 'I'm sorry, who?'

Egg looks slightly mystified by the question. 'The Pasta Rasta. The artist who makes everything out of pasta.'

I sit back on my haunches, tossing my next pasta piece onto the wrapping paper.

Farrell glances at my artwork and cracks up. 'Looking good, Amber!'

'He does it live on YouTube,' Egbert adds. 'He even has a rap... *My name is Rasta and I love pasta, I stick it onto wood and I stick it onto plasta.*'

'I have to see this!' Farrell says, digging out his phone from his pocket. He's practically in stitches before the video has come on and Egbert seems bemused by the success of his contribution. 'I think he's beaten you to it,' Farrell splutters. 'Time for a new concept!'

Exactly, there's no point carrying on now.

Farrell holds his phone up to my face. Contrary to what his name would suggest, Rasta Pasta is a skinny little white boy who looks like he should be in school. He might be a weak lyricist, but I have to admit, his use of macaroni and spaghetti is alarmingly good. His work has an incredible symmetry to it.

'Sod this. It's time for plan B.'

'What's plan B?'

I take Farrell's phone and enter two words into the search bar. CUTE KITTEN. As the videos pop up I turn to show him. Judging from the twitching corners of his lips, it's clear he's waiting for a punch line.

Egg is still in the room. His curiosity is palpable. I put my hands on my hips and look at him.

'Egg, how do you feel about getting a kitten?'

He raises his eyebrows. 'The Egyptians considered cats to be demi-gods.'

Right.

'How do you feel about getting a demi-god?'

His eyes glaze over. 'I could write a new book. *The Eggsistential*

Life of Cats.'

Farrell looks up from the video of a cute cat flushing the toilet. It has nine million hits. My cat is also going to have nine million hits for being equally cute and intelligent. I will dedicate a website to him and the advertising money, which will flood in, will get me out of this rut I'm in, because becoming an artist is going to take too long.

'Why don't we go to the pet shop and have a reckie? See what's out there?'

My best friend is gawping at me and I'm reminded of my dreadful outfit. Obviously I won't be stepping outside the door like this. I do have my pride. He doesn't have to worry on that score.

'I thought you were becoming an artist for this bloke? What's the kitten for?'

'I wasn't doing it *just* for this bloke. I was doing it for me. I'm bored of being a temp going nowhere...'

'And the kitten?'

'It's part of the plan.'

Farrell starts laughing. He thinks I'm joking again.

'So are you coming to the pet shop with me and Egg or not?'

I sense Egg straightening up with excitement. He hasn't left the house for a few days. It's an expensive world out there.

Farrell looks worried. 'Did you just snort the Copydex or were you always this mad?'

'Insanity is essential if you want to succeed in this life Mr Farrell Kennedy,' I say, feeling more decisive than I ever have in my life.

Chapter 4

I'm expecting the new email in my inbox to be yet another funny YouTube video from Farrell. When I see it's from Elliot Frinton-Smith I feel a rush of excitement. Elliot is a client and all I should be expecting is an order of canapés and a query about the cost of delivery. But the way I look across the office to check Vicky hasn't got her eye on me would suggest I'm hoping for a lot more than that.

Dear Amber

Mission accomplished. He knows my name.

Thanks so much for your kind email. I'm sorry I didn't get back to you sooner.

It's fine, my darling, you were worth waiting for.

Montague is concerned food might be too much of a distraction.

Is he the Artist? Or a ghost of some Shakespeare character who never gets hungry?

He's also worried people will drop crumbs everywhere. There's always so many scroungers at these events who only come for the free drinks and have no appreciation for the artwork!

Who would do such a thing?! Such Neanderthals!

I bite the corner of my lip, simultaneously blushing with shame and wanting to laugh out loud. But Elliot hasn't finished.

Even if people manage to pop the whole canapé cleanly into their mouth there's still the issue of smell. I don't suppose you can suggest some of your less-aromatic options?

I look over at my colleague.

'Vicky, bit of a funny one... Elliot wants to know if we have canapés which don't smell...'

She doesn't even look up from her screen as the list rolls off her tongue.

'The quail eggs, the spinach and mushroom pizzetta, the feta and olive tart, the dolmades vine leaves...'

On and on she goes. When she finally finishes I realise I should have been taking notes.

'Wow, you know so much, Vicky. Did you always want to work in catering?'

I love to know how people got where they are, especially if it was their childhood dream.

'No, I hate cooking,' she says, flatly. 'I wanted to be an air hostess.'

I lean forward, feeling curious. 'Really? So what happened?'

'I needed some money, so I got an admin job. I did a few different short contracts and then I came here and Flamingo asked me to stay because I was good. So I did.'

She looks suddenly so dissatisfied that I feel it my duty to relight a flame of possibility in her life.

'You still could train to be an air hostess, though... there's still loads of time. I bet you'd be really good at it.'

Her brow furrows. 'I think it's too late for that.'

'It's never too late. Forty is the new twenty!'

'Well forty-six isn't. Now are you going to email that man or analyse my life?'

'Sorry, I just meant if you still wanted to you could, that's all...'
I'm really not making much progress with our friendship. I feel that until Jan returns and they can confer about how useless I am, Vicky will continue to feel threatened by my presence. I wonder if she replaced someone all those years ago as a Flamingo temp. I don't know why her revelation has made me feel so disappointed.

27

It's not like I'm in danger of being asked to stay, and if I was I'd just say no. I'm not going to let paying the rent get in the way of discovering my greater purpose in life. If only I knew what it was, so I could get cracking on it.

'Go on then, email him,' she says.

I'm surprised she doesn't want to write to him herself.

Dearest Elliot

I quickly delete 'Dearest' and replace it with the more contemporary 'Hello'. His very name, Elliot, transports me into a BBC period-costume drama, something by Jane Austen. Oh what a handsome couple we would make! I close my eyes and loosen my neck before turning back to the mail.

Hello Elliot

Sorry to hear you are so busy.

How Sorry? Very sorry or plain sorry? Just sorry. Being over sorry might sound unprofessional.

I understand your concern about messy eaters, however please be assured our canapés are made with that very thought in mind and can be consumed in one bite, if not less.

I consider this last statement and decide it gives the impression our canapés are a bit on the mean side.

... and can be consumed in two bites, at the very most. With regards to fragrance, I imagine you don't wish for any of our squid or prawn delights. Below is a list of less aromatic options, which I hope will prove suitable for your occasion.

The End.

I delete 'The End' as I'm not writing a novel and round it off with the standard 'Kind Regards', which to me sounds like another phrase dragged out of an Austen novel. Then, feeling impressed by my own efficiency, I press 'Send' and abandon my desk in search of lunch. Vicky acknowledges my departure with a grunt about wishing she had time to eat.

Lunch on my first day was intimidating because the kitchen was full of men who all stopped what they were doing to stare at me as I picked food from the staff buffet. My nerves meant I ended up eating a mixture of mango chutney, pork chops and ice cream. I felt so sick. Since then I've grown in confidence and am now able to walk into the kitchen with my head held high.

Before I even make it to the kitchen, I come across Andrzej. He's squatting beside a bulging hessian sack, smoking a roll-up and rubbing his face in his customary anxious way.

'What's the matter?'

He looks up and his eyes are red, as if he's been working in a mine. He shakes his head, too emotional to speak and my eyes rove towards the sack.

'What's in there?'

'That woman...'

'What woman?'

There's no way a person could fit in there, unless they were chopped up.

'Not a bloody woman!' he growls. 'Bananas are in there. Fucking bananas that Vicky is telling me I've got to throw away.'

I regret stopping to talk to the chef now. I'm not quite sure how to round off the conversation. It doesn't seem right to mutter, 'Oh well, never mind,' when he's so clearly upset. For some reason I feel compelled to offer him a solution. How bad can these bananas be anyway?

I gently tug a corner towards me and peer inside, expecting the pungent stink of overripe fruit. But no, I'm greeted by bunches of friendly, yellow bananas that look just right to be eaten and smell distinctly of...lemons, actually.

'But they're perfect.'

Andrzej nods his head furiously. 'That's what I told her, but she says they are too risky.'

The only way a banana is risky is if a bank robber pretends it's a gun and everyone believes him.

'Don't throw them away, I'll take them off you.'

Egg will be happy. I can already picture him spreading chunky

29

banana on toast, as if it were a meaty pâté.

'All of them?'

'If you don't want them.'

'No I don't like bananas.'

'Alright I'll take them.'

I purse my lips as I lift the sack and I sense Andrzej watching me closely for signs of weakness. I'm not expecting it to be as heavy as it is but the important thing is that I can lift it and that means I can carry it on the bus home. I leave the sack where it is while I serve myself up a stomach-approved combination of chicken, rice and peas. The kitchen is bustling and stressful so I eat quickly at the end of the long aluminium table and mind my own business.

Outside again I find the sack of bananas has been left unguarded and I decide the best thing to do is carry it upstairs to the office. I make quite a fuss of hoisting it over my shoulders and grunting as I push through the door. I want Vicky to be aware of the volume of food that she was prepared to let go to waste. Maybe I'm just a lowly temp, but I'm a lowly temp with principles. People are dying of hunger and here we are merrily chucking away bananas, perfectly good bananas that smell as clean as soap.

I haven't even made it to my desk before Vicky snaps to attention.

'What are you doing with those?'

'I'm taking them home to eat.'

She narrows her eyes. 'Did Andrzej tell you he found them on the street?'

No, he did not. But I'm not going to admit that so she can laugh at me.

'So what?'

My expression is one of nonchalance as I sit down behind my screen. My brain, however, is buzzing. What on earth is a sack of bananas doing on the street? I mean there could be a bomb in there. I stare at my screen while listening out for a *tick tick tick*... But all I can hear is Vicky muttering and rustling pages. A catering firm is hardly going to be a terrorist's prime target, is it?

'Dogs could have peed all over them,' Vicky says.

Yes!! A new email from Elliot Frinton-Smith has just landed in my inbox.

'Have you even smelt them?' Vicky says, in an accusatory tone.

'Yes, they smell lovely.'

I open the mail.

Hi Amber

Just like that, the formality has gone.

'Doesn't that worry you? I mean, they smell too lovely... too clean... too...'

I wait for her to finish but she doesn't and I look up wondering what has stopped her. She's glaring at me with a meaningful look, but I'm not sure what the meaning is.

'They smell like BLEACH!' she cries.

Vicky is on edge because she's hungry. If anyone is in need of a banana, it's her.

'I'm sure they're fine.'

Egbert and I will peel them obviously. I can't be bothered to explain this to her because I want to read what Elliot has to say.

If it were me I'd be all for the crustaceans. I just want you to know that.

I straighten up in my seat, feeling chuffed that he cares what I think at all. The next few lines are taken up with an apology and a begging for forgiveness for wasting my time so horribly.

Montague has now decided not to have any consumables at the show because he fears it will corrupt the sensory experience of his work.

No consumables? He can't possibly mean no wine either. If Montague's art is as pretentious as *he* sounds the only way people are going to be able to appreciate it is if they're completely wasted. I reply at once.

No wine either? It seems a shame. I suppose it will guarantee there'll be no scroungers!

His reply comes within seconds.

Believe me, I'm working on Project: Persuade Him. Talking of wine, I hope you'll let me take you out for a glass soon. Tomorrow evening?

I stare at the screen with my heart in my mouth. His confidence blows me away and I find myself rereading his email to make sure I haven't transferred my daydream onto the screen. A warm, happy feeling spreads over me as the invitation sinks in and I bite my lip to stop the silly grin that threatens to give me away.

Of course I want to go out with him, but there's the small of issue of me lying to him about being an artist. He's going to see right through me. Should I come clean now? What if he retracts his invitation? I think *I* would if someone had lied to me before we'd even gone on a first date.

Another mail lands in my inbox. It's another YouTube link from Farrell and I automatically open it. A little white ball of fluff peers up from out of a box with big, blue Disney eyes. Farrell probably thinks I've given up on my plan to get a kitten after our expedition to the pet shop ended with the owner trying to bully me into buying a pair of African snails instead. But I know it's only a matter of time before my own feline friend is twerking to half a million fans, unaware of how adorable he is. We were going to go this week but perhaps it'll have to be the weekend now.

Dear Elliot

I was intending to buy a kitten tomorrow evening, but I'd be happy to postpone this new responsibility if you can promise a few crustaceans with my glass of wine. They're feeling terribly offended at the moment.

Kind regards

Amber

The trouble with emails is that they never feel real to me. I feel like I'm play-acting. I feel as though I can write any old nonsense because there isn't really a person reading them on the other side. And yet replies keep coming back.

You shall have all the crustaceans your heart desires.

Best

Elliot

And if I were in a Jane Austen novel I would cry out for the smelling salts to calm my beating heart.

Chapter 5

By the time I've lugged the sack of bananas up the hill to my house, I'm sweating, panting and making empty promises about joining the gym. Too lazy to dig through my handbag for the house keys I press the bell. Egg opens the door dressed as an ancient Egyptian mummy and almost pokes my eye out with the long pointed beard on his mask as he pushes it up onto his head.

'I know, don't say anything, completely inaccurate,' he says, looking disgruntled.

I have a feeling he's talking about the mask. Personally I think his jeans are the problem.

'They want me to shave off my beard, but I'm arguing that I could be a foreigner travelling through Egypt...'

He breaks off and I follow his gaze down to the sack at my feet.

'I had to rescue some bananas,' I explain.

He nods, as if it were the most normal thing in the world.

'That's good of you.'

He takes my bulky luggage without question, and I follow him into the kitchen. There's something different about it. He's cleaned up. The counter, which traps crumbs to its surface like a binge-eating Venus flytrap, has been wiped clean. And there are new additions. On the floor beside the washing machine he's laid down a wicker place mat and on it are two gleaming metal bowls. I point at them with my mouth open and Egbert looks at me sheepishly.

I sit down at the table and that's when I see the books: *The Cat Whisperer*; *The Book Your Cat Would Want to Read*; *Cats: Fit, Fun and Furry* and finally, something close to Egg's heart, *Test Your Cat: the Cat IQ Test...*

'I'm just preparing,' he says. 'Can we get our furry friend today?'

It's the first evidence I've seen that Egg can get excited about something living.

'I'm knackered. Look at all those bananas I had to carry home,' I say, pointing at the sack. 'Completely free, I couldn't pass them up.'

Egg opens the top of the sack and looks in. His frown is disconcerting.

'Why do they smell of bleach?'

'They don't smell of bleach!'

He shrugs, never one to fuel a confrontation.

'We can make banana bread,' I say in a huff. I just have to entice one of my bake-happy friends to come over. It will give them something to post on Instagram.

'But we'll get him tomorrow won't we?' Egg says.

Elliot's proposal of wine and shellfish springs into my head and I feel nervous and excited.

'I can't do tomorrow. Let's leave it till the weekend, okay?'

Egg is crestfallen. He looks mournfully at the feeding bowls, which I now notice have 'Fido' written across them in bubble writing.

'I've got a date tomorrow,' I say, and just saying it stirs the butterflies in my stomach. It's not as though I haven't been on any dates recently. I've made full use of the free trials on several dating sites. The problem is until you pay up they only seem to offer you the duds. There was Joe, who was allergic to nuts and humour, and Mike, the Game of Thrones fans who admitted he couldn't go out with me if I didn't watch it because, 'what would we talk about?'

Elliot is neither a blind date nor a friend of a friend, and my expectations are much higher. His Oxbridge confidence is a little intimidating but I'm not exactly a shy, retiring little thing either.

'Alright, the weekend it is,' he sighs.

A normal housemate would want to know the gossip. They'd want to know who I was going on a date with and how he'd asked me out. But Egg's not interested. Now he knows we won't be getting a cat until the weekend he's probably going to disappear into his room and study different attitudes towards facial hair in Ancient Egypt until the moment he needs to shine.

I spend the rest of the evening Googling contemporary artists, only coming out of my room to rustle something up for supper. As I wait for the water to boil for my spaghetti, I contemplate the sack of bananas, which is taking up far too much room in our tiny kitchen. I take a bunch out and hold it up. Such strange things. Do we ever really see them? Or does giving them the label 'banana' blind us because we already assume we know everything about them?

I'm really going to have to start eating them.

I should eat one now as an aperitif.

But I don't.

Later, after my insipid bowl of spaghetti and tomato sauce, I find myself staring at the bananas again. I should have one for dessert. I could chop one up over a natural yoghurt. But I don't. The damned spirit of Vicky is whispering in my ears that one dreaded word over and over: *Bleach! Bleach! Bleach!*

Vicky is already in the office when I arrive the following day. She gives the impression that she has been there all night. There are some people who love to look exhausted so other people will feel sorry for them. They stop wearing make-up, sigh regularly and remark on how little they've eaten and slept. I am not one of these people. The worse I feel the more make-up I wear. I believe you can trick yourself into feeling good.

Today I don't need too much cosmetic disguise as I'm feeling great. I have a hot date and I can almost taste the expensive wine on my tongue. I've revised my artists, touched up on my conversational French, *'Oh là là, ce crustacé est exquis!'* and I've also learnt three different breeds of horse because my gut is telling me he loves horses. Number one is the Appaloosa, which is basically like a Dalmatian if it were a horse, two is the Black Forest from southern Germany and not to be mistaken with a Black Forest Gateau (*'Oh là là, ce gateau est exquis!'*) and third is the Banker Horse, which is a descendant of the domesticated Spanish horses and probably resides in the Cayman Islands. I've probably done a bit too much homework for this date, but I got carried away.

Elliot is coming to collect me after work. No one collects you in London. You always take the bus or the tube and meet somewhere in the middle. If it goes well you stay out until the last tube. If it goes really well you miss the last tube and take the night bus, and if it goes really, really well you take the night bus home together after buying a portion of chips to share from the nearest kebab shop, which is full of people who've had the same romantic idea. Having someone collect me makes me feel like I'm in an American movie.

Well, it doesn't really. It doesn't at all. I'm sitting in a chilly office in the bowels of King's Cross writing out labels for the *smoked salmon canapé with green olive grapefruit tapenade,* which I've abbreviated succinctly to 'salmon'. I'm not sure what tapenade means, but in my head I've got a little salmon tap-dancing upstream and if I knew the truth I'd be missing out on such a cheerful image.

'Mr Frinton-Smith didn't make an order then?' Vicky says.

I look up, surprised. Has she been looking through my emails? I should have erased them. I'd completely forgotten we all share the same unimaginative password: *Flamingo1*

I suddenly feel hot and flustered.

'Uh...no, actually he didn't...' If she has, then she'll have seen that my sales pitch was on the weak side. 'His friend was worried

37

food would interfere with, um, the sensory experience of his work...
something like that.'

'Typical, of course,' she says, knowingly. 'It's always the ones
with the big act that let you down. He probably doesn't have a
penny. It's all show.'

'Do you think so?'

I've imagined Elliot living in some plush pad in Chelsea ordering
breakfast from Fortnum and Mason, and speaking fluent Spanish
to his Honduran cleaning lady. Spanish that he picked up from
his gap year volunteering in Central American orphanages. I try
placing him in a council flat, eating pot noodles in front of a
broken television. I'm not convinced.

'He's got the voice, but did you see his jeans?' she says. 'They
were full of holes.'

'But they were probably "designer holes".'

It's for the people that can afford to get decorators and will
never come close to wearing out their own clothes.

'Well, I don't know,' Vicky says, unwilling to accept my theory.
'But I don't expect we'll see him again.'

'Mmm.'

I look at my watch. Five long hours stretch ahead of me before
I'm to be collected by Mr Frinton-Smith himself. That's quite a
lot of time to keep it all to myself. I mean, so far only Egg knows.
And Dee. And Maggie. And anyone on Facebook who has guessed
something is up from my infuriating status update: *Five-hour
countdown! Excited ;)*

'What is it?'

Vicky is looking at me with narrowed eyes. She suspects something. My 'Mmm' evidently gave too much away.

'Nothing,' I say, without conviction.

'You're going to see him, aren't you?'

I don't need to answer. My face gives it all away.

'That's so unprofessional!' she cries.

'But he's not a client.'

'Jan wouldn't like it.'

'Jan isn't here.'

Then a miracle happens. She starts to smile and she leans forward on her arms as if she's going to tell me a secret.

'I think a little coffee break is in order, don't you?' Ah, the power of gossip. Vicky has been stand-offish because she knows I'll be gone soon and doesn't see the point in investing her time in getting to know me. That's the downside of being a temp; no one can be bothered to find out who you are. You've got to win the permanent staff over somehow, either with gossip or with cake. Or better still, gossip *and* cake. I'm not convinced this is the beginning of a beautiful friendship. Vicky is too uptight for that. But it's a step in the right direction.

Chapter 6

Unless you shave it off entirely, short hair is a pain in the arse. It requires more blow-drying, spraying, gelling, pinning than hair down to your knees. That's why I've been trying to grow mine back ever since I got it lopped off at university. Finally it's tickling my shoulders again and slimming out my face, which looked as round as a baby's with short hair.

Only people who are stunningly beautiful can get away with a shaved head. People who have defined jaws and big beaming eyes and big luscious lips. Anne Hathaway pulled it off; so did Natalie Portman. I'm not ugly by any means, but I do need my hair to make my face work. I've got what you'd call a soft face. My cheeks are round; my lips are full. I wore braces for ten years, which sorted out my crooked teeth, but after all that time my lips instinctively twist to one side rather than open when I smile. As for my eyes, when people ask what colour they are, if they're blue or grey, I say it depends on the weather.

I've never had issues with the way I look. In school when we discussed what plastic surgery we'd have, I only said ears so I wouldn't come across as being too vain. Great ears; that's another thing you'd need if you shaved your hair off.

At five to six I pull out my compact mirror to top up my mascara and put on some bright cherry lipstick. I exchange my black pumps for my thrice-worn ridiculously high red heels. They are suede and beautiful and should be inside a glass cabinet and not on my feet. I've already spent more on blister plasters and jelly pads than the total cost of the shoes.

In theory I'm against heels because they're anti-feminist. Once you've got them on, you can't do very much except stand in one place and look pretty. But in practice, I'm a hypocrite because when I put them on I feel like a goddess.

'Oh wow,' Vicky murmurs. 'They really are gorgeous.'

She'd look a little alarmed by my description in our coffee break and in retrospect I can see how they might have sounded a bit like drag-queen shoes. But now her admiring look is enough to put my mind at ease. Any minute now and Elliot Frinton-Smith will be riding in on an Appaloosa with a Black Forest at his side, all saddled up and ready to... I don't know, hunt foxes?

'I'm going to see if he's outside,' she says.

'No, don't!'

But she doesn't listen to me.

My stomach lurches when she returns a second later.

'He's here! He's just pulled into the car park! And guess what he's driving?'

I can't possibly anticipate what she says next because I've no idea what it is.

'A BMW 507 Roadster! You lucky bitch!'

My eyes widen with excitement. 'Is that good?'

I'm imagining chrome alloys, tinted windows and a bumper that could annihilate an elephant at 10 km per hour. Poor elephant.

'Oh my God, it's going to be so wasted on you!' she moans. 'It's a 1959... A beauty...'

I've never been into cars. But it's more than that. I don't actually like flashy cars. To me they look like a massive ego on wheels. If you've got so much money then go on holiday or adopt a tiger.

I push open the door and step outside just as Elliot Frinton-Smith is getting out of a pale- blue classic sports car, looking like an old-fashioned film star. I mean it's a CLASSIC convertible, which has totally different connotations from the sort of vehicle I had in mind. This isn't the car of a man trying to compensate for a shortage elsewhere.

Oh it's a beauty, but completely impractical. It's basically two tiny seats attached to a long bonnet that rolls up on each side like the front of a black cab, ending in vintage round headlights and a chrome-plated bumper. There's only room for two people and a very small dog.

'Amber, there you are!'

His handsome face breaks into a delighted smile.

'Hello!' I say, feeling self-conscious.

I cross the gritty tarmac and I'm doing well until some loose gravel makes me totter a bit too energetically towards him. He catches my arm and I steady myself as he leans forward to kiss my cheek. My heart is pounding. One or two kisses? If only Britain could decide on some etiquette for greetings. At the moment it ranges from a conservative handshake or a kiss, to a clumsy hug or odd little wave at close proximity.

One kiss. Like I thought.

'You're looking gorgeous,' he says.

'You don't look too bad yourself.'

It sounds like something my Dad would say. I turn my eyes to the car, feeling awkward.

'1959,' he says, with a wink.

'Couldn't you afford a newer one?'

He bursts out laughing and I smile with relief.

'I won't tell you about the engine then...'

'Thank you.'

He opens the door and I slip into the creamy leather seat. The roof is down and the anticipation of feeling the wind in my hair makes me excited.

'There's a poncho on the back seat if you get cold,' he says.

Slightly tempted, I look behind and see a brightly coloured

creation probably made by an indigenous tribe in Peru.

'From your travelling days?'

'Um, no, I think it's H&M, actually... it's my sister's.'

'Oh.'

'Between the treks in South America and the camel rides in the Middle East I had to practically burn all my travel gear to get rid of the stink. What about you?'

'Oh yeah same...all ashes now...' I don't know why I feel the need to lie, because the truth is I didn't do a gap year. 'All ashes except for these shoes.'

For some stupid reason I think it's alright to hoist one foot up to show off my shoe.

'Oh I had those too,' he says, with a straight face. 'Great for icy terrain. At one point I took them off and used them as ice picks.'

He grins and I laugh. Inside I'm dancing. I think he may be *the one*. Not only is this man gorgeous and sophisticated and rich but he also has a sense of humour. And if he isn't *the one*, I'm going to try my best to make him *the one*!

'So, where are we going?'

He looks a little guilty. 'Don't be mad...'

I feel my toes clenching in my shoes, readying myself for disappointment.

'What is it?'

'There's been a little emergency at the gallery,' he says. 'Do you mind if we pass by?'

'Of course I don't mind,' I say, shooting him a big smile full of understanding.

If we're going to be married and live happily ever after, I'm going to have to find out how he makes a living sooner or later!

Seriously, as long as we go on a date I don't mind what errands we do first. What I don't want to have to do is admit to the nosier members of Facebook that my much-anticipated date finished before it even began.

Elliot doesn't say much as we drive. He puts on the radio and we listen to moody British ballads on X-fm. Occasionally he turns up the volume for a song, but then he lowers it again. It feels so good to be in a car, whizzing through London, the wind in my hair. I just wish I had some huge sunglasses and a scarf, but next time I'll be prepared. Next time? I wonder if I'm getting ahead of myself.

'So, you've got a sister?' I ask.

'Yep, and a brother. Both older.'

'You're the baby?'

'Yep. Just out of my nappies.'

'Thanks for that image.'

He smiles. 'What about you?'

'No, I'm an only child...'

'What was that like?'

'Um... fine.'

'Do they dote on you?'

'I suppose, like normal parents, I mean they care what I'm doing...'

'That's good.'

I laugh, 'Why? Don't yours?'

He breathes out and gives a non-committal shrug. I realise I must have hit a nerve. Ten minutes into the date and we're already getting to the deep issues. I consider that progress.

'My parents have always been busy people.'

I wait for him to expand, but instead he leans forward and puts the music up. It's alright. It's not that easy to talk with all the noisy traffic. There'll be plenty of time to swap life stories in the restaurant.

'We're nearly there,' he says.

Not long after he pulls up into a small parking spot on a quintessentially Mayfair street of smart red brick. We get out of the car and I wait on the pavement while he pays for parking on his phone. A happy feeling spreads over me as I watch him. He has the healthy glow of those who love the great outdoors and

44

can afford to use it as their playground. His body has been toned through rock-climbing and skiing, rather than being created in some superficial gym environment. I bet he could be with any girl this evening. But he's not; he's with me!

'All done,' Elliot says, breaking into a brisk walk.

'So, what's the emergency?'

'Montague is having one of his bloody episodes.'

Before I can ask him what sort of episode, he abruptly stops outside a shop front concealed by a black metal shutter. In smart gold writing against a dark-grey background the sign announces: The Earnest Taylor. Elliot's expression is grim, his teeth are gritted and his jaw is twitching furiously.

'He's not here?' I say, unhelpfully.

He aims a little grey object at the top of the shutter and clicks a button. There's a mechanical groan and it starts to rise.

Elliot folds his arms and watches as the gallery space slowly becomes visible.

'Oh yes, he's here.'

And there he is. A slim, young man with a pencil-thin moustache lying stretched out on the floor, legs and arms spread out like a starfish. A passerby does a double-take as he walks past.

'Damn it Montague!'

There are random objects on the floor, but the walls are bare and it looks as though a removal van has been and gone. Elliot heads for the door and fumbles with a set of keys. I squint through the window and make out a few eggs in a bowl and a chunky carrot, which appears to have been attacked by a stapler. It looks like a surrealist's murder scene.

Our footsteps echo around the room as we enter. Montague doesn't move.

'Alright, get up,' Elliot says sharply.

Not a twitch.

I get a sinking feeling as my eyes wander over the pale-faced artist and travel across the miscellaneous rubbish on the floor.

There's supposed to be a show taking place here in two days and unless Montague himself is the artwork, it looks as though it's not going to be ready in time. There is a tiny chance this could be a portrayal of an alternative Cluedo, where the candle stick has become a carrot, the billiards room is an art gallery, and the murderer is not Colonel Mustard but the destructive nature of the artist himself.

It wouldn't be the first live art I've seen. In one exhibition I went to there was a teenage girl sitting on top of a ladder wrapped in a white sheet with her face painted white. She was 'the space between'. People had walked around the ladder *umming* and *aahing* in appreciation, as if it made perfect sense. It might have been more thought-provoking if she hadn't spent the whole time playing Candy Crush Saga on her phone.

I suddenly feel very irritated. It's Montague's fault that I'm not tucking into a plate of seafood and a glass of Rioja right now. NOT house wine, cheapest on the list, but Rioja for God's sake! Elliot must be harbouring the same sort of emotion as me. He walks over to him and places one foot on either side of his waist. His nostrils flare with quiet tension and then he bends down and tries to wrench Montague up by the arms. His friend continues to play dead, although I no longer buy the charade because he's visibly wincing.

'Get up!' Elliot growls. But he's unable to make Montague put weight on his jelly legs.

'Shall I get some cold water?'

Montague's eyes snap open at the sound of my voice. Elliot chooses that moment to let him go and he falls with a bang onto the hard laminate floor.

'Ouch you bastard!' Montague cries, sitting up and clutching one spindly arm. He's wearing a plaid blazer with patches on the elbow the colour of tea stains. He looks as if he's stepped out of the 1940s with his quiff and that moustache. Judging by his lean-ness he's on a war diet too.

He looks at me suspiciously.

'Who are you?'

'I think I'll be asking the questions!' Elliot snaps. He waves a hand around the room. 'What the hell is going on? You said it was under control.'

Montague throws him a look of contempt. 'You can't control art.'

'I *can* when I've bloody spent five thousand pounds hiring the venue!'

So it isn't his gallery then. Of course it isn't. It would cost a fortune to own a gallery in this part of town. Elliot is rubbing his mouth anxiously and pacing up and down the room. Montague gets to his feet, crosses his arms and throws me a murderous look.

'The private view isn't until Thursday,' he grumbles 'I don't see why *she* should be allowed to see it before anyone else.'

'See what? There's nothing here.' I say.

'Amber, I'm so sorry about this. I had no idea the situation was this bad.'

Elliot's tone says it all. He's going to say, *maybe another time...* And suddenly I feel so bitterly disappointed. I put on a brave face because that's what I'm good at, but I'm gutted.

'It's okay,' I say, clutching my bag to my side. 'I understand.'

'I can drive you straight home, it's the least I can do... unless...'

A glimmer of hope. 'Unless what?'

He scratches his neck and looks embarrassed. 'Unless... you want to help? I mean you're an artist and Montague could obviously do with some help...'

'I don't need help,' Montague says mournfully. 'I need divine inspiration.'

'Well we haven't got the budget for that!'

My brain is buzzing. Should I stay and risk them finding out that I'm a fraud? Would they even find out? It's not exactly Michelangelo's workshop in here.

'Arguing isn't going to get us anywhere,' I hear myself say. 'Montague, can you tell me what you're trying to do?'

Montague folds his arms and sighs while Elliot shoots me a look of gratitude.

'Well... I wrote a brief.'

'Yes, what the fuck happened to it?' Elliot cuts in.

'As I said before, you philistine, I can't control my art. I went off in different tangents... initially it was about the collision of man with nature, nature with man...'

'Okay, so what do you have now?' I say.

This space needs filling and I have a feeling Montague is a man of words, rather than action.

'I did several oil paintings, but I don't know if I like them any more...'

'Why don't you show us?'

Montague points to the boxes in the corner.

'Oh for God's sake!' Elliot shouts. 'Move! Get them out! Don't you know Amber and I are supposed to be having dinner together. The least you can do it show a bit of willing.'

Looking remorseful at last, Montague goes over to the boxes and retrieves a canvas depicting an orange explosion. Perhaps it is an actual orange. I can't be sure. It's fiery and not wholly terrible. Something you might find in the lobby of a hotel.

'You don't like it,' he says. 'I knew it.'

'No, I do,' I say, hurriedly. 'I'm always lost for words when I see something I genuinely like.'

'What about you, Elliot?' Montague challenges him.

'Me? I'm going to get us a bottle of wine... I'm so sorry Amber, I'm so embarrassed.'

Montague frowns. 'What's that supposed to mean?'

'It's fine,' I say.

This is the kind of evening where you bond with someone. Perhaps after a few glasses of wine even Montague might grow on me. But I doubt it.

'Red or white? I won't be long.'

'White,' I say.

'Red,' says Montague. 'I can only drink red.'

'I wasn't asking you.'

Elliot gently touches my back before he leaves and shoots me another look of apology. I smile back, and with my eyes communicate my sympathy. We'll laugh about this when we're alone together next.

Once Elliot has gone, Montague and I examine the objects around us. There are eggs, an avocado, a Tupperware container, a heavy-duty stapler...

'What about the enslavement of nature?' I suggest.

It's not exactly original, but if it has worked before it will work again. This is exactly the sort of concept that people love to brood over with a glass of Chardonnay.

'You could have a plinth in the centre with a single egg in a Tupperware,' I say. 'Then along the side, shelves with... I don't know, perhaps an avocado in a bowl...

'Trapped,' Montague says, nodding.

'Exactly. Trapped. And then you've got the carrot...'

'I can get more carrots.'

'Yes. Lots of carrots would be good.'

When quality is lacking then quantity becomes important.

'And we can hang them from the ceiling, condemned to be sliced, diced, chopped and should we want to, even STAPLED!'

I clap my hands together and Montague jumps.

'Sorry... I got excited. What do you think? Can we do this?'

'Yes,' he says, rubbing a finger along his moustache. 'Actually, this was my original idea, of course I remember now, yes, the egg in the Tupperware, the bowl, the carrots...'

Unbelievable. I wish Elliot was here to hear this. I feel quite indignant.

'Well now you've remembered you probably don't need my help any more. I'll tell Elliot that we can go to dinner.'

I take out my phone and notice I've got a missed call.

'No, don't go,' Montague says. 'I do need your help... you're

49

obviously good at this sort of thing...'

Bibiana Fuentes. Her name surprises me. Since she moved back to Argentina a couple of years ago our communication has consisted of sporadic emails and approving 'likes' on Facebook.

When I first met her at university she could barely speak a word of English, so conversation had been a bit stiff. But she was friendly and generous, always offering to cook for everyone. I had felt sorry for her, all huddled up and shivering in her layers of jumpers, so far from home. She hated the cold. She missed her family, her boyfriend, proper meat, the sun... Wine made her English better, made my non-existent Spanish exist and by the end of that first term we were having deep, meaningful conversations late into the night.

I dial my voicemail and listen for her message.

Hi Amber! It's me, Bibiana! I'm moving to London! Can you believe it? So I was wondering if I could stay with you for a few days? Please, please, please? I'll be very quiet and helpful and I'll cook you whatever you want, unless it's horrible British food, haha! Anyway let me know! Email me, text me, I don't accept pigeon! Okay maybe I do, not very often, actually not at all, they're always crapping, is that how you say it? Crapping? I used to think that meant hunting for craps at the beach... ANYWAY, call me! Or text! Email!

She sounds crazy, and a lot more fluent than I remember. It'll be great to see her again and fun to hang out with another women for a change. I can tell her about this, about Elliot, and about Montague, who is now looking at me anxiously.

'You're not going are you?'

I consider the gallery around me. If this was my space I'd have so much fun with it. I'd use colour to spice it up, stop it looking so sad. God, I hate sad stuff. I hate the concept I've given him. Nature can't be shut in a box of Tupperware. It would push through it, crush it with its winds and rains and snowstorms.

'No... I'm staying.'

He looks relieved. 'Thank you.'

Montague is welcome to claim my idea, because I'm going to work on a better one.

Chapter 7

'Wednesday is the best day to go to the pet shop,' Egg announces when I get home from work. 'Everyone else will be at the cinema because it's "two for one".'

I don't need much more persuading. Even Farrell is up for it.

We stare into the tank at the soft little bodies curled up and sleeping in the folds of a fleecy pink blanket. Only one of the kittens is wide awake and eager to play. He's a little tabby cat with a white belly and paws that look as if they've been dipped in white paint. He's so fluffy he looks as though his natural habitat should be the snowy peaks of the Andes and not the warm, slightly moist pet shop environment in East London. He puts one paw on the glass and looks up at us with his big black eyes, and we all know he's *the one*.

At my side there's an audible intake of breath from Egbert. He clutches my sleeve.

'Please, Amber, please.'

In that moment I want him as much as Egg does.

'He's adorable,' I whisper. I look over at Farrell, who's staring at the little kitten but with a worried expression on his face. 'Isn't he adorable?'

'He's going to get bigger, you know.'

Trust Farrell to try to dissuade us. But it's too late. Egg and I are completely smitten. The little kitten bounds over to his sleeping companions and jumps on top of them. They squirm and try to bury themselves deeper into the blanket but he's so desperate to play. We just have to get him. This tank is too small for such a free-spirited creature, any longer in there and he'll think he's a fish.

The pet shop owner, who has been eyeing us cautiously from the counter, decides to risk her time on us and comes over.

'He's twelve weeks old,' she says.

I nod and try to look as if this information means something to me.

'That's a good age,' Egg says, looking satisfied. After all the reading he's done, I wouldn't be surprised if he's already worked out the kitten's IQ. 'He's had all his vaccinations, has he?'

'Absolutely.' She proceeds to tick them off with her fingers. 'FIV, feline enteritis, feline chlamydia and, of course, feline respiratory disease, more commonly known as cat flu.'

I grimace at the images these diseases evoke in my head and, for a moment, the bundle of fur is rendered a little less cute. But then he tries to chase his own tail and my heart melts again.

The conversation moves from disease to diet (unfortunately he's not going to help deplete our stock of bananas) and then to the myth of cats having nine lives. Egg wants to know if the pet-shop lady has ever resuscitated a cat.

'Oh, I could write a book with all the stories I've got,' she says, and begins to dictate it to us.

While Egg nods with interest, I sidle off to look at the guinea pigs.

'So...' Farrell says, grinning, 'How was the date?'

'Well... it wasn't exactly a date.'

There was wine. Check. There was conversation. Check. But mainly between me and an egotistical artist, and not the date himself.

'I mean it was supposed to be a date, but we ended up putting up an exhibition. He's an art curator and the artist was really behind...'

53

Farrell moves over to peer into a cage where a baby rabbit is kicking up a cloud of sawdust.

'Sounds like he was after free labour.'

'No, it wasn't like that. Elliot was so apologetic...'

'Elliot?' he says, and he exaggerates a stiff English accent. 'Elliot... Sir Elliot...'

I feel my face reddening and I turn away, pretending to be suddenly very interested in a small tank that seems to have nothing in it.

'The show is tomorrow, so obviously he had to make sure it was done.'

'Strange though, isn't it? Why did he ask you out if he was so busy?'

'Because I'm irresistible.'

Farrell smiles. 'Ah, of course.'

Elliot didn't say he'd call so I shouldn't be disappointed that he hasn't. He just told me to come on Thursday. Tomorrow. My heart does a little summersault at the thought.

'He's got a sports car, you know,' I say. I can't help sharing this juicy morsel. I've never been out with someone who owns a car, let alone something as impressive as what he was driving.

'Good for him,' Farrell says. 'That's what you need in a man.'

'Actually I think sports cars are a bit stupid because they cost a ridiculous amount of money and you can't fit anything in them. If I had the money I'd get a people-carrier.'

'Why not a bus?'

'A bus would be ideal.'

I try to imagine Elliot driving a bus and smile to myself.

'There's nothing in there, you know,' Farrell says.

'What?'

Farrell nods his head at the tank I'm still staring into.

'How do you know?'

He taps his finger on a little white label in the corner, which reads: *Nothing in here!*

We look at each other and burst out laughing. And suddenly I've such an urge to tell him all about Montague and the stapled carrots.

'You should have seen us trying to hang up these...' thinking about it just makes me laugh harder.

'What?' Farrell asks, laughing before he's even heard the story.

'Carrots!'

'You were hanging up carrots? Real carrots?'

'Yes!'

'Why?'

'Because it's art!'

'Carrots are art?'

'And the avocado...'

'You hung up an avocado?' he splutters.

I explode laughing. 'No! We put it in Tupperware!'

'Why?'

'Nature, Farrell, nature is trapped in Tupperware.'

'What? All of it?'

We're in hysterics now. It takes the stern stare of the pet-shop lady to shut us up and even that doesn't fully work. You always want to laugh more when you're supposed to be quiet.

Egbert's expression is solemn as we approach the counter.

'Sorry Egg... we were just discussing art...'

'So?' my housemate says, ignoring my apology, 'Are we going to take on this huge responsibility?'

I look over at the little kitten, who's still involved in an exciting game of chase with his own tail. One thing's for sure, if he keeps that up, he'll be a YouTube sensation.

'Why don't you think about it?' Farrell says.

Egg looks at me with pleading eyes. I don't know why it's my decision. It's not as if I own the house. We aren't entirely sure we're allowed to have pets and we don't want to disturb the landlord, who has been living in the middle of French nowhere since Egg moved in ten years ago, and has no idea that the houses on our street are now worth double the rent we're paying.

'We're taking him,' I say firmly. 'Today.'

Egg looks as if he's about to hug the pet-shop lady, but then remembers he doesn't hug strangers.

'I expect you'll be wanting a travel bag for him,' she says brightly. She strides up the aisle and picks up a soft blue case.

I ignore the knots in my stomach as I hand over my credit card to pay. It'll be alright, I think, because I'm going to be a famous artist soon. I just need to get my head around how I'm going to make it happen.

We spend the entire bus journey home arguing over names for him. Egg likes the sound of King George but Farrell says he won't come over any more if we name him something so fecking English. He prefers a good Irish name like Malachy or Dugan. At least we all object to Hello-Kitty.

Farrell doesn't seem all that eager to go home so I invite him in to share a pizza. Obviously he's more enamoured by our little ball of cuteness than he cares to admit. We unzip the travel bag in the kitchen and our new housemate peers out.

'What about Fido?' Egg whispers. 'I mean that's what it says on his feeding bowls.'

'Why are you whispering?' Farrell whispers. 'He's not asleep.'

Slowly he steps out onto the lino. The fluffy tip of his tail curls over his head as if it's too heavy to hold up.

'Rupert!' I say.

They don't immediately reject it like they have done for most of my other suggestions. I can see them trying it out for themselves.

'Because he's furry like a bear. Rupert Bear.'

We're all staring at him but he doesn't seem bothered at all. I lean down nearer to him.

'What do you think? Do you feel like a Rupert?'

He crouches down, then in an ambitious move, leaps up to catch a strand of my hair. I move back just in time to avoid his baby claws.

'Yes Rupert,' Egg says, looking pleased. 'He likes that.'

And that's that. We suddenly have a Rupert in our lives. Egg chooses to give him the tour of the house and Farrell and I sit waiting for the pizza to cook.

The trip to the pet shop has temporarily distracted me from my phone. I'd just thought that maybe, after saving the day yesterday, Elliot might have sent me an email or something. Just a little echo of last night's sentiments. *Sorry, thank you, our next date will be better,* that sort of thing. But the only mail I'd got was from a woman wanting to know if there were nuts in the chicken satay's peanut sauce and a man asking if we sold any exotic birds other than flamingos.

I'm just feeling a bit insecure. I'm worried I'm going to turn up tomorrow and Elliot will be too busy to talk to me. I'll have to mingle and pretend I'm some great artist. I can just imagine the inspired conversation.

Hello, I'm Amber.

Well, hello there Amber, and what do you do?

I'm an artist, actually.

Oh, wow, have you done anything I might have heard of?

Um... the Coliseum?

You did that? THE Coliseum.

No one is that stupid. The artists I've come across might be wacky but they're nearly always well educated. I'll have to explain that I'm so avant-garde that I haven't hit anyone's radar yet.

I suddenly notice Farrell is looking at me closely.

'You alright?' he says.

'No, not really.'

I suddenly feel so depressed I might cry. I slump down on the chair beside him. Farrell has made an origami boat out of a serviette and I take it off him and turn it over in my hand. I remember him saying it calmed him down.

'I just don't know what I'm doing with my life. I did a tourism degree thinking it would take me around the world, but all it got

57

me was some crappy interviews for even crappier paid jobs... I've probably forgotten my French by now!'

'*Non, ce n'est pas possible ma chérie*'

'What? See! I have forgotten it.'

'No, it's just my French-Irish accent.'

'Oh.'

'You've just got to be patient. You'll find your thing.'

'I don't know if I will...'

'You're brilliant as you are. Don't try and be something you're not.'

I roll my eyes. 'Is this book you're writing secretly a self-help?'

He looks down at the floor and I could swear he's blushing. 'Actually I've been meaning to tell you...'

'What?'

'I'm doing a reading at this prose-and-poetry night. I'm doing some poetry this time, but next time I think I'll read out my first chapter.'

I let out an enthusiastic cry and squeeze his arm. 'Yes! I've been telling you to get your writing out there forever!'

'I know. You've been a bloody pain in the arse,' he says, grinning.

I slap his arm. 'It's for your own good.'

He cocks one eyebrow. 'So?'

I suddenly realise what he means. He's asking me if I'm coming. And of course I want to go. It's Farrell, for God's sake, my best friend. But Montague's show is opening tomorrow and I really want to see Elliot. I haven't felt like this about anyone for so long and I'm worried that if I don't go nothing more will happen between us. He's not going to pass by the catering firm if he doesn't have a show to prepare for.

'I've got this thing but yes...Yes! ... What time?'

'8.00...'

Damn, damn, damn! There's no way I can make both of them.

'That's so great,' I gush. 'So great.'

'But it's alright if you can't come... but you can, right?'

And at that moment the oven starts beeping, saving me from making any more promises I can't keep.

Chapter 8

Come on, Amber, look as if you're enthralled by it. You're a journalist working for *The Art Review*... if that is a real magazine. It doesn't matter. Look intelligent.

In front of me, on an Ikea shelf, is a transparent Tupperware. Inside is a pallid little egg and a dark-green avocado. The piece is called *Trapped*. It's a masterpiece, obviously. Why else would so many people cram in here to look at it? It can't possibly just be down to the free wine.

A young woman in a tiny red kimono dress and towering wedges bursts out laughing. I steal a look and catch her friends showering her with adoring smiles. Montague comes up behind her and puts a possessive arm around her waist. A photographer snaps at them and she poses as if she's used to the fuss. Montague surveys the room and I try to get his attention, but he seems to look through me. When he starts nibbling on his girlfriend's ear; I turn around, feeling awkward.

It's strange how alone you can feel in a room packed with people. I look at my watch. It's seven o' clock. If I go now I'll have plenty of time to catch Farrell's reading.

Elliot is still deep in discussion with an older man in a light-grey suit, who is leaning to one side, as if propped up by an imaginary wall. I have so far failed to do as he instructed and say hello. He hasn't been alone for a second, and I haven't wanted to butt in. I was hoping he'd come to me.

As I'm looking at him, he catches my eye and my hurried smile feels more like a grimace. He waves a finger at me; a sign he'll be free in one minute. I feel a flush of pleasure. There's still time. We can make contact, maybe arrange a proper date and then I'll say I've got to go.

A man in purple spandex leggings and a floaty shirt covered in tigers sidles up beside me. His girlfriend is half his height and is swamped in a baggy vintage Mickey Mouse t-shirt that looks so tired my Mum would have ripped it up to make dusters. I shoot them a tentative smile and then move on to the next... to the next what? How do you describe a group of suspended, stapled carrots? Is it an installation? A sculpture?

'It's so symbolic, isn't it?' the man says in a nasal voice.

He's talking about the Tupperware containing the one avocado and one egg.

'Totally,' the Mickey Mouse Girl agrees.

'There are all these couples so utterly different, who, like, co-exist in such a small space...'

'Metaphysical space, right?'

'No, physical space. Normal space. Space space.'

'The final frontier?'

'No! *Here* on earth.'

I bite my lip to stop a smile and hover in front of the carrots, wanting to hear what they'll say about them. But someone else gets there first.

'Fucking shit isn't it?'

The voice belongs to a young man with waxy black hair who is standing beside me with his hands in his pocket looking amused. He's wearing a black shirt with the sleeves rolled up and dark jeans.

'Well I would've used a lot more carrots,' I say.

He laughs and offers me his hand.

'Matt Costa,' he says, and then with a roll of his eyes. 'Art reviewer.'

'Amber.' I'm impressed, even if his hands are a little clammy. 'So is "Fucking shit, isn't it?" going to be the title of your piece?'

He smirks. 'It would be if it were my fucking choice. Fancy a fag? I need to get out of here for a minute.'

I glance behind me and discover that Elliot is now having an animated discussion with a girl in a pink wig. I ignore the twinge of disappointment in my stomach and smile at Matt.

'I don't smoke, but some fresh air would be great.'

We pick up a glass of wine each on the way out and stand in the last rays of sunshine. A lot of people have had the same idea. In this city famous for disappointing weather, sunshine is a rare treat and when it comes everyone feels a pressing need to stand in it and soak up every drop.

Matt takes a moment to check his phone and it gives me a chance to look at him properly. The shadows under his eyes hint at late nights. I'm guessing it'll be a mix of long hours in an office followed by exhausting parties to let off steam. He sucks on his cigarette as if it's providing him with the oxygen that's keeping him alive.

'So what are you doing here?' he says, glancing up briefly from the text message he's writing.

'Oh, Elliot invited me.'

'Elliot Frinton-Smith,' he says, with a tight smile.

I take a sip of wine and wish I would stop blushing at the mention of his name.

'Do you know him, then?' I say.

'I see his face everywhere I go.'

I detect a trace of scorn in his voice and wonder if he's jealous.

'I'm sure he'll offer me something for a good review...'

My eyes widen involuntarily. 'Do you take bribes?'

'Depends who's asking.'

'I'm asking.'

He laughs, 'I was joking. I'm just suggesting he has more money than sense...'

I wonder how much money.

'So what do you think is the meaning behind the carrots?' I say.

His eyes narrow as he takes another deep drag and he starts speaking before he's breathed out all the smoke, stabbing his cigarette in my direction.

'It means people will buy into anything if you can make enough noise about it.'

I nod my head emphatically. This is what has been going through my head for the last few days.

'I mean, take Crocs,' he says.

'The shoes or the animal?'

'The shoes! I mean I can't believe people fell for such plastic shoes... it's like putting your feet in a kid's toy.'

I sense he's about to launch into a long rant and I'm keen to bring the conversation back to art.

'So, do you think anyone could do what Montague's done?'

Matt shrugs. 'It's an added bonus if you've got friends throwing money at you... but yeah, I think if you make enough noise about it...'

'Publicity?'

'Yeah publicity, bad, good, it doesn't even matter. I mean just look at the kind of people who are celebrities these days... all you have to do is lip sync to Madonna and air your tits on YouTube.'

'Would you help me?'

'I don't think you need me, you just need a video camera and maybe a little...'

He glances at my chest, his expression a little doubtful. My hand flies up to cover my already well-covered breasts.

'Were you going to say padding?'

He laughs, his cheeks reddening. 'Well there's a lot of competition.'

'Now you've given me a complex.'

'You're going to need a few of those if you're going to be

a celebrity. You've got to have something to cry about in the interviews.'

'I'm not going to be like that!'

'Of course there are other routes.'

'I know, I was talking about art!' I say. 'Will you help me? As an experiment?'

'What do you have in mind?'

I'm not sure yet, but I feel something brewing and I sense Matt might be a good person to have on my side when I'm clearer about what it is I'm concocting.

'I can't say yet.'

'Then neither can I.'

'Do you have a card?'

He grins as he digs into his shirt pocket and retrieves a stiff, black card.

'What about yours?' he says.

'I forgot them.'

'Mistake number one.'

Elliot has seen us and is coming over.

'Oh thank God, I thought you'd left,' he says, making me feel deliciously wanted.

He moves in between us and his hand lightly brushes my back as he greets me with a kiss and then offers Matt his hand.

'Go on then, what do you think?'

Matt tips his glass towards him. 'Congratulations.'

Elliot nods his head, satisfied, then turns to me. His eyes flit to the card in my hand and he tenses a little.

'I'm sorry, I've completely ignored you,' he says. 'Why don't I introduce you to a few people?'

Beyond Elliot I can see Matt is looking highly entertained. He thinks I'm a fraud now. But then he's a fraud too, pretending he's into conceptual art but actually hating every minute of it.

'It was good to meet you, Matt.'

'You too, Amber.'

Elliot's hand stays on my back as he steers me back into the gallery. It's an abrupt end to our conversation and I feel a little rude abandoning Matt. But I can tell, too, that Matt won't be alone long.

'Get in touch about your project,' he calls after me.

With Elliot's full attention on me I no longer feel like the outsider. Another glass of wine in my hand and we merge with the Montague-and-kimono-girl group. To my relief they aren't even talking about art at all but what they thought of the last Spiderman film.

My eyes flit to the carrots hanging in the distance. Five is not enough. He should have covered the ceiling with them. It would have looked completely insane. No one would have been able to take their eyes off them. Quantity. For great impact you need quantity. Take Antony Gormley's life-sized bronze cast of himself. If there had just been one, it would have gone unnoticed by the majority of Londoners. But there wasn't just one, there were thirty-one of these sculptures positioned around the city; some on the tops of buildings. It was eye-catching and alarming. So many people did double-takes thinking they'd just spotted a suicidal man about to jump. It was incredibly memorable.

What I need is a lot... of something.

'If it wasn't for you he'd probably still be lying on the floor,' Elliot says, in my ear. 'You must think I'm an idiot for taking him on.'

'His paintings are very...' I'm scrabbling for a clever word. 'Good.'

'Most of them were sold in the first ten minutes.'

'You must wish he'd done more.'

He smiles. 'Oh I'm happy... I do it for the love. It's exciting not knowing what he'll come up with next... like reading a mysterious book.'

Farrell. I look at my watch and I feel the knot in my stomach. It's 7.30. There's no way I'll make it now.

'Don't say you have to go?' Elliot says.

'I feel guilty... I was supposed to be at a friend's reading...'

'Oh dear. Reading what?'

'Poetry.'

Elliot leans into my ear. *'She walks in beauty, like the night ... Of cloudless climes and starry skies; And all that's best of dark and bright, Meet in her aspect and her eyes: Thus mellowed to that tender light, Which heaven to gaudy day denies...'*

'Wow...'

I wasn't expecting a poem to be whispered in my ear. It would be romantic if we were alone under a moon-lit sky instead of surrounded by people. I wish we were.

'I was going to be an actor. I'm very good at memorising lines.'

'You can still be one,' I say. I could watch his face all day.

He wrinkles his nose. 'No, I don't think so. After RADA, I acted in a couple of low-budget films and it was excruciatingly boring. The amount of takes that have to be done... everyone thinks it's so glamorous, but it's not. It's actually very dull.'

A big man pushes into our group and slaps Elliot on the back.

'Elliot Frinton-Smith! How the devil are you?'

I step to the side because the man, whoever he is, seems to have an inbuilt loudspeaker and his voice is hurting my eardrums. I dig out my phone, which I'd put on silent and with dismay see the three missed calls and two messages.

Where are you? Are you alright?

'This is Amber,' Elliot says, and I quickly drop my phone back into my bag, to shake his fleshy hand. 'Amber, this is Thomas Fitzpatrick, art collector....'

'It's just fantastic isn't it,' he gushes. 'I mean the texture of those carrots.'

'Well, they are *real* carrots...' I say.

Elliot shoots me a funny look.

'The contrast of the organic world and the man-made, such conflict captured so succinctly,' Fitzpatrick continues, spittle flying as he enunciates every consonant with feeling. 'I don't know where he gets his incredible ideas.'

From me.

'I know, it's just wonderful,' Elliot says.

I look at his expression, of genuine admiration. Or is he acting? I'd prefer to think he was acting than that he genuinely believes Montague is brilliant. To me the show looks like what a desperate parent might do to entertain a small child who's just had all his toys pinched. But I can't get away from the fact that Elliot spent five grand on this venue. How much does that mean to him? Is it the equivalent of a hundred quid for me?

'So, Amber,' Fitzpatrick says. 'What do you do?'

It sounds like a challenge and I wish I could rise to it with some fantastical invention that would dissolve the glue under his toupee.

'I, um, I'm working for a catering firm at the moment...'

I see his eyes glaze over.

'It's research,' I say, scrabbling to get his attention back and be interesting. 'For a... an art project I'm doing...'

Elliot looks impressed. 'I didn't know you were undercover.'

'Yes... it's going to be big.'

I'm never going to be able to show my face again.

'Well, big-ish...'

Fitzpatrick is looking intrigued. 'Oh?'

In fact the entire group seems to have come to an end of their separate conversations and are now all focused on me.

'I can't tell you much... but it'll be very...'

My confidence is ebbing fast. My mouth feels dry and I take a sip of wine.

'Come on, Amber, give us a clue,' Elliot says.

'Yes, we all want to know what we've got to look out for,' Fitzpatrick booms.

Now it feels as if the whole room is straining to hear me. I want to sink through the floor. My brain is buzzing wildly. I think of Rupert painted in different colours. I think of Egg doing a handstand. I think of pasta twirls and glitter. I picture Farrell made of plasticine, solid words coming out of his mouth and I think of Andrzej doing breast stroke in a bowl of garlic. I don't know what goes on in other people's heads but this is how mine works. It darts from one thing to another. And just as I feel people losing faith in me, my thoughts land on the sack in my kitchen.

Of course! That's it. It's the only thing I have in abundance. Quantity. Impact...

'Bananas,' I say. 'That's the clue. Bananas.'

It's not what they're expecting and judging by the titters of laughter, not everybody is convinced. But that doesn't matter now. What matters is I've finally got a plan.

I hear questions being raised about my project. What sort of bananas? What will they be made from? Was there a significant event in my life marked by bananas?

I bat away as many questions as I can, but they keep on coming.

'I've got to go...' I say to Elliot.

He searches my face, looking for a clue. 'Will I see you again?'

I want to shout YES! YES! YES!

'Of course,' I say. 'You promised me dinner remember?'

My smooth reply is undermined when I bump his nose going in for a kiss goodbye. He smells delicious and I have an urge to cup his face and give him a proper snog. Instead I smile as I say goodbye to everyone and congratulate Montague one more time.

It's good to get outside and feel the warm summer air on my face. Finally, I'm fired up. I know what to do and the night is still young. Not young enough to make it in time for Farrell's reading, though.

I ring my best friend on the way home, but there's no answer. I'm sure he'll understand when I tell him about my epiphany. In fact, maybe he was secretly relieved about it. If he'd really wanted me to come, he wouldn't have left it until the day before to invite me.

I get off the bus one stop early and head to the 24-hour corner shop famed for selling everything. If I can't get spray paint in here, then I can't get it anywhere at this time. They just have to have it. The anticipation makes my heart beat faster. I'm afraid that if I don't carry out my plan tonight, then I'll think better of it in the morning. In cases like this, spontaneity is crucial.

Chapter 9

The corner shop is called 'Rose's Food and Wine Market'. It's where I go when I can't face the battle of shopping in a bigger supermarket, which, let's be honest, is most days. It's got everything you need, with boxes of vegetables collecting dust outside and inside, all sorts of unusual ingredients from Turkey and beyond. It's a dodgy but charming place, which sells khat under the counter and confectionary off the top of it.

The shop is owned by a thin, Somali man with a coarse beard and an eye patch. He doesn't look much like a Rose. A deep scar continues beneath the patch and runs down his cheek, deep and white like lightning. He runs the shop with an army of young men, who enjoy asking for IDs. They hand over the booze regardless of the person's age after they've had a good laugh at their photo.

When I arrive there's a group of them sitting with their friends on the curb outside, faces hidden under dark hoods. A mobile phone in a pint glass blares out a tinny accompaniment to their low mutters. I sober up as I cross the road. A little voice tells me to go home, but I charge on.

I walk around the shop once, half hoping to find spray paint sitting comfortably in between the baked beans and tins of tuna. At the counter, one-eyed Rose is looking at me suspiciously.

'What you looking for?' he barks.

'Spray paint?'

'Wha'?'

My finger presses down on an imaginary nozzle and I wave my arm in the air.

'Spray paint.'

'For graffiti?'

'God no! For bananas, but yeah, it's the same sort of paint...'

His one eye narrows. 'You police?'

I burst out laughing, but shut up quickly when I see the rage in his eye. I can imagine it's only a small glimpse of what he's capable of feeling.

'No, I'm just an artist working on a project.'

He softens and the good side of his face smiles.

'Why didn't you say so? What colour you want?'

'What colour do you have?'

'What colour you want?'

'Blue?'

'No blue.'

'Red?'

He shakes his head.

'Green?'

'Why you want green? It's unlucky colour.'

I'm starting to feel tired. The alcohol is losing its hold on me and I'm feeling a pull towards my bed. Maybe I should just hold this thought until the weekend.

'Oh... never mind... just leave it.'

'Wait! Don't go!'

He goes out to the back room and comes out with a can with a transparent lid. On it there's a yellow sticker. My heart sinks. What's the bloody point of painting bananas yellow? My mind scrabbles for a solution. Couldn't yellow on yellow symbolise people's different layers of identity? That Russian artist Malevich who painted 'White on White' got away with it. In fact he got away with it so well it became a movement. Maybe my yellow on yellow could be a post-movement.

'You don't like yellow?'

I shake my head miserably and he starts shrieking with laughter. He calls out to a boy stacking shelves at the back of the shop.

'Hassan, she doesn't like yellow!'

The boy comes over and when he sees the spray can, a big smile dimples his chubby cheeks.

'Quick! Call them, call them!' Mr Rose shouts, followed by a torrent of Arabic, which flies straight over my head.

Soon there are about five boys standing around me wiping tears of laughter from their eyes and slapping each other's back.

'You don't want yellow?' he says for the second time.

'No...' I say, feeling humiliated and confused.

'Well then you don't get yellow.'

And he holds up the bottle for everyone to see and he picks the edge of the yellow sticker with his nail, catches it between two fingers and then whips it off. Below the yellow sticker is another sticker, which is bright, fuchsia pink.

'See! You don't like yellow! So I give you pink!'

The boys are in hysterics.

'Yes, pink, that's better,' I say, feeling like an upset child who has just been offered a consolatory biscuit. I should be annoyed that I was nearly conned, not relieved that I've got what I wanted after all.

I'm surprised at myself for not paying up at once and getting out of the shop as quick as I can. My confidence has returned and I hold up a finger and tell Rose to wait while I scan the fridge for the cheapest bottle of wine. I cross the line at £2.99 Lambrusco and pick up the next best thing. I've got to wake up early tomorrow, but I need something to get me through this night-time challenge.

'You famous?' Rose says, as he puts the wine and spray paint into a plastic carrier bag.

I hand over a crumpled twenty-pound note; money I shouldn't be spending and muster a bright smile.

'Yes... I'm the one who does the colourful bananas.'

71

There's a slight twitch of recognition in his face and he nods slowly. 'I think I know you...'

'My name's Amber. Amber Thompson.'

Perhaps it's because I deliver the line as if I'm James Bond, but instead of frowning and telling me he's never heard of me, his face lights up. 'Yes, I know you, you're the one who does the colourful bananas!'

I don't know if that's the publicity Matt Costa had in mind, but I feel pretty good and pretty damn famous as I walk home, and I'm only just getting started.

Chapter 10

I arrive home to find the door Chub-locked, which is strange because Egg has already had one reenactment meeting this week and I can't think what else he could be doing. In the kitchen I notice there's still food in Rupert's bowl and his litter tray has been emptied. So far Egg is doing a great job of cleaning up after him.

'Rupert? Where are you Rupert?'

I pick out a bunch of bananas from the sack and sniff them gingerly. It has to be said; they do smell of bleach. Such a waste! At least it would have been a waste if I hadn't rescued them.

'Don' you worry ma'leetel ones,' I coo at my bananas in my best French accent. 'I weel show you off to the world! You weel not 'av died in vain!'

Feeling a renewed energy I unscrew the bottle of chemical Chardonnay and take a cheeky sip from the bottle before rinsing out a glass and using that. I kick off my tan heels and consider the dress I am wearing. My navy Audrey Hepburn number is perfect for a posh Mayfair art show, not so good for painting in. But I can't be bothered to get changed. 'Egg! If you're here don't come in!'

My voice is momentarily muffled as I pull my dress over my head and then fling it across the back of a chair. I stand in my underwear in the kitchen, feeling wild and exciting. My underwear is a matching set in lacy pink, which I wore just in case. It seems a pity no one will see it now.

I call out for Rupert as I unlock the door to the patio. Our little housemate is probably asleep in Egg's room. Egg's had such a head start getting him used to his company. I'll have to put some hours in or else I'll be like the distant father that watches over the cot, yet another bedtime missed.

We only use the tiny patio space off the kitchen for hanging out the washing on the handful of sunny days in summer, but tonight it will be my studio. The outside sensor reactive light switches on as I place my bananas in the middle of a paving slab and shake the aerosol hard, enjoying the rattle of the ball bearing.

The memory of working on that theatre set at university comes flooding back. It was hard work spraying all those candy-floss trees, but I loved seeing them come to life, so tantalising in their colourful coats. *Charlie and the Chocolate Factory meets Heart of Darkness* was set in a Congo full of licorice lizards and sugar-coated butterflies. The play was terrible. Pretentious nonsense. But I loved working on that set. I shut my ears to Eva's bitching and I sprayed to my heart's content.

I'm about to press the nozzle when I realise that I'm going to be scraping paint off these tiles for the rest of my life or else face a massive charge from the landlord to take them back to their grimy, brown colour. Damn it! I hurry back to the kitchen to get a black bag to slide under the bananas. Then I step back and take one more thoughtful gulp of wine. I have already delayed enough. I am now quite drunk but also very insightful. Those bananas are speaking to me. They are telling me that they don't want to be lumped into this one huge category of BANANA. These bananas are individuals who have received a long and substantial education from the sun and the rain and earth. They don't want to be eaten without this journey being acknowledged. If that means I have to paint them as brightly as an exotic bird then I bloody well will. And once I've done that I'll make sure that they perch on the highest... perch... in London... which is... oh shit, it's the Shard.

74

I swap wine for aerosol can and start shaking it as hard as I can. I stop, narrow my eyes and begin to spray. With a satisfying whisper the paint spreads quickly over the soft yellow skin. I draw the can back when it begins to grow too thick in one area. I squat down to fill in all the ridges between each banana. I look up, wondering where I might be able to dangle the bananas so that I can evenly cover the bottom of them. I'll need a hook. As I'm standing there in my knickers and bra, considering my small but significant dilemma, I hear the unmistakable sound of the front door slam shut. I stand still long enough for the light to switch itself off.

What to do? Do I continue to stay as still as a statue in the dark until Egg has disappeared upstairs? I strain to hear his footsteps. He seems to be lumbering up and down the corridor in his clunky Doc Martins.

Then I hear him call my name.

'Amber?'

He calls it faintly, as if he's assumed I'm asleep.

Now go upstairs, I think. Go on!

I hear the sound of his key turning in the lock and I let out the breath I was holding. I know he'll go upstairs now.

In the darkness I make out my glass of wine. I squint at the floodlight above the door, daring it to catch my subtle movements as I lean slowly, so slowly, forwards. Then I freeze because I swear I've just seen a movement in the kitchen. My heart starts pounding. Hold it! Hold it! Then I hear a thud. Why hasn't Egg put the light on? And if it's not Egg, then who is? Are we being burgled?

I slowly place my other hand on the can and direct it at the patio door as if it were a gun. My legs are bent and beginning to ache.

There's another bang and then a footstep, and then suddenly the floodlight turns on, flooding my pasty body in unwanted light.

The first thing I see is Egg with his mouth open, about to bite the top off a pepperoni stick. The first thing he sees is his half-naked housemate preparing to spray him with paint. I don't know who is more shocked, but I'm guessing it's him

75

'You're eating meat!' I cry, dropping the can and throwing my arms around myself.

His eyes are huge plates. He doesn't even know where to begin with where I've gone wrong.

'It's art! I'm finding my inner artist!'

Egg just blinks.

I point at his pepperoni stick and he looks down at it as if he's only just seen it.

'I couldn't resist!' he says, hugging it to his chest. 'She gave me red wine! I'm like an animal when I drink red wine!'

He flops down to the floor, his long legs folding up like a grass-hopper's and starts to whimper. There is no doubt in my mind that someone has got Egg drunk; he would never have done it all by himself. The fact that I know Egg is drunk must mean that I'm not as drunk as I thought. Feeling smug, I reach for my glass of wine and polish it off.

'S'alright Egg. Protein's very good for you. You have to eat it.'

'But I've spent my week's allowance...'

'Thas' crazy! How much was it?'

'Three pounds fifty.'

I reach down and squeeze his shoulders. 'Don't worry Egg, I can lend you three fifty.'

'I just couldn't help myself...'

'S'alright, tomorrow's another day...' and tomorrow suddenly seems horribly close. 'I really should go to sleep...'

I leave him on the step and make my way upstairs, but before I make it to the top, his words slap me in the face. '*She* gave me red wine' – had he actually uttered those words?

My feet hammer down the stairs and I grab my coat off the hook by the front door to cover up before returning to the kitchen. Egg pops the last of his pepperoni stick in his mouth and gets up off the floor.

'Egg! What girl?' I cry, breathless with excitement and lack of exercise. 'What girl gave you wine?'

He looks confused. 'I left you a note.'

'What?'

'In your bedroom. I told you.'

'What did it say?'

'Bibiana Fuentes.'

I clap a hand over my mouth. She'd given me the date of her arrival in an email, which I'd scanned briefly and then forgotten.

'I opened the door to her and I was holding Rupert and she almost had a heart attack,' Egg says.

'Why?'

Rupert is cute and fluffy. What's to be scared of?

'She's allergic to cats.'

'Oh no! What happened? Has she gone to a hotel?'

Poor Bibiana.

'No, no, I took her over to Farrell's,' he says. 'That's where I've just come from. She opened a bottle of wine to say thank you.'

I'm staring at him like an idiot. In my head I'm trying to picture Bibiana in Farrell's house. Where is she going to sleep? Farrell's room is a box and to sleep anywhere near Danny wouldn't be safe as he plays football in his dreams and wakes himself up kicking.

But it's good news! I should be massively relieved that she didn't have to go off to some expensive hotel. But I don't. I feel really guilty. Not only have I let Farrell down by not coming to his reading, I've made it worse by offloading a guest onto him. And as for Bibiana, the least I could have done was be here for her when she arrived.

'It's okay,' Egg says. 'They seem to get on very well. She made Farrell feel better.'

'Wasn't he feeling well?'

Egg shrugs. 'He was quiet... Are you going out somewhere?'

I wrap my coat tighter around me and shake my head. The only place I'm going is bed.

When Egg isn't looking I smuggle the bottle of wine under my coat and head upstairs to my room. As I enter I catch a waft of something awful. It's a sharp, bitter pong that stings my throat and makes me want to gag. I press my hand over my nose and turn on the light.

There's movement under my duvet and then a hopeful, 'miao.'

'No nono... shitshitshit!'

I pull back the covers and Rupert stands up and pads to the end of the mattress. Immediately I see why his litter tray downstairs is empty. It's because he's found a much more luxurious one in the form of my bed. I look at the little, brown poo on my recently cleaned white sheets. How can something so small smell so bad?

'Egg,' I call. 'Egg!'

I hear him outside my door.

'You have to rub his nose in it and then carry him downstairs to the litter tray so he learns,' he says.

'Oh Rupert...' I say sadly, looking at his little pink nose and his white moustache. 'I'm glad that's not how I was taught.'

I take another gulp of wine and resign myself to the fact that it'll be a while before I can fall asleep.

Chapter 11

My alarm is like a dentist's drill tearing through my brain. It's loud from the start, high-pitched and fills me with panic. It comes from my phone, which must be in the pocket of some article of clothing trailing across my bedroom floor. I sit up and the contents of my head lurch into place with some delay.

It's a bad one.

I try not to look at the empty bottle of wine perched on my desk, laughing at me from the other side of the room. The reek of cheap white wine wafts up my nostrils. It must be my breath. My tongue is furry with regret.

I roll out of bed without grace and scramble to find the source of the horrific sound. When, at last, I find it I panic-tap the screen until it stops. I know there's a high chance it will start up again in five minutes. Exhausted, I crawl back under my duvet and wait for the throbbing in my head to go away. But it doesn't and it's not going to either.

How many times do I need to learn this lesson?

Drinking is bad.

Drinking is bad.

Drinking is bad.

Why doesn't it sink in?

I feel a light pressure as something drops onto my duvet. The pressure moves across my stomach and up to my neck. I pull my cover down a few inches and Rupert steps onto my mouth and sniffs my hair. I splutter and nudge him off me.

'Miao,' he whines and tries to mount my arm.

'It's alright for you, you weren't poisoned last night.'

I pick him up and stroke his beautiful, soft fur. He pads at my hair like a baby intrigued by everything. It's a brief moment of oblivion, me and Rupert against the world, and then memories of the previous night kick in. Did I really spray-paint bananas in my knickers? I flush with shame as I remember Egg standing in the doorway gawping at me. It doesn't make me feel any better that he was eating pepperoni in secret. It's not as if I had money on him lasting very long on lentils.

He said he'd been drinking.

'Miao.'

Then I spot Egg's crumpled note in his spidery writing on the floor; confirmation that it wasn't just a dream. Bibiana had arrived yesterday evening and Egg had taken her to Farrell's before her allergies could erupt. And I hadn't been there for anyone.

Rupert wriggles out of my grasp and walks along the mountain ridges that are my legs. He turns, lets out one more disappointed 'miao' then jumps off the bed.

I throw off my duvet and try to ignore the stabbing pain in my head. What I need is a brilliant excuse. I need to have tried to get home in time but was delayed, not just by a traditional signal failure on the tube but something epic.

Foxes on the track?

My alarm goes off again, cutting short my pathetic brainstorm. The problem with an EPIC excuse is that unless it has been featured on the front page of this morning's newspapers no one is going to believe it.

It looks as if I'll have to go with uninspiring plan B, which is to run over to Farrell's and apologise to them both. I'll make sure Bibiana had a good night's sleep. Where *did* she sleep? I really hope

Farrell didn't feel he had to give her his bed. There's nothing wrong with the sofa, which is cosy, soft and worn, like an old slipper.

In the bathroom I guiltily swallow two Nurofens and tell myself that this is the last time. From now on, I'm going to be focused. I look in the mirror and flare my nostrils.

Amber Thompson, there will be no more drinking until you've achieved something significant! The world is your oyster and you must eat it before it goes off and gives you a stomach full of regret and a mind full of mediocre memories!

My inner pep talk continues as I dowse myself in shower gel, as if soap could wash away my hangover. Thank God make-up can at least mask it. Men are so unlucky. They can possess all the tools in the world but none of them can conceal an immature evening.

Downstairs in the kitchen, I'm confronted with my mutant bananas. Rupert sniffs at them once and then jumps back and hides under the table as if they've stung his nose. I pick them up and spin them around from their long stalk. In spite of everything, the artificial lighting, the inappropriate painting attire and the impaired judgement caused by fermented grapes, there is hardly a speck of yellow skin peeping through the paint. That's if you don't turn them over and look at the bottom, of course, which wasn't quite as successful.

A smile tugs at my lips. They are vibrant and alive. They genuinely look like happy bananas.

'Now what to do with them, Rupert?'

Rupert remains under the table until the bananas have disappeared into a carrier bag. Only when he's sure they've gone does he come out to inspect his food bowl. I fill it with dry pellets, feeling sorry for him, because it looks likes the insipid fibre you add to cereal to fight constipation. As for me, I make do with the only thing in the cupboard, which is a packet of salt- and-vinegar hula hoops. Then I grab my bananas, throw my handbag over my shoulder and hurry up the road towards Farrell's house.

It's early. Not early for the nine-to-five crowd, but it might be early for Farrell, who starts work at the local bookshop at 10 a.m. I don't consider this until I'm standing outside his door, about to ring the bell. It's 7.37. Some people would have jogged around the block, listened to the news, walked the dog and cooked porridge by now.

I ring the bell.

It's unusual for me to feel nervous about seeing Farrell. I'm worried he's angry with me, or worse, disappointed. Standing on the step waiting for the sound of footsteps I find myself really wishing that my foxes-on-the-track excuse was true. All through our friendship I've been the one nagging him to raise his profile as a writer and he's always dragged his heels, and now that he finally does something, I don't show up.

I'll make it up to him. Maybe I could buy him one of those fancy artisan notebooks with the paper that feels as if it's been recycled five times, covered in sand, then bound in a scrap of ancient leather. Or perhaps just a pen? Although, knowing Farrell, he probably only uses a particular pen, something ethical and handcrafted by Celtic shamans.

I straighten up as I see a shadow behind the glass panes. I hear the sound of the latch and then Farrell appears in the doorway in a baggy grey t-shirt and tracksuit bottoms, groggy-eyed and with his hair standing on end. He looks so adorably dishevelled that I want to cuddle him.

'Amber, what're you doing here?'

He rubs the sleep out of his eyes and starts heading back inside, leaving the door open for me to follow.

'Good morning to you too,' I say with forced brightness. The thumping in my head has faded to a dull beat, like someone banging the drums with a teddy bear.

The kitchen is joined onto the living room with a small wooden bar separating them. I climb up onto a stool and look around, taking note of the empty sleeping bag stretched out on the sofa and a fresh mould in the pillow. Farrell moves about the kitchen making coffee on auto pilot.

'Sorry I thought you'd be up...'

'I normally am, but your friend got me drunk.'

'Bibiana?'

'Why? Should I be expecting another guest?'

'I'm so sorry, Farrell! I wish she'd called me, I completely forgot, you know what I'm like with emails. I read them once then I forget everything they said.'

Farrell doesn't say anything as he measures out the milk into two big mugs to heat up. He didn't start drinking coffee until a couple of years ago but now that he does, he takes it very seriously.

'And then Rupert, I never thought it possible for someone to be allergic to Rupert.'

I'm aware that Farrell is not adding to the conversation.

'Was she alright?' I ask.

Bibiana has never been one to keep her feelings to herself. Perhaps she gave him an earful about how inconsiderate I am. Did he have to apologise on my behalf all night?

'Better than alright,' he says.

'Oh...that's good then, isn't it?'

He leans against the counter as the microwave whirs behind him.

'She was really lovely. We had two bottles of wine.'

'Two? Egg said only one.'

'We had another once he'd gone. He's such a lightweight. You should've seen him. I think he's in love. He told her she was the perfect Cleopatra.'

I laugh out loud. I feel as if a weight has lifted off my shoulders.

'Brilliant! If she's Cleopatra then he doesn't have to be an Egyptian, he could be Caesar... or Mark Antony... although they probably didn't have beards either, did they?'

The microwave pings. Farrell removes the mugs and pours in the coffee. I become aware of the huge clock on the wall ticking loudly. I've got to get a move on in a minute, but I don't want to go. I want to curl up under a blanket on Farrell's sofa and laugh at people's seventies haircuts on daytime TV. He puts the coffee in front of me and I wrap my hands around it and take a tentative sip. It's deliciously hot and milky. Life suddenly feels much better.

But as I rest my mug back down I become aware of the tension in the room. Farrell is holding his mug very stiffly, his lips are pursed and he seems pensive. He looks at me and then down at his coffee, as if he was about to say something but decided not to. But then he looks at me again.

'Why did you say you were going to come, Amber?'

My stomach clenches. He's upset with me and I feel horrible.

'I'm sorry. I really wanted to. But I had to go to this show and I got caught up... you didn't exactly give me much notice.'

'But you knew you weren't coming. You *knew*. I just don't know why you couldn't just have told me. I expected Phil and Erica not to show but you...'

I'm about to ask why they didn't make it either but I stop myself. Phil would have been caught up at the bookshop, while Erica, his old uni friend, is so flaky I doubt she even offered an excuse. She missed his birthday party last year and didn't text him an apology until a month later. Her excuse? She fell asleep. That's quite some nap.

'I'm so sorry, Farrell...'

'I felt like an idiot all on my own with my stupid little reserved table.'

'Oh God, I didn't know.'

He shakes his head. 'Was it Elliot's show? Is that why you didn't come? I hope you at least got a date out of it.'

I feel my cheeks redden. 'Actually I did.'

'Good, I'm glad,' he says. But he doesn't sound very glad.

There's a sound coming from one of the bedrooms; a creak of floorboards then the sound of a zip.

'Is that...?'

I don't finish the question because my answer appears in a silky pink dressing gown.

'Amber!'

Before I can take her all in, she's smothering me in a bear hug. I react a little slowly, but then my arms find her neat little waist and I can feel her boobs pressing against me. To be honest, it's a bit too energetic for my fragile state. She draws back and I'm struck by how different she looks.

'Amber! I can't believe you have a damn cat!'

She's also got a slight American twang.

'I know I can't believe it either. We only got him a couple of days ago!'

Her hair is still long and jet black, but she's straightened away the frizzy halo she used to have and acquired a severe fringe, which is cut in a perfect straight line across her forehead.

'You look amazing,' I say.

She lets out a little laugh and I can see she's blushing. 'It's my eyebrows. I finally plucked them. I can't believe what hairy caterpillars I used to have! So embarrassing!'

'No they weren't!'

Yes, they were. They had always dominated her face. They're now neither caterpillars nor the angry pencil-thin variety either.

'Look at you,' she says, touching the ends of my hair. 'It really suits you longer like that. You don't look like a boy any more.'

'Thanks a lot.'

'What?' Bibiana laughs. 'Much better to look good now than in university. Oh my God, it seems so long ago. You have to tell me everything, EVERYTHING!'

It's not just her eyebrows that have changed; it's her entire body language. She's not hunched up like she used to be and the dread has left her eyes.

'So, come on, are you married, divorced... how many kids do you have?'

'No, no and none.'

'Boyfriend?'

I smile. 'No.'

85

'Liar! Farrell said you went on a date.'

'Exactly. One date...'

'Would you like a coffee Bibiana?' Farrell cuts in.

'Call me Bibi; only my grandmother insists on calling me Bibiana,' she says, and then she hesitates, tapping her fingers against her lips. 'Actually I was thinking of getting one at your bookshop if that's okay?'

Farrell looks chuffed, 'Yeah, of course.'

'Farrell's told me all about the bookshop and it sounds so cute. Isn't his idea about doing readings there great? I'm so gutted I missed yesterday. I love poetry, don't you?'

'Uh, yeah,' I say, unconvincingly.

'Liar,' Farrell says, not catching my eye.

'Oh my God, would everyone stop calling me a liar please?'

Bibiana cackles with laughter and Farrell shoots me a half-hearted smile. Forgiveness?

I look at the clock, which is moving too fast. I'm going to be late, but I can't tear myself away from the cosy kitchen. I feel I'll be missing out if I go. I want to hang out in the bookshop too.

'I wish I didn't have to go to work.'

'Pull a sickie then,' Bibiana says. 'One more lie won't kill anybody.'

'I can't... If I don't go, I don't get paid.'

'Boo!'

'What are your plans, then? What are you doing here?'

'I'm moving here. I've decided London is the place to be.'

'About time.'

I want to know what her accommodation plans are, but I don't want to sound as though I'm trying to get rid of her. Not that I've got much influence in the matter now that I've got Rupert. But Farrell must be feeling a bit claustrophobic. He loves his space. He likes to be able to get up in the middle of the night and write the first thing that comes to his head.

'I've got some job interviews lined up, so fingers crossed,' she says.

'What sort of job are you looking for?'

'Marketing.'

'I can't believe you're here,' I say.

'Yeah,' she smiles. 'It's going to be awesome. I want to see all of London again properly. And I've also promised Farrell so many things.'

'Oh yeah?'

They look at each other and burst out laughing.

'When I get drunk I always promise to make people so many different types of Argentinean food,' she says grinning.

I smile but I feel a little excluded. 'So, are you looking for a place?'

'I've found somewhere already. Unfortunately the tenants still need to move out...' she shoots Farrell an apologetic glance. 'Farrell said I can stay here meanwhile.'

Oh God. I look at him to read the subtle signs of 'I'm going to kill you Amber' but he sips his coffee and appears perfectly calm.

'Are you really that allergic to cats?' I say, hoping for it all to have been a terrible mistake and actually it's dogs she can't cope with.

'I blow up like a balloon.'

'It's fine, Amber,' Farrell says.

'But I was really looking forward to some girly times.'

'I know, sucks right? But we can always include Farrell in our girly times.'

'Yeah, I'm used to it.'

I turn to Farrell. 'What about if you take Rupert and Bibi stays with me?'

He does that face; the one where he's laughing and frowning at the same time.

'To be honest,' he says. 'I'd prefer to have Bibi.'

Bibiana flushes with pleasure and then she puts an arm around me and kisses my cheek.

'We can still go out together! It's all going to be alright, you'll see!'

But it doesn't feel alright as I'm running to catch the bus ten minutes later.

I'm late for work, my head is pounding, my stomach is in knots, I've got a bunch of bright-pink bananas in my bag which I've no idea what I'm going to do with and I feel like I'm going to throw up.

Chapter 12

I only get half a seat to work as the woman beside me has huge jelly buttocks that spill into my territory and tremble with every vibration of the bus. Still, it's better than having an elbow in my face, which was the alternative. I dig out my mobile to text Farrell because I've had an idea. My parents live just outside London, an easy distance by train, and I know they'll be happy to put Bibiana up for a few weeks. They have a guest room, where she'll be much more comfortable. Sharing with a man is always a bit awkward. You end up doing that weird bra under t-shirt maneuver because there's no lock on the door.

After I send the text message I scroll through my list of contacts until I hit Elliot Frinton-Smith. I couldn't resist putting in his surname, even though I don't know any other Elliots.

Last night I left the gallery so abruptly as if at any moment my dress was going to turn to rags and my non-existent car turn into a pumpkin. I just want to make contact, so he doesn't think I'm not interested. I'm staring at my phone composing a message in my head, when it vibrates in my hand. Immediately my stomach tightens with anticipation. I want it so much to be him.

Are you serious, Amber? I finally get a hot lady sleeping in my bed and you want me to send her to your Mam's?!

It takes me a second to realise the message is from Farrell, not

Elliot. I'm slightly taken aback at first and then I smile, because I can imagine his cheeky grin when he wrote it. I text him hurriedly back as my bus pulls up to my stop.

FINALLY - You said it! To be honest I thought you weren't into the ladies any more.

I'm fifteen minutes late already and as soon as I'm off the bus I start to run. My phone vibrates and I can't resist slowing down to take a peep.

You know me, I'm a romantic writer. I was just waiting for the right one.

The problem with text messages is you can't always be completely sure of the tone. I'm assuming Farrell is being sarcastic but if he'd added a winky face then I'd know for sure. I mean, he could actually be smitten. Egg already is, apparently.

Farrell and Bibiana? I'm not sure I can see them as a couple. What if she turned into another Eva? The few tantrums Bibiana had in our halls went down in university history. I'll never forget the way she tore into Steve when he failed to wash up one evening. It was uncomfortable because he was the cleanest of the lot of us. He didn't defend himself, which made it even more awful. I think he was either afraid of her or in love with her. Of course she apologised, but it was too late; the damage was already done.

But it's unfair to judge Bibiana on what happened at university. We were all idiots then. Perhaps she'd be good for him. She's affectionate, generous and always full of energy. She'd crack the whip, make sure he finished that novel once and for all, because I'm sure her interest in his writing is genuine. It's just that I can't help thinking that Eva was passionate about Farrell's work once too.

It began with that play and Eva insisting on daily meetings with him so she could gain real insight into his script. Then she would swan in late, when we'd already been painting the set for hours, and would go on about his talent and his vision. It all went downhill once they started going out. She was critical of him when he doted on her, suspicious when he didn't. He couldn't win. It was exhausting to watch. I spent a long time wanting to slap him out of it. No, I couldn't go through that again.

I catch my breath as I turn into the dusty street where Flamingo Catering's offices rise up like a giant grey portaloo and I'm surprised to see a police car badly parked across the entrance. As far as I know, the police don't use our catering services.

I push open the door to the office feeling nervous because I'm late and I'm not in the best frame of mind to come up with a convincing excuse. Foxes on the track won't cut it. They know I come by bus.

Everyone turns around to look at me. There's Jan, Andrzej, Vicky and a boyish-faced policeman. The room is so small it feels like a sold-out concert.

'There she is!' Vicky says, as if they hadn't noticed.

What have I done? Why are they looking for me?

'I'm so sorry I'm late, the bus took ages.'

Jan is fresh back from her walking holiday. Her arms and legs have increased in bulk and her cheeks bear the ruddy marks of windy weather. She could hoist a sheep off a cliff. She could hoist me off a cliff, too.

'Is it the same bus route you normally take?' she asks.

'Uh... yes.'

'Well the distance can't have changed, so you probably just left at the wrong time.'

She turns to the policeman, who's studying me anxiously and my moment to deliver a mouth-dropping explanation passes me by.

'This is the woman you need to speak to.'

My mouth is dry and I'm gagging for a glass of water.

The policeman nods at me. He doesn't look much older than twenty. He's got small features packed into the middle of a chubby, round face as smooth as a baby's bottom.

'I'm Special Constable Jamie Perkins.'

I'm not expecting what he says next.

'I'm here about some bananas.'

I just stare at him. The bunch of spray-painted bananas in my bag seems to grow heavier. I can feel them coming to life, calling for help, 'We're in here! She's the kidnapper! Save us!'

Andrzej is refusing eye contact and is examining a freckle on the back of his hand, rubbing it gently as if to see if it might come off.

'Bananas?' I say. Am I going to be arrested for possessing a bunch of stolen and now adulterated bananas?

'The sack,' Andrzej growls.

The policeman looks uncomfortable.

'We were doing a special operation to catch some dealers who have been frequenting this area...'

He can't be serious.

'Banana dealers?'

Andrzej mutters obscenities under his breath.

'Drug dealers,' the policeman says.

I'm too hungover for this. I want to sit down, but the policeman is blocking the way to my desk.

'There was a small camera monitoring the area, hidden in the sack, that you apparently removed.'

'I didn't remove anything,' I say, feeling irritated. 'Andrzej guilt-tripped me into taking them all home so they wouldn't go to waste, but we haven't been able to eat any because for some reason they smell of bleach.'

'Oh why are you looking at me?' Andrzej cries. 'Who do you think I am? Heston Blumenthal?'

'No one is blaming you!' Vicky snaps.

'I can't even cook with garlic these days, let alone bleach,' he says, throwing a dirty look at Vicky, who responds by folding her arms and quietly seething.

'Could it have been the work-experience boy?' I say.

I notice the policeman is looking increasingly embarrassed.

Andrzej smirks, 'Well, if you pay peanuts you get monkeys.'

'So because he isn't getting paid, he's allowed to poison everyone?' Vicky cries. 'Actually, that bit was us,' Constable Perkins admits at last. 'We thought the bleach might preserve them.'

Andrzej shakes his head at the officer, making it clear he thinks the man is an idiot. I'm inclined to agree with him.

'Why didn't you just use something more durable?' I ask. 'Like coconuts?'

'Amber!' Jan snaps. 'For heaven's sake, just answer the constable's questions, please, so we can get on with our day.'

The policeman clears his throat.

'We will be analysing the success of our project and will be making amendments.'

How can they be analysing the success of their project, when the project is leaning against a cupboard in my kitchen?

'Please madam, can you confirm the camera is in your possession?'

'I'm not sure. I haven't checked.'

'Will you please check?' he says, sounding a little desperate now. I wonder what trouble he's in for orchestrating such a silly operation.

'Yes... Would you like the bananas back, too?'

'No, just my camera.'

'That's a pity.'

'I would advise you not to eat them.'

'I've no intention of eating them,' I say. 'Although if I had and was feeling sick, would I get compensation?'

The policeman bristles. 'Madam, you stole them.'

I open my mouth to protest this point as the phone starts ringing. Vicky answers and we all turn to look at her, even the policeman, as if the caller could possibly have information about the missing camera, which was left unguarded in a sack of fruit.

Vicky glances warily at me. 'Who shall I say is calling?'

Jan holds out her hand to take the call. Everyone who doesn't want to talk to Vicky wants to talk to Jan. Usually it's a salesman making sweeping statements about how our lives would be transformed if only we changed our telephone lines, electricity, gas, credit cards...

'Actually it's for Amber...'

It can't be. I'm the temp. No one wants to talk to the temp.

'It's Elliot,' she says. 'Elliot Frinton-Smith.'

I can feel my face burning up.

'It..it... must be about the goujons,' I stammer.

I squeeze past the policeman and Andrzej. Jan folds her arms and watches me closely. My heart is drumming in my chest as I take the phone.

'Hello, Flamingo Catering,' I say stiffly.

'Amber! It's me, Elliot. Gosh, is that your phone voice?'

'Yes, it is.'

This is excruciating. I simply have to pretend he's a client. It's bad enough that I'm twenty minutes late to work. Vicky doesn't know where to look. Yesterday for a brief moment she was on my side, but with Jan in the room she's no longer an ally.

'Are you alright?' he says.

'Yes, I can send you another menu.'

'I'm not ringing up for a bloody menu, Amber. I thought that was obvious.'

There are butterflies in my stomach and I have to bite my lip to keep a serious face.

'That's... great,' I say. 'Have you got... any... special requirements?'

'Wow, Amber, I just thought we'd see how it goes.'

'Yes...'

'Yes? Okay... well I've got two theatre tickets for tonight...' in the background I can hear a phone ringing sharply.

'Tonight?'

'Oh, sorry, I'll have to call you back.'

'Email me!'

The line goes dead and I hand the phone over to Vicky who returns it to its receiver and looks at me with open curiosity. Jan coughs. I swallow and turn around to face her.

'Now that you've made plans with your boyfriend, can we get

on with some work please?'

Jan must have heard every word. I want to sink through the floor.

'I'm sorry...' I say, miserably.

The policeman takes my details and gives me his card.

'Ring that number as soon as you've found it and please bring it in tomorrow.'

'But tomorrow's Saturday.'

'Monday, then. Just make sure it's there, will you? That camera means a lot to me.'

Andrzej leaves with the policeman. I don't know why he was in the office anyway, except that he likes to know everything that's going on. I let out a deep breath and return to my computer station. It's not been a good morning, but I've got away with it and now I just need to use the rest of the day to mend my reputation. I click open my mail and smile when I see Elliot has written to me.

Dear Amber,
You sounded very odd just now. Have you been held hostage and unable to talk? I suppose if you are, then you're unlikely to answer this email. Let me know. I'd really love to see you tonight but if you are being held hostage that would really scupper my plans.
Yours
Elliot

I let out an involuntarily giggle and clap a hand over my mouth. When I glance up, I see Jan glaring at me.

'What agency are you from?' she says, coolly.

A wave of dread washes over me. Not that question, anything but that question. I stare at her unable to speak.

'I'm... I'm with a few.'

'I see,' she says.

I can't lose this job. I need this job. Up until now my track record has been impeccable. The temp agency loves me! What am

I supposed to do if I haven't got any work coming in? Everyone knows that looking for a new job is a job in itself. Plus you always need previous experience and how are you supposed to get experience if you can't get the job unless you've got some?

No, I can't lose this job. I'll run out of money in no time. I can't even move back into my parents' place because they've converted my old room into a mini gym. I'll have to sleep on a yoga mat and vacate it for Mum's early-morning sun salutation. If the temp agency drops me, my independence will be well and truly over.

Jan doesn't say any more and after that she leaves the office.

Chapter 13

Leicester Square Station is a madhouse on a Friday evening. Tourists assemble at every exit and consider their next move with the urgency of Zen monks. I'm one of the Londoners struggling to keep tabs on a soaring temper as I'm jostled up the stairs. My hangover keeps coming back in waves.

Only tourists and people from the suburbs go to Leicester Square. I'm coughed out onto the street and dodge the oncoming human traffic, which is loaded with cameras and maps and leather bum-bags. Some people are dressed up for the evening; others are dressed up for safari, in khaki trousers covered in bulging pockets. I don't understand why people wear survival gear on city breaks. They're staying in a three-star hotel in Russell Square, not a hammock in the Amazon.

I see Elliot standing on the corner of the street, looking like a real city boy in his fitted grey suit and pink shirt. If I'd known we were meeting I would have worn something more attractive. In my black knee-length skirt, white shirt and ballet bumps I look like a waitress. Elliot sees me and his face relaxes into a smile. I feel the tickle of butterflies in my stomach. He waves and my own smile grows.

For the next few seconds I'm like a salmon trying to swim against the current and then I burst through into his small corner of calm. He takes my hand and pulls me over and he's a head above me and looking down at me with misty, brown eyes. I'm expecting a peck on the cheek, but he goes straight for my lips. It's so bold and sexy and I go from being nervous to feeling completely aroused. His hand caresses my cheek and I feel myself slipping out of the chaotic street.

When he pulls back there's a mischievous twinkle in his eyes.

'Hello,' I say, stupidly.

'Hello to you, too.'

He offers me his arm like an old-fashioned gentleman, and I hold on.

'Come on, let's grab a drink at the bar before it starts.'

I'm buzzing with excitement as we manoeuvre through the crowds. My head, which felt so heavy on the tube, is now as light as a balloon. I can't believe we just kissed like that in the middle of the street. People must have thought we were lovers who hadn't seen each other in years!

We need to kiss again to make sure that did just happen. We're bound to kiss again. I mean once you've kissed once, you can't *not* kiss, can you?

I clutch my oversized handbag to my side as I squeeze past a hoard of noisy Italian school children. It's only then I feel the strange lump and remember I'm carrying a bunch of spray-painted bananas.

What if someone at the theatre wants to check my bag? I'm going to look like a complete clown if they confiscate them in front of everybody. I look around for a rubbish bin as we speed-walk towards the theatre. But the only one I can see is on the other side of the road. Even if it was on the right side I'm not sure I'd throw them away anyway. I have a big plan set out for them and it seems heartless to toss them out before they've had a chance to shine.

Of course you can take bananas into the theatre! It's not like taking in your own wine, is it? But you can never be sure in an ancient country like England. There might just be some little known anti-banana law that was established in the fifteenth century when infected bananas caused mass outbreaks of nose-bleeds. I know, for a fact, there's still a law in place that states people suffering from bubonic plague are not allowed to hail a taxi.

'You never told me what we're going to see,' I say, dismissing the increasingly ridiculous scenario in my head.

'I couldn't risk you saying no.'

'Why would I say no? Is it that bad? Tell me! What are we seeing?'

'Don Carlos.'

It doesn't sound like a comedy, which is a shame. I could do with a laugh after the day I've had.

'It's an opera...'

'Oh...'

And by 'Oh', I really mean 'No!'

'Damn, you hate opera, don't you?'

'No, I love it!'

'Really?'

'Yes!'

I hate opera.

'It's supposed to be a really fantastic version,' he says, cheerfully. 'Ground-breaking, even.'

This morning all I thought I was capable of was crawling back into bed. I didn't think I would be saying 'yes' to a gin and tonic in an antique theatre in central London. Hair of the dog, I think, before taking a refreshing gulp, inwardly celebrating avoiding a bag check on the way in.

'Did you catch your friend's reading yesterday?'

'No... And to make it worse, a friend arrived from Argentina to stay at my house and I wasn't there to meet her either... And because she's allergic to cats and I've just bought a kitten, my housemate had to send her over to my friend's house... the same friend whose poetry reading I missed.'

Elliot looks intrigued, which is a relief. I was half-expecting his eyes to glaze over and for him to nod with fake interest. That's what my last date did. He spent the whole time looking over my head at someone else.

'Where does this poet live?'

'Up the road from me.'

'That's useful to have a poet up the road,' he muses.

'Is it? A plumber would be useful, an electrician maybe... but when do you have an emergency that requires a poet?'

He smiles and sips his drink. Then something dawns on him.

'Has he ever written *you* poetry?'

'Me?'

'Yes, you... People still write each other poems, don't they?'

'Do they? They only send me text messages.'

'Don't tell me no one has ever written you a poem!'

I shake my head. I've already lied about being an artist, taking a gap year and loving opera. I think that's more than enough. Now I'm picturing his study with a mahogany bureau filled with scrolls tied with red and purple ribbon. How many girls have poured out their hearts to Elliot in ink and tears?

Roses are red, Violets are blue, Elliot darling, I've fallen for you!

'I've never even seen any of Farrell's poems,' I say, with a shrug.

Does he think less of me now he knows I've never inspired anyone to write a poem about me?

Elliot looks intrigued. 'Never?'

I'd quite like to sit down. My legs are aching, even though I've been sitting down all day long.

'No, just his book... He's been writing it ever since I've known him.'

Farrell used to show me odd pages, pulled out at random, without any context to anchor me in. His writing was elegant, but when I admitted that I hadn't got a clue what was going on, he would instantly withdraw into himself and say it was obviously rubbish, then. It was a relief when he stopped sharing his writing with me. I never knew how to talk about it without offending him.

'He could be writing about you, you know,' Elliot says, looking conspiratorial.

I let out an unattractive snort. It's Farrell's snort. That's what happens when you hang around with the same person too much.

'No way, he'll be writing about the meaning of life...'

Roses are red, Violets are blue... but why are the Roses red and the Violets blue?

'Poetry can have so many layers of meaning, though,' Elliot says.

'That's what I don't like about it.'

He looks surprised. 'You don't like mystery?'

'It's not that. I don't like confusion. If it's important, then you should say it clearly.'

The bell rings to let us know it's time to take our seats. We're in the Royal Circle, which sounds promising. There's a pile-up on the stairs and we sip our drinks as we wait for people to move along.

'Have you ever slept together?' he asks.

No! Of course not!'

'I just thought if you had then he's bound to have written about you.'

Before I can answer, the queue starts to move.

'You should ask to see his poems and see how he reacts.'

'No!' I say, glaring at him. 'To all of that.'

And 'No' to him talking about me sleeping with my best friend. The idea should torment him because he fancies me so much. Can we just get back to the part where we're kissing, please?

'Can we change the subject?'

'Absolutely,' he says, with mock seriousness. 'It's really none of my business what you do with your local poet.'

'I'm going to pour my drink over you if you say 'poet' again!'

'Can I say say "poets"...plural?'

'No!'

But I'm laughing now because there's no way I'm wasting this ridiculously expensive drink.

An usher takes our tickets and shows us where to go. I relax a little when I discover we're in the middle of the front row of the

Royal Circle, which offers a perfect view of the stage and looks over the seats below. I sink into the soft, red velvet seat and discreetly slip out of my shoes. I just need a blanket around my legs and someone to turn the lights off and I'll be in bliss. A power nap will get me through the rest of the evening. The energy from that one kiss is already starting to fade.

The lights dim and the soft touch of his hand on my bare knee takes me by surprise. I glance at him. He's staring straight at the stage. The red curtains are still drawn, but we hear the distant roll of drums and then deep male voices chanting. Smoke creeps under the curtain as it slowly lifts. His hand is still on my knee. The low voices of men are growing louder and stronger. It's Latin. *Ominus. Dominus. Very Ominus.* Bang. Bang. His hand seems to grow heavier with every passing moment and I can't concentrate on anything else.

Why am I so tense? *Ominus. Dominus.* He must have spent a fortune on these tickets and yet I just wish we were chatting over a watery pint, instead of sitting here watching hooded monks walking in circles swinging incense burners.

Maybe I haven't really admitted to myself how much this morning's encounter has affected me. I was accused of stealing police property. For all I know the camera is recording the activities in my kitchen this very minute. It won't be particularly exciting; only Egg walking around in his pants chewing on contraband pepperoni, while talking incessantly to Rupert.

Bang. Bang. *Ominus Dominus...Rather Ominus....*

What's bothering me really is that Jan threatened to fire me. Why else would she have asked me what agency I was from? The weight of that question makes me sink lower in my chair.

Elliot's hand is now gently massaging my knee. It stops and then moves a little way up my thigh. My heartbeat quickens and I put my hand on top of it, to stop it rising any further.

He leans over. 'I'd write you a poem if I slept with you.'

I almost laugh out loud. 'Is that supposed to be romantic?'

'Shssssss...' someone hisses from the row behind.

'Sorry that came out completely wrong,' he whispers back.

The monks file out and the curtains start to come down again; the shortest scene in living history. I can sense Elliot's agitation. I don't blame him.

'I don't want you to judge me on that line.' He leans in closer. 'I blame the pressure of being in this historic hub of creativity...'

'It's too late...' I say, enjoying his discomfort. It's nice not to be the one putting my foot in my mouth for a change.

The man behind us leans forward. 'If you don't be quiet, I'll call security.'

That shuts us up. Elliot leans back in his chair and I close my eyes and try to block out a woman's voice, but there's so much drama in it, it takes me some time.

I dream I'm in my bed under the soft duvet. I smile to myself as Rupert pads along my legs and curls up on my tummy. The best news is that the following day is Saturday and I'm going to sleep so much. I'll sleep until my eyes open. So cosy, so warm...

I jerk to attention as someone grips my arm. I look about me, blinking in the dark and my heart is racing and it takes me a second to remember where I am.

'You were snoring,' Elliot whispers.

'No I wasn't...' I say, mortified.

He smothers a laugh. I don't understand how he could possibly find my sleeping funny. These tickets must be at least fifty pounds each. I am officially the worst date ever.

I rub my face and open my eyes as wide as they can and stare at the woman with the heaving bosoms who's lamenting her life in Italian. How on earth could I have slept through this?

'Shsssss....' comes the man behind me, anticipating Elliot, as he leans over again and says something that makes my heart leap for joy.

'Fuck this, let's escape at the interval and get something to eat.'

The rush of relief is nudged aside by the guilt I feel at

abandoning this opportunity for cultural enrichment. I've been brought up to think of opera in the same way as I think of Brussels sprouts; unpleasant but probably good for you.

'We can't,' I whisper back. 'You bought these tickets...'

'Oh don't worry about that, life's far too short.'

My guilt is alleviated quickly and I start to cheer up. I even start to enjoy the opera. And yet, when the interval comes, we step outside the door and I feel the evening finally begin. We hand the tickets to a tourist couple passing by and they are flabbergasted by the opportunity and thank us in broken English, shaking our hands till our wrists ache.

Elliot offers me his arm.

'Ready?'

I nod. 'Ready.'

Chapter 14

Tucked away in a narrow Soho street we've found a French bistro with a free table.

'Is this alright?' Elliot asks.

The air smells as if it has been seasoned with fresh herbs and my mouth waters as I breathe it in.

'It's perfect.'

Above us the wooden beams have been stained to look old and the walls are distressed white. Candlelight flickers over animated faces and the long, narrow room is filled with conversation and the tinkle of cutlery. Our table is in a corner separated only by a few inches from a couple engaged in a silent attack of two steaks, which I sense might represent their relationship.

A waiter hands us the wine list and menus and then delivers the specials in a thick foreign accent.

'Did you get any of that?' I ask, once he's gone.

'Yes. He said avoid the pot noodles as they're not in season'

I laugh. 'No specials for us, then.'

'We may as well just give up and go home.'

'Are you trying to get out of having dinner with me again?'

He grins. 'Thank you so much for the other night. The success of that show was down to you pinning up all those carrots. I really appreciate it.'

'It was a success then, was it?'

'Not financially, but it was good publicity for Montague. He's just had a table commissioned for the lobby of a hotel in Japan.'

I imagine four carrots supporting an Ikea shelf.

'Has he made many tables before?'

'No. He'll get a carpenter to do it.'

'But he'll design it.'

Elliot looks uncertain.

'What's he doing if he's not designing it? *I'm* very good with carrots. Can *I* design it?'

I love the way he laughs; as if he's been holding it back, then suddenly bursts.

'I think they specifically said no carrots.'

'Avocados then. I can work magic with an avocado.'

The waiter interrupts to take our drinks order and to light the tea light in the red jam jar. Elliot runs a hand through his silky hair as he looks over the wine list. He asks me if I'm alright with the Bordeaux and I nod, as if I had a preference.

'So why do you do it?' I ask.

'Why did I become an art curator?'

'I was talking about helping Montague, but go on, your question covers it.'

What I want to know is, does he work with Montague because he thinks he's genuinely talented or is it some elaborate joke?

'I think it was seeing how useless my artist friends were at marketing themselves. I mean, they'd make an incredible sculpture, or paint a great picture, and then they'd just shove it into storage. I couldn't bear it.'

'So you became an art curator to help your friends? How very noble of you,' I tease.

'No, not noble... I like to organise things and see a project through. Working with Montague is a nightmare but it keeps life interesting... I like that he's so liberated. I'm hoping it will rub off on me.'

I smile and hope that nothing from Montague ever rubs off on my future husband.

'Liberated or crazy?' I muse.

The wine arrives and once Elliot has approved the bottle, the waiter pours it with great elegance.

We raise our glasses and as we smile at each other across the table I feel there's an unspoken promise of adventure in the clink of our toast.

'To your future project,' Elliot says.

You are my future project!

'And to yours!'

The waiter takes our order. We both want the steak with the pommes frites; the latter are classed as extras and probably charged per chip. Elliot wants his steak rare and 'still mooing'. The waiter laughs as if this is an original description.

'God, I sound like my Dad,' he mutters afterwards. 'It's a complete lie, too. I would be pissed off if he brought me a live cow.'

He sets his glass down and presses his fingers against the base, jerking it forwards and back until there's a whirlpool in his wine. I expect this is some trick to aerate the wine and extract the hundred and one subtle flavours. If I copied him I'd probably need something to extract the hundred and one stains down my shirt.

'What is it anyway?' he says. 'Your future project?'

I think of the bananas in my bag. My future project is supposed to begin tonight. Luckily my mobile starts to vibrate, saving me from answering. I dive under the table to grab it. Normally I would have ignored it, but I need to buy some time.

'Amber! Are you home yet?'

It's Farrell and I sense I'm in trouble again.

'Bibi is cooking something delicious. Oh, man, if you could smell it... Hang on.'

I hear a voice in the background.

'She says it'll take another half an hour...'

'What?' I feel a wave of dread. 'But no one told me and now

107

I'm out.'

'How long do you think you'll be?'

'No, I'm out having supper.'

'What?'

He can't believe it and now I'm kicking myself for not giving either of them a call at lunchtime. I'm officially the worst friend ever!

'But you haven't seen Bibi properly since she's arrived. I assumed we were all going to have dinner together!' he lowers his voice. 'She's cooked enough for the Last Supper!'

I laugh nervously. 'Wasn't that just wafers and wine?'

He doesn't reply.

'Sorry, not funny, I'm really sorry. I'm terrible, I'm with a friend, it was very last minute... can you put Bibi on?'

Elliot smiles guiltily at me.

A second later Bibiana is shrieking down the phone. 'AMBER GET YOUR ASS HERE WOMAN! NOW! NO EXCUSES!'

I wince as the volume of her voice kills off a frequency. 'I'm really sorry! I'm on a date.'

'I don't care. Bring him with you. Farrell thinks I've cooked too much. I think he's too skinny.'

'I really can't. We've already ordered.'

'I hate you,' she says.

'I love you too.'

Elliot raises his eyebrows.

'We'll catch up tomorrow, I promise.'

'Fine. Are you going to sleep with him?'

My cheeks are ahead of me, burning bright red before I've even digested her question.

'Actually, don't tell me,' she says. 'I like surprises.'

'Let's talk tomorrow.'

'Fine. Bye!'

I hang up, my cheeks still flushed. 'I'm so sorry about that.'

'The poet?'

'Yes, and my friend.'

'Are you supposed to be somewhere else?'

'Maybe, but I don't want to be.'

Bibiana will forgive me for this. So will Farrell. They're my friends, after all. Surely they want me to find love and happiness.

'Anyway, they were getting on perfectly fine with each other yesterday...'

This morning Farrell has seemed happy enough to have a '*hot lady sleeping in his bed*'. Meanwhile Bibiana hadn't made any complaints about staying with him. They probably don't even want me to be there, so I'm not going to feel guilty.

'I'm relieved. I thought it might be your back-up call to get you out of this date.'

I laugh. Isn't it obvious that I'm madly attracted to him?

'No, I was pretty sure I wouldn't need one of those tonight.'

The chemistry between us makes our tea light flicker wildly as we look at each other. Okay, I know it's the draft, really, as the door opens and closes. But the chemistry is as real.

The waiter appears with our steaks, interrupting the moment and then refills my glass.

'That's not to say I've never done it before... I've been on some terrible dates.'

He brightens and I recognise a fellow gossip.

'Go on, tell me the worst...'

'Well... there was one guy who I'd had a crush on for ages.'

'You've got to set the scene... how long ago?'

'Two years ago. He worked in Costa about twenty minutes from where I was living.'

'Not a high-flyer, then. Was he good looking at least?'

I laugh. 'He was called Joao and he was a Brazilian Capoeira dancer, so you can imagine what his body was like...'

He rolls his eyes. 'Yeah, yeah, whatever.'

'So after months and months of going out of my way to buy coffee, he finally asked me on a date...'

The couple beside us have started to talk to each other and Elliot leans in so he doesn't miss what I'm saying. It feels so good to have his undivided attention.

'Where was the date?' he says.

'In a restaurant.'

'What kind?'

I smile. 'I love that you care.'

'I don't. I'm just a snob.'

I stick my tongue out at him. 'Well, whatever. It was just a Pizza Express off Oxford Street.'

'Oh God. How imaginative.'

'Shut up or I won't tell you!'

He waits with one eyebrow raised.

'So I'm really excited and I'm thinking, this is *the one*...'

Shit. I probably shouldn't have said that. I'll scare him off!

He frowns, but otherwise seems unfazed. 'Really? In Pizza Express?'

'Look, I'm exaggerating for effect!'

'If I'd known Pizza Express was all it took...'

'SO!' I say, feigning exasperation. 'We sit down at our table and he gives me this huge smile and he says...'

'I'm gay?'

'Nope.'

'I used to be a woman?'

'Nope.'

'I'm married?'

'He says...' and I hold up my hand and put on my best Brazilian accent, 'What is your relationship with Jesus?'

Elliot leans back in his chair smiling widely. In reality, Joao and I had talked about London for at least ten minutes before he had thrown out this question.

'It's a valid question. What did you say?'

'Well obviously my heart sank... I knew we weren't going be on the same wavelength after that.'

'Did he try to convert you?'

'Yes. It was awful. He picked holes in every part of my life. He asked me if I was sure I wanted alcohol. He didn't call it wine, no, *alcohol*. Oh and at one point he said that he couldn't go out with someone who wasn't a virgin.'

Elliot's grin grows, encouraging me to go on.

'So I suggested we should end the night soon and go our separate ways because I wasn't a virgin.'

'You're not a virgin?' he gasps, and acts like he's getting up to leave.

I ignore him. 'Then he said, he could forgive me if I turned to Jesus.'

'That's quite a commitment to ask after half a date.'

'I know, he should have left it until date two.'

I polish off my steak and wash it down with the rest of my wine. This is without doubt the best date I've been on for ages. I feel relaxed and happy.

Elliot pours more wine into my glass. I think I should probably have some water, but I can't be bothered to ask for it.

'So tell me what's it like to be an artist?'

My happy feeling fizzles and I feel the onset of panic. I've got to steer the conversation away from art as fast as possible.

'It's good... well, hard... a slog really...'

I'm thinking of Dee, who dropped out of law school to become a musician. I imagine the lifestyle of an artist might be similar to that of a musician; uncertain, full of ups and downs, a bit of a gamble.

'But what about the freedom?'

Dee works harder than any of my friends to pay her way. I wouldn't call that freedom.

'Artists still have to pay bills.'

'Money is so tedious.'

'Only a rich person would say something like that.'

Oops. The wine has loosened my tongue. Is this the third or

fourth glass?

'Not necessarily.'

'I don't think you'll hear some poor sheep herder in Bolivia saying money is boring.'

'Ah, no, but then they're poor but happy, aren't they?' he says, grinning as he sips his wine.

'Oh shut up... Wait, you probably believe that, don't you?'

The couple beside us glance at me warily. What? Too loud?

He's teasing me, I know he is.

'If they're so happy, why don't you go over there and join them?' I challenge. 'You could become a sheep herder too.'

'I think you mean llama herder... or is it alpaca? Which one's the softest?'

'I don't know, you're the well-travelled one.'

'Where did you go on your gap year, then?'

Shit, shit, shit... come on Amber, you're unravelling!

'I didn't get to Bolivia,' I say, my cheeks burning.

'Stopped at Peru, did you?'

I nod my head. Technically if I don't say 'yes' it's not a lie.

'I bought a great alpaca jumper out in Cochabamba... I think I got it down to ten pounds...'

'You haggled?'

'If you don't haggle they think you're an idiot.'

I feel a mixture of relief that we're no longer talking about art or my gap year, but I also feel a little ruffled that a rich boy like him would haggle with a poor alpaca farmer. Generosity is a key quality in a partner I think.

'You know, if I hadn't been conditioned to this lifestyle I might well go,' he says. 'It's too late for me. But what about you?'

'I have a fully functioning toilet in my house which I'm very conditioned to.'

Elliot smiles. 'Are we agreeing to stay in London then?'

'For now.'

'That's good. Bolivia is a bit of a commute and I'd love to see you more often.'

'We'll see about that...' I say, struggling to conceal my delight. 'Ouch.'

I smile. To be honest I can't remember a date when both parties have been so frank about their intentions. We are like one mind as we choose the cheesecake and two forks. When it comes we demolish it strategically, with smiles and innuendo.

As I expected, when the bill comes he won't let me near it. He pays with a card and we head outside to find Soho buzzing with Friday night revellers. The night is young, but judging by some of the drunken shrieks and floppy body language many won't last much longer. It's not a particularly warm summer evening but people spill outside onto the street semi-naked and pretend they're in Lanzarote. Seeing how packed the bars are I feel a wave of tiredness. I feel as if my hangover is back, or maybe it's tomorrow's come a bit early.

I don't think I can face battling for a post-dinner cocktail, only to have to stand holding the freezing glass in my hand whilst shouting at the top of my voice to be heard over the music.

'I'm not sure I can face that crowd,' he says, with a laugh. 'Am I getting too old and boring?'

'To be honest, I feel exactly the same.'

'I fancy something much more...' he curls his fingers through my belt loops and draws me towards him. 'Private.'

His lips press against mine and I feel his tongue slide between them. I draw back at first, wanting more lip than tongue. But he's going for the big film kiss. It's a bit awkward as I'm acutely aware of disgruntled pedestrians being forced to walk around us on the pavement.

I slip my hands under his jacket and run them over the taut muscles of his back. His tongue is slowing down. That's better. I don't want another bar. What I want is to be transported out of these noisy streets to some luxurious hotel room with feather pillows and sheets made of Egyptian cotton.

What I don't want is to go home to Egbert and cat poo.

He pulls away and the question in his eyes makes my heart beat quicken. It's a first date; I know I shouldn't. But I look into that handsome, confident face and my will power weakens. I want to take that shirt off and run my hands over his sun-kissed skin.

Sod the bananas. Sod everything. I haven't felt the touch of a man in nine months and I'm feeling a strong urge to mount his Appaloosa and ride off into the night!

Then again, if I don't do anything with the bananas nothing will ever change. And I've got to do something or Elliot will soon find out I've lied about being an artist.

'So...' I say.

'So.' He takes the tendril of hair that's fallen from my ponytail and pushes it behind my ear. 'So where do you live?'

'Me?'

He nods.

'Uh... east.'

'Shall we get a cab there?'

No! He can't come to mine! My bedroom is a disgrace, with a week's worth of clothes strewn across the floor and God knows what else. Plus there's very little in it to suggest I'm an artist.

'Oh, you don't want to go to mine, no, no...' I say, waving a hand dismissively.

What if Rupert has contributed something stinky to the pile-up? Then there's Egg, who might be potty-trained, but won't necessarily react favourably to this unannounced visitor.

'No, I was thinking more along the lines of... yours?' I say.

'Mine? The problem is it's a bit of a bombsite at the moment... I'm having some things done to it...'

'That's alright by me.'

White dust must be better than cat shit.

'No, really, it's not,' he says. 'But can't we go to yours?'

His hands are on my hips again and he's kissing me. His warm tongue runs along mine and it would be so sexy if I wasn't picturing

Egg in a loin cloth. What if he's having another reenactment meeting? There's no way I can let Elliot witness that.

'My housemate's got this thing,' I say, pulling back.

'What sort of thing?'

'An acting thing...'

He frowns. 'So he's an actor?'

'Sort of.'

'And he's got lines to learn?'

I nod.

'Can't we just be quiet?'

'He's shy...'

'A shy actor? That must be tough.'

'It is.'

A flicker of disappointment crosses his face. We've already told each other we don't want to battle for another drink. We could change our minds, though, couldn't we?

'Well, we could go for a drink...' I say.

He looks at his watch. 'I don't know, we don't want to ruin it.'

I think he just did, by saying that.

'I'm sorry. That came out wrong,' he says. 'It's just I'm supposed to be running with a friend at the crack of dawn tomorrow. I'm doing the London Marathon next year and we're taking it pretty seriously.'

'Wow.'

Let's just add marathon runner to the list of why this man is amazing.

'You're not angry?'

'You just bought me a delicious dinner, I'm furious.'

He offers me his arm. 'Come on, I'll walk you to the station.'

But we only get to the end of the street before I let go.

'Actually, I'm going to walk...'

He looks astonished. 'To East London?'

'No, to a bus stop...'

'Oh.'

I can tell he doesn't fancy the idea and I'm fine with that as I've got a mission to carry out; a mission I was very close to giving up on.

'Go to the station,' I say. 'I'll be fine.'

Our goodbye kiss reassures me that we'll see each other again and I'm in a great mood as I make my way to Trafalgar Square. The wine and the kisses have put me in a very generous mood and I forgive him for bartering with the alpaca trader. At least he bought a jumper. In fact, I'm sure he single-handedly boosted the Bolivian economy.

Enough. Now is not the time to speculate on my future with the handsome Elliot Frinton-Smith. No. Now is the time for focusing all my energies on my career as an artist.

I feel nervous and excited as I reach the National Gallery and head down the stone steps into the iconic square. It's growing dark and the fountains are illuminated by floodlights. Watched by their parents, two small children perch on the edge of one of them and dip their hands in the water. Here and there tourists pose for photos.

My heart thumps in my chest as my task draws nearer. There are people sitting on the benches around the edge of the square and others taking photos of the huge bronze lions that are seated at the base of Nelson's column. I walk with purpose towards the monument.

There are three huge steps between the ground and the column and I clamber up to the top. From there, I look out across at the square. I am in between two of the lions. It must be one of the most-photographed places in London. Even now, there are people squatting and squinting, hoping for the best angle of an image that has been perfected on a hundred postcards.

Taking a deep breath I reach into my bag and pull out my bunch of spray-painted bananas, which are a little worse for wear, but still predominantly pink. I set them down and the huge step seems to swallow them up. There's nothing more I can do now.

I feel like a criminal fleeing a crime scene as I jump down the steps and head off. I don't stop to take in the reaction of the photographers. I don't look back until I'm on the other side of the stone balustrade that surrounds the square.

I watch a Japanese tourist approach the first step, then turn to his friend and point up at the bananas. My heart is in my mouth as he holds up his iPad. A moment later he starts tapping away at his glowing screen.

Of course! He must be sharing it on Twitter!

This is how it all starts.

One little click.

Chapter 15

I wake with a jolt as a bright light cuts through my dream. It's so blinding it hurts to open my eyes. Someone is shining a torch in my face. Beyond the glare I make out Egg's silhouette.

'Who *are* you?' he says.

'What the hell are you doing? Turn that off!'

He lowers the torch and I rub my eyes and sit up in bed. It must be the early hours of the morning. Outside my window I can see it's still dark.

'Are you MI5?'

Is he drunk? Is this some pot-induced paranoia fit?

'MI6...7? 8!'

'What are you talking about?!'

'Tell me!' he pleads. 'Who are you working for?'

'You know who I'm bloody working for, Egg. I complain about the agency on a regular basis.'

'So you *are* a secret agent!'

'Yes, I'm a secret temp agent! It's very hard to get work because no one knows who I bloody am.'

Egg looks unhappy.

'Of course I'm not a secret agent, you nutcase! Do you think my bedroom would really be this messy if I was?'

'Then *why*, Amber? Are you working undercover for the tax

office?'

He's lost it. All those books have finally got to him. His brain has been chewed up by theories and spat out. Any minute now and he's going to start checking my cupboards for aliens. I snatch up my phone, which for once is on my bedside table and the clock tells me it's four in the morning.

'Okay Egg, what have you taken? Should I be ringing the hospital to get your stomach pumped?'

He holds my gaze for a moment then his face crumples and he flops down at the end of my bed with his head in his hands. I don't know much about drugs. I don't know how I managed to go through university without ever coming into contact with any, but I did. My friends and I didn't need much. We were content with beer and tequila shots. I probably should know what it means to take acid. In my head I can't separate it from the horrible burning stuff that can melt human flesh like an ice cream in the sun. How people swallow it remains a mystery to me.

'I couldn't sleep...' he says. 'I was just lying there thinking and thinking...'

He hesitates, his attention turns to the rubbery strands sprouting from the end of his torch, which he starts to pick at.

'Come on, spit it out.'

'I was thinking about Bibiana.'

'And?'

'I asked her out.'

So this is the irrational behaviour of a broken-hearted man.

'She said yes.'

'What? ...Really?'

He looks puzzled. 'Why are you so surprised?'

'Well... I thought she'd said no and that's why you were thinking about it.'

'Why would she say no?'

It's too early for this. He could have at least made me a cup of tea to make this more bearable.

'What's the problem, Egg? Don't you know where to take her?'

Did she really say yes?

'I'm taking her to the British Museum so she can get a feel for who I am... and a feel for Egypt...'

I nod my head as if the very act might shift my thoughts along a bit quicker, because I'm confused. Why are we talking about this at four o'clock in the morning?

'So what does this have to do with me being a secret agent?'

He sits up and flashes the torch in my face again. This time I'm awake enough to snatch it off him. I switch it off and we're plunged into gloomy pre-dawn light. I turn my bedside lamp on and I turn to look into his pale face, part-masked by his ginger beard. I wonder if he's going to trim it a bit. At the moment he looks like a radical Scottish imam.

'As I was saying, I was thinking and thinking...'

'Yes, I got that.'

'And then I decided I may as well make something rather than lie there thinking about the same thing over and over, so I went to the kitchen and thought, Amber keeps saying we should eat the bananas...'

I clap my hand over my mouth. Of course, the toxic bananas!

'They've made you hallucinate?'

He frowns. 'No. I didn't eat any. I dug my hand in to get one but then I found...'

'What?'

All I can think of is, 'more bananas'.

'I found your spyware.'

And then it comes, the memory of that uncomfortable morning...Policeman Perkins! The camera!

'Oh my God! I was supposed to ring him straight away! What have you done with it? I've got to hand it into the police!'

Egbert leaps off my bed and holds his palms up. 'I didn't do anything! You can never prove it!'

'It has nothing to do with you or whatever you've done. Wait, what have you done?'

'Nothing!' He looks sheepish. 'Perhaps some tax evasion here and there, when I was younger, nothing big, the print on the form was too small, it was unavoidable really...'

'Whatever. It turns out the sack I took home was part of a bloody police operation.'

He looks incredulous. 'You sabotaged a police operation?'

'Maybe, but it was a pretty stupid one. I probably did them a favour.'

In the silence that ensues I realise that I'm wide awake and unlikely to fall back to sleep easily. If Egg was a reasonable human being he would apologise for the intrusion and leave. In turn I would forgive him and slide back under the covers. But neither of us follows these obvious paths.

'Well I'm glad you're not an agent,' Egg says. 'Now I can go back to making banana bread for Bibiana.'

'What about the bleach?'

'It'll be alright if they're cooked.'

'Well don't use them all because I need some too.'

I throw off my duvet and get out of bed. From the pile of clothes on my floor I retrieve a baggy hoodie, which I use for a dressing gown.

The point of being an artist is to avoid the monotony of an office timetable. Four o'clock in the morning is as good as any to get on with a project.

'Here's your spyware,' Egg says, passing me a small camera.

I pick it up and stick my tongue out at the lens.

'They might be watching,' Eggs says.

'Pulling faces isn't a criminal offence.'

There's no light on. The batteries must have run out ages ago. I text the number Perkins gave me to confirm I've found it and turn my attention to my bananas.

Outside on the little patio, I hang up a bunch on our clothes dryer and blast paint at it. It doesn't take long before I'm bored of the colour pink and take a trip to one-eyed Rose. He doesn't seem to find it at all strange that I require materials at 5 o'clock in the morning. He's done the night shift and has probably seen every possible permutation of drunkard going.

I'm expecting another colour lottery with a dusty can disguised as yellow paint, however my previous visit seems to have inspired him to increase his stock and I'm treated to a range of lime green, powder blue and red. I hand over my credit card and take home all three.

While I spray merrily away outside, Egg mashes bananas and talks to Rupert. There's something magical about working when so much of the country is asleep. It's peaceful and the light is watery and gentle. Birds shift in the neighbour's overgrown shrubbery, flapping their wings as the branches buckle and bounce. Without the hum of rush-hour traffic, their song carries so clearly. In a city of eight million it's quite something to experience these moments of tranquility. If you're lucky you can escape it without leaving it behind.

I take a break from spraying and look up at a passing plane, shielding my eyes from the glare. Those tourists are the lucky ones. They've caught London enjoying a rare hot summer. They won't have to go back home confirming the rumour that the English capital is always rainy and grey. Though the sun has yet to fully rise in the sky, it's already obvious that it's going to be a scorcher. It's great news for my bananas as it means they'll dry quickly and I'll be able to carry out my plan. This afternoon I'm going to deposit them across the city.

Chapter 16

'I'm so sorry about the other night,' I say to Bibiana.

We're sitting outside a café pretending we're in Paris and not a dusty high street in Dalston. We've finally got away from everyone to have a real catch-up. Farrell is at the library working on his book and Egg is at home giving a private lecture on the role of cats in 40 BC Egypt to Rupert.

'Come on,' she says, plucking a cigarette from her pack. 'You were on a date; you don't need to be sorry. How did it go?'

That warm, happy feeling from last night bubbles up again.

'It was great!'

'Where did you go?'

The memory of the opera makes me groan. 'Oh it was so embarrassing... First we went to the theatre and I fell asleep.'

'Amber!'

'I know, and then he took me to dinner.'

'Did you manage to stay awake for that? Because that's not what I meant when I asked if you were you going to sleep with him...' She narrows her eyes. 'Did you?'

'No, you know me, I'm a good girl.'

'Yeah, right...'

'Well, we wanted to... but his flat's a building site apparently and I didn't want him to come to mine in case Rupert had pooed in my bed.'

She wrinkles her nose. 'That's so disgusting. You know that bloody cat is keeping everyone away, don't you?'

'In hindsight Rupert did me favour. I'm glad I didn't sleep with him on our first date.'

'So you'll see him again?'

'Yes. Definitely. I've got a good feeling about this one.'

She raises an eyebrow. 'Oh, really? When do I get to meet him then?'

'I don't know; give it a month!'

'What does he do?'

'He's an art curator.'

She looks impressed. 'Cute?'

'Gorgeous.'

'Have you got a picture?'

'No.'

'You should have taken a sneaky one.'

'How?'

'Oh yeah, I forgot you were sleeping the whole time.'

'It was five minutes of the entire date...'

'That's five minutes too much.'

I laugh. 'True... What about you anyway? Any men mourning your departure from Argentina?'

'The whole country is in mourning. But I don't want a man. This year it's going to be about me getting a life for *me*. I mean, everyone's doing exciting things, aren't they? Have you heard? Jess has only got herself a translation job in the fucking UN... Helen's setting up her own design company... what's Dee doing?'

'She's still working on her music...'

'Okay, but everyone else is doing amazing stuff.'

I think about my bananas and wonder if I should tell her about my plans. She carries on talking about everyone who used to sleep in our halls. The coffee arrives with a chocolate brownie to share. I break bits off, aware if she doesn't stop talking I'll end up eating the lot.

'What about you, Amber?' she says suddenly.

'Me?'

'Farrell said you were searching...'

'Did he really?... Searching for what?'

'Meaning... purpose...that kind of thing...

'Oh God. That sounds serious.'

She smiles, 'you can't be a temp forever.'

'I could.'

'But do you want to?'

I let out a deep breath. 'The advantage of being a temp is that I don't have to commit to one boring job. I get to do two weeks of a boring job here and then one day of another boring job there... it makes life less boring...'

'But you're not working towards anything... doesn't that worry you?'

'Sometimes... but what am I supposed to be working towards exactly? A slightly dull but stable job? A mortgage? I want to do something more exciting, I want my life to be less predictable.'

'Well, do something about it, then!' Bibiana says, clapping the heels of her hands together, causing ash from her cigarette to float to the table. 'Not all jobs are boring. There are loads of great opportunities out there, but you've got to break out of this little safe cycle you're in.'

'It's not a safe cycle.'

'It is. It pays well enough and it doesn't involve much responsibility.'

'I sound like I'm living the dream.'

'Except you're totally bored and deep down you know you could be doing more with your life.'

'Not that deep down... more on the surface really.'

'You've got to think about what you love doing, what you care about...' I think of my bananas and suddenly wish so badly that they were the answer.

125

'I'm going to do something about it.'

'Good. I don't like people who moan about a situation and never do anything to change it.'

'Who does like those people?'

She leans back in her chair and pushes her sunglasses up onto her head. The sun came out for a while but now it's back behind the clouds. She stubs out her cigarette and then pops a piece of brownie in her mouth, chewing on it thoughtfully.

'He's lovely, isn't he?' she says.

I think of Elliot. She's never met him. 'Who?'

'Farrell.'

Oh. Of course. Her wonderful host.

'Remember when Eva broke up with him? I think you wanted to punch her in the face.'

'No I didn't. I wanted to punch *him* in the face for being such a wuss about it.'

'He's a writer. He's sensitive.'

I stick my fingers in my mouth and mock vomit.

'What?' she cries, laughing.

'Writers are just normal people. He was a wuss and it was really annoying.'

'He's considerate and calm ... and cute.'

Does she fancy Farrell now? I flare my nostrils at her. 'I thought you said you didn't want a man.'

'What?' she laughs. 'I don't. I'm just saying... he's got a lot going for him, you should set him up with someone.'

'I don't know anyone.'

Half my friends are already paired off. The other half aren't suitable. It's up to him to find a girl because my days of matchmaking are over.

'And he's fit,' she says. 'Like healthy fit.'

'No, he's not.'

'Well he runs...'

'Since when?'

This is the first I've heard of it.

'In the morning, he jogs...'

'Shut up!'

I'm surprised. I thought I knew everything about Farrell.

Bibiana sips her coffee and looks smug. I take a bigger lump of brownie and suck on it. In my head I try to imagine Farrell jogging. Does he wear shorts or a tracksuit? What music does he listen to? Miserable but lyrically beautiful ballads or pumping work-it baby dance music? If he listens to dance, then I don't know who he is any more.

'What time are we going?' she says.

'Where?'

'The British Museum.'

'*We*? Egg seemed to think it was just you and him.'

She laughs. 'He's so funny.'

'I don't think he means to be.'

'We're all going. You, me, Egg, Farrell... or have you got another date to go to?'

I sigh. 'Not yet.'

The British Museum is as good a place as any to plant a spray-painted banana.

'What are you thinking?' she says.

I may as well tell her my plan. If I'm serious about it, I'm going to have to talk about it sooner or later.

'I'm thinking about bananas.'

I wait for her to make some joke, but she doesn't. She looks at me curiously.

'Is this some crazy art project? Farrell said you were trying to come up with some whacky idea...'

'That's exactly what it is.'

She grins. 'Excellent. Tell me, then, what exactly are you up to?'

Half an hour later she's appointed herself Head of Marketing of the London Bananification Project and outlined several plans of action. She's talking social media strategies, viral content, social lead generation, brand management, blogger outreach... She's ticking acronyms off her fingers as if she's reciting some very long and incorrect alphabet. It's ages before I can get a word in edgeways.

'So basically, you want me to join Twitter?' I say.

She looks at me in despair. 'Oh my God, it's a little more than that babe.'

'Well I'm already on Facebook...'

'It's lucky I don't have a job right now because you need all the help you can get.' It's one thing to dabble in an idea, knowing that you could technically pull out at any moment and not let anyone down. Having an employee invested in the idea is another matter entirely. Okay, so she might be an unpaid volunteer, but I know Bibiana and I can tell she means business. Things have just got a lot more serious. Half of me wishes I could rewind the conversation back to the part where we were just talking about dating, the other half is thrilled I won't be able to back out now.

Chapter 17

We travel to the British Museum by tube. I sit opposite Bibiana, who flicks through a thin London guidebook. She has reapplied her make-up and her dark eyes are thickly lined with kohl, which makes them look huge. It occurs to me that she might just be one of those people who could look good with a shaved head. Then again she is lacking symmetry on the nose front, which a bit leaning tower of Pisa. Anyway, she can't know how excited her dark eyes must have made Egg. She looks quite the Cleopatra.

As well as being the future historic Queen of Egg's social life, Bibiana is also delivering on her job as marketing director. I am now signed up on Twitter as @lookabanana. Originally I wanted to be @LondonBananas but then realised it would limit me. Successful people always think big. I've since imagined the Statue of Liberty thrusting a giant, purple banana up into the sky. The other reason I didn't get that name was because it's already been taken by someone who photographs banana skins in urban settings. I followed them last night and they didn't give me much of a warm welcome.

@LondonBananas another copycat has joined the melee. Don't mix us up with @lookabanana #keepingitreal

After I'd got over the shock, I finally managed a reply.

@lookabanana Not a copycat. I'm more into bringing bananas to life rather than focusing on their death and decay.

I wanted to add a hashtag #getoveryourselves, but I was worried that would provoke an online war, and I want @lookabanana to be the peaceful strand of the banana appreciation movement. @LondonBananas didn't respond and I like to think they felt bad about being so hostile. I look over at Egg to check how he's coping. He's sitting beside Bibiana with his eyes closed. He's imagining buffalo pastures, endless open space. He hates the tube. Beside him is Farrell, who has put off shaving for another day and has a bristly stubble. Personally I think it's getting too long. He's got such good lips; full, defined, the lips of moody male models. Why would you want a beard to distract from such a feature?

My best friend's in a good mood and keeps winking at my bag and laughing.

'We should put a bunch on a mummy,' he says.

I've been thinking the same thing all morning, but I can't see how we'll get away with it. The mummies are one of the main attractions in the museum and people are always huddled around them.

'There's bound to be security,' I say.

There are a few furtive glances my way from passengers near by. Everyone's very edgy on the tube. Discomfort can be created using keywords including 'security', 'bomb', 'terrorist' and 'vomit'. Phrases such as 'whose bag is that?' And 'there's a busker playing the banjo heading our way,' also make commuters unhappy.

'We'll create a diversion,' Farrell says. 'Then we'll plant it.'

The woman reading her book beside him doesn't move her eyes from the page but they grow significantly wider.

'I don't know,' I say. 'I think it's better to put them where there are more people. It'll have more impact.'

The woman steals a glance at me. I smile brightly back at her and she scowls. A disapproving scowl is what tube passengers resort to when something really terrible is happening. The norm is to stare vacantly ahead and pretend nothing is wrong.

'Outside, then,' Farrell says. 'Where everyone sits near the pillars and has their lunch.'

The British Museum looks like an Ancient Greek temple with its rows of huge stone columns and decorative carved pediments with statues dressed in bed sheets. As expected on a Saturday afternoon, the place is packed with tourists. Half of Japan, styled by Burberry, is posing at the gate for photos. There are teachers yelling at school children in foreign languages. Most of them are too old to chase pigeons but are doing it all the same. Smaller kids toss crisps at the birds, then run away squealing.

I hold back as Bibiana and Egbert head up the stone steps to the entrance.

'Go on ahead, I'll come in a bit,' I call after them.

Farrell turns to look at me.

'What are you plotting?'

In an ideal world I'd fly up to the top of the building and balance a bunch of bananas where the roof meets in a point, high up above the crowds. Some people would think it a publicity stunt by a supermarket; others the start of the apocalypse. As long as they notice them I don't really mind what they think. I'm hoping the general public will establish a concept for me.

'Shall I just leave them on the steps?'

There are people walking up and down all around us. Despite the width available, people still feel compelled to tut and mutter under their breath as they divert past me.

'You don't want people stepping on them.'

'They'll definitely notice them that way.'

'For about five second and then they'll be ruined and no one else will see them.'

'What do you suggest, then? Shall we throw them at people?'

'No, Amber, of course I don't think we should throw bananas at people.'

131

'Come on, let's put them at the bottom of one of the columns. At least they won't get stepped on.'

When we get to the top of the steps we find that Egg and Bibiana have disappeared inside. I pass the bananas over to Farrell and ring my housemate.

'We have a lot of history to get through,' Egg replies grumpily. 'We're in Mesopotamia. We can't wait.'

Farrell doesn't look too disappointed by our abandonment. In fact, I think we're both pleased to avoid a private tour with the man who knows everything.

'Right,' I say, taking the bunch off Farrell and placing them swiftly and without ceremony at the base of the column.

'Is that it?' Farrell calls, as I stride off.

Plant and run is the way I do it. No fireworks. No fanfare. It would be better if I had a special plinth with smoke coming out of it. Couldn't I use dry ice? I turn around and Farrell bumps into me. I grab his arm and pull him over to a column further along.

'Now we watch,' I say.

'Have you done this before?'

'In Trafalgar Square.'

'When were you there?'

'The other day.'

'No way! With Elliot? Is he nuts too, then?'

I blush. 'No. I was alone.'

'I guess littering isn't first-date etiquette.'

'It's not littering. It's art. I'm littering the city with art.'

He snorts with laugher. 'You keep telling yourself that.'

A few people have noticed the bananas. Some stop from a safe distance and squint at them. They nudge their friends and their partners, nod their head at it. There's vague interest, slight confusion, but little willingness to get too involved.

'Come on, take a photo someone...'

Farrell is laughing quietly beside me. I watch a woman with curly red hair bend right over and stare at it for a full minute.

She's wearing a colourful headscarf and enough leather necklaces around her neck to open a stall. I think she looks like a potential message-spreader. She just needs a little more encouragement.

'Go over, Farrell,' I say suddenly. 'Quick! Go over and take a picture!'

The woman is straightening up. She's coming to the conclusion that maybe a bunch of red bananas isn't such a rarity in such a diverse city as London.

'Please, Farrell! Go over! Create some hype!'

'Why me?'

'I can't go; I'm the artist! I'm anonymous!'

'You owe me one.'

The woman with the headscarf turns to look at him as he sidles up beside her. He says something that makes her laugh, then he digs his phone out of his pocket and fiddles about with it before squatting down and holding it steady to take a picture. The woman moves back a step but looks as if she doesn't want to leave. She starts fiddling with the clasp on her small leather satchel. Yes! She's getting her camera!

Egg and Bibiana might be getting an education, but Farrell and I are pulling off a publicity stunt, and in this dog-eat-dog world we're the ones who won't be going home hungry.

But the feeling of triumph is short-lived. Before the woman has even taken her camera out of its knitted sock, a hunched figure appears who makes my heart slump. He's wearing a high-visibility waistcoat over his green overalls and he's dragging a broom behind him. Without warning or apology he reaches for the bananas and starts to walk away with them.

'Excuse me...' Farrell calls weakly. But he doesn't make a move. He's not the one who's emotionally invested here. He wasn't outside at stupid o 'clock this morning spray-painting them. I hurry after the dustbin man calling at the top of my voice.

'Wait! Man with the bananas! Wait!'

He turns slowly and looks at me, then at the bright-red bananas in his hand. He has thick grey sideburns that spread over his cheeks like Sherlock Holmes. I can imagine him with a pipe.

'Why did you move them? They're an installation!'

I'm breathless from my brief run and my heart is beating fast. There's no turning back now. It's all or nothing. Did I ever think it could be any other way?

'They're bananas, love,' the man says, his lips curling.

'No they're not! Look! They're red!'

'If my wife dyes her hair red, is she still my wife? Or should I prop her up against a pillar and call her an installation?'

He starts walking off towards his small rubbish trolley.

'Well, actually, some people *would* do that!' I call after him. 'In fact I think it's quite a good idea! Wait!'

He doesn't wait.

'They're mine, give them back!'

He holds them above the wide mouth of his rubbish bag, which is fastened to a metal frame and he savours the power as I stand there squirming.

'Are you admitting to littering the British Museum, Madam?'

'It's not littering! It's art!'

'I'm a litter specialist and this is litter. Now how would you like to pay your fifty grand fine?'

My choked laughter causes the deep trenches of his scowl to deepen.

This is theft. He has stolen my bananas!

'I don't know, maybe I'll pay with my library card, do you take library card? Or maybe my bus pass? Or can I pay with coupons? What about Paypal?'

He grits his teeth and hurls the bananas into his rubbish bin.

'Count yourself lucky, Madam,' he says, before gripping the handle of his trolley and moving off.

'I don't know how you sleep at night!' I cry. 'You work at a temple of culture, but you wouldn't see culture if it slapped you in the face!'

Someone grips my arm.

'Amber, calm down!'

Farrell is looking at me as if I've gone mad. Then he nods his head at the people taking photos of me standing there as red as the bananas that have just had their opportunity to shine snatched from them.

'I think they all got it,' he says, and he starts to smile. 'I think your little display might have just got those bananas on the map.'

I see what he means. I suppose the kerfuffle might have increased their visibility. I don't want to get my hopes up, but maybe it wasn't a complete flop after all.

'So what next, my fair artist?' he says.

'Big Ben?'

He gives me a cheeky wink. 'I was thinking more along the lines of a pint.'

'I could work with that.'

Bibiana and Egg can fall in love amidst the scattered remains of old empires and Farrell and I will approach culture from the other side, in a traditional pub with wooden beams and couches that smell of stale beer.

As soon as we're on the other side of the museum gates I feel much calmer.

'I can't believe what you shouted at that poor man...' Farrell says. He flares his nostrils and mimics my stupid voice. *'I don't know how you sleep at night! You wouldn't see culture if it slapped you in the face!'*

'Oh shut up.'

'Well, I'll hand it to you, you are passionate!'

'He was right, you know... they are just bananas...'

'We're all just bananas sometimes.'

I laugh and link my arm in his. It feels good to be out with my partner in crime.

135

Chapter 18

In the pub we choose a table by a window that looks out onto the British Museum. It now also looks out onto a bunch of lime-green bananas that I've perched on the window sill. A random pub doesn't have the same clout as Big Ben or Buckingham Palace, but it's better than keeping all the bananas in my bag, where they were getting bruised and losing their colour. The front of the pub is a bit too picturesque, frankly. With its abundance of flower baskets and hanging ivy my little organic installation is likely to be overlooked.

Farrell rests our pints on the table and beer dribbles down the side of the glasses adding a ring of history to the wood. He slides along the bench on the other side of me and turns to check on the bananas as he sips his beer. I've reminded him about the elephants that were once all over London. It's the same principle. We've got to surprise Londoners, make them stop in their tracks and want to share.

'We need a list of places where we're going to put them,' he says.

'Agreed.'

I pull a serviette from under the cutlery on the table and he provides the pen. I write down the first place that occurs to me.

No.1 Downing Street.

'It's number 10,' Farrell says.

'I'm making a list.'

'Then you should put number 1, 10 Downing Street.'

I roll my eyes in mock exasperation.

He grins, enjoying himself, 'If you're going to involve me in your crazy projects then I need some say.'

His smile is contagious.

'Fine.'

I add a 0 to the 1.

'Next?'

No. 2 Buckingham Palace

'I don't know, Amber, isn't that treason?'

'Why should you care? You're Irish.'

'Fair enough.'

No.3 Houses of Parliament.

'Are we trying to make a political statement?'

'Yes. Just don't ask me what it is.'

No.4 Big Ben

'We could swap the clock hands for two bananas!'

How would you fix bananas onto a smooth clock face? Gaffer tape? They'd be too small, though, we'd have to make bigger bananas. What about using plantains?

'You're thinking about it, aren't you?' he says.

'Of course I am... don't we know someone who works in Big Ben?'

Farrell pulls out his mobile phone. 'Yeah, of course, my man Tony. I'll just give him a buzz to see if we can pop over now.'

I reach for the phone, laughing, and grab it off him. 'It was a fair question! How am I supposed to know what contacts you do or don't have?'

'Just so you know, I've got no friends in Buckingham Palace either.'

'Not even a cleaner?'

'Nope.'

I look down at my serviette notebook and add a fifth location.

'That's risky. What if the ravens peck at them and get poisoned? You know what they say will happen if the ravens leave the Tower?'

'That pigeons will replace them?'

He looks at me solemnly. 'No, that the crown will fall and Britain with it.'

'Well, as before, why should you care? You're Irish.'

'Good point. I don't give a flying fuck.'

'And anyway if they bury the poisoned ravens within the Tower, then they haven't actually left it.'

'Well their souls have and maybe that's enough.'

I take a large gulp of beer and review our list. It's not going to be easy.

'Have you told them we're here?' he asks.

'Yes, I texted them.'

'Egg must be having the time of his life,' Farrell says grinning. 'Poor Bibiana.'

'Oh she can handle him.'

'I'm sure she can. She's good fun, isn't she? I don't remember her much at university... wasn't she really quiet?'

His selective memory never ceases to surprise me.

'You don't remember her temper?'

He looks surprised. 'Not really.'

'I bet you remember Eva as an angel as well.'

'Eva wasn't so bad.'

I glare at him. The hours I spent consoling him in a pub just like this. We had our own special recovery-from-Eva corner. He would pour out all the crap she'd done and said during the week. I'd confirm that, yes what she'd done and said was crap and he shouldn't take it. And then he would say yes, it was crap, he would do something about it. And then the following week we'd be in the same corner.

'It wasn't her fault. If I'd had some balls back then she wouldn't have been such a bitch.'

'Finally, you've seen the light.'

'I wonder what she's doing now.'

'No, stop it now. I've wasted enough of my life talking about Evil Eva.'

Farrell laughs. 'Fine...fine...'

I say it without thinking. 'How's the book going anyway?'

It's like asking someone with a terminal illness if they're feeling better. I regret it immediately. Okay, so writing might not be quite as bad as that but it does seem to make him tired, melancholy and, like a terminal illness, it never really goes away.

'Actually, it's going well...'

Wow. That's the most positive answer I've had in years, now I need to get him off the subject before he talks himself into a black hole.

'That's good, then.'

'I mean I don't know how good it is...'

Too late, he's off.

'I mean, I've been working on it so long that I've lost perspective. It could be amazing or it could be complete shite.'

'You can't please everyone.'

'No, I know. But no one likes complete shite.'

'Rubbish! People *love* complete shite! Send it off, Farrell. Just send the bloody thing off to an agent! You said yourself that every writer has to get at least ten rejections before they get an acceptance.'

Farrell's bad taste in girlfriends isn't the only recurring topic of conversation in our friendship. Literary rejection is another popular one. I know that C.S. Lewis had 800 rejections before he sold anything, Rudyard Kipling was told he didn't know how to use the English language, and the author of *The Great Gatsby* was told his book would be much better if he'd only lose the Gatsby character. I haven't read any of their books, so there's a big chance I might agree with the editors that rejected them, but that's not the point.

'Who says I haven't sent it off already?'

That stops me in my tracks. He winks at me, a cheeky grin on his face.

'Have you?'

'Yes. But please don't keep asking me if I've heard anything, okay. If I do, I'll tell you.'

'Fine.' I raise my pint glass, 'To your book finding a sympathetic agent!'

'And to your bananas making the evening news.'

We clink glasses and I glance out the window to check on my bananas. I'm disappointed to see that two men have placed their beers on either side of the bunch and are occasionally tapping their cigarettes over it as if it were an ashtray.

'So where shall we go first?

Farrell drains his pint. 'I don't know about you, but I'm going to the bar. Same again?'

I respond with a dramatic sigh. 'This is not going to buy the baby a pram, is it?'

'Good job we don't have a baby, then.'

'Fine! Same again.'

While he's at the bar I find myself grinning to myself. I'm not the only one that has selective memory, I suppose. Farrell had some rough moments back at university, but most of the time he was fun to be around. That's why we're still friends.

I can't help thinking, though, that things won't be like this forever between us. I mean, when he gets a girlfriend we're bound to hang out less. It's inevitable. I'll also want to spend more time with Elliot if things get serious. I just hope the people we end up with don't ever resent us being such close friends. It would make me doubt the person I was with if they didn't get on with Farrell.

I look out the window and indulge myself in a daydream where we're both dressed up as Beefeaters, the famous guards of the Tower of London. Farrell redirects the tourists while I deactivate the burglar alarm and reach for the crown jewels, which I'm to replace with blue bananas. I don't get to finish the job as the sound of my mobile interrupts my reverie. I think I see Egg's name flashing on my screen.

'We're in the pub across the road,' I say.

The well-spoken voice that replies gives me butterflies. 'You're going to have to be a little more specific than that.'

'Elliot?'

'Amber.'

Farrell returns with the pints and sets them down.

'Have they reached the mummies yet? Ask if there's much security.'

I shake my head at him. I hate having phone conversations in front of other people. It's like sharing a toilet cubicle. Why do girls do that?

'I missed you last night,' Elliot says with such ease he could be talking about the weather.

There's a pause where I'm not sure if I'm supposed to say I missed him too.

'We were idiots to go home so early,' he continues, 'I sat in my pyjamas and watched television until 2 am and then I was completely knackered for this morning's run. I would've been less tired if we'd got pissed. So what do you say, do you fancy a mooch around Notting Hill?'

'When?'

'Today, now... carpe diem or carpe afternoonem, at least.'

'That would be so nice.'

Farrell nods at the window. I follow his gaze and see that a young girl with pink hair is taking a picture of the bananas. She looks very serious as she checks her screen and then abruptly walks away.

'Definitely a blogger,' Farrell whispers.

I give him a thumbs-up and feel excited. I can't possible abandon the project, even if a stroll around Portobello market with Elliot sounds so idyllic.

'I can't today. I'm out with some friends.'

'Oh I thought you might... I didn't expect a girl like you to be free all weekend.'

He sounds more matter-of-fact than disappointed.

'But how about tomorrow?'

I don't want him to lose interest.

'Can I let you know later?'

'Yes, of course.'

'Great.'

I get off the phone with a funny feeling in my stomach. Like rejection. But how can it be, when he asked me out? Am I being oversensitive or did that feel like he was just flicking through his contact list to see who might be free?

Farrell pushes a pint towards me and I muster a smile.

'Where were we?' I say, looking down at my silly serviette.

'The Tower of London, poisoned ravens, the fall of Britain, the Irish Empire... then some bloke asking you out.'

'Ah yes.'

'And you turned him down.'

'My bananas are very important to me.'

Farrell reaches for my hand and looks at me solemnly. 'And if they're important to you, Amber, then they're important to me.'

Then he lets go of my hand, gives a funny little laugh and downs half his pint.

Chapter 19

Almost an hour later, Bibiana and Egg arrive at the pub. I sense Bibiana is pretty annoyed with us for abandoning her and can only imagine the lectures Egg has delivered on each artifact. I hurriedly explain that we decided to have a strategy meeting about my new mission to become a cutting-edge artist. It doesn't seem to mollify her. She plucks the serviette out of my hands, takes one look at it then chucks it disdainfully across the table.

'Prehistoric savages used more modern systems than this! Where's your laptop? Where are your charts? You can't just leave rotting fruit at different landmarks and hope for the best.'

'She's right. Even the *Homo habilis* had a strategy for survival,' Egbert says knowingly.

'They weren't advanced enough to make a serviette though, were they?' I point out, feeling clever and quite tipsy.

'The bananas need to engage with people,' Bibiana continues. 'People need to feel something or else they will just walk past them, especially in *this* country where everyone is too scared to even talk to each other. Half the people here will pretend not to notice because it will make them feel uncomfortable!'

I feel slightly defensive. We're not *all* scared to talk to each other. The other day on the bus somebody sneezed and I said 'bless you'. By London standards, that's quite a bold conversation-starter. We didn't progress to a conversation, alas, but we could have.

'You need to make them friendly,' Farrell says.

'Exactly!' Bibiana agrees.

'Shall I draw a smiley face on them?'

Egbert starts to nod, but Bibiana is not amused.

'NO!'

'I think that's a "no",' Farrell says.

He's also quite tipsy, which is his own fault. I suggested we get a half instead of that third pint.

'Your bananas need to be ambiguous, but they need to engage,' she says. 'You need to introduce them to the public.'

I'm baffled. Does she mean I should learn to be a ventriloquist? Does she want me to stop people on the street and, with a banana perched on my arm, deliver a message in a squeaky banana voice: *Hey mister, I'm a banana, nice to meetcha! Do you wanna be my friend?* Now it's my turn to think NO! If I wanted to be a presenter of a kiddies' shows then I'd be wearing a banana body suit, wouldn't I?

'I'm not doing a banana voice,' I say firmly.

Bibiana looks at me as if I'm a complete idiot.

Egbert tries out a robotic voice, 'Activating vocals – I'm-a-banana-I'm-a-banana-I'm-a- banana.'

Farrell slaps his chest because the beer has gone down the wrong way and he's laughing and choking at the same time.

'You don't need to talk like a banana,' Bibiana says. 'You introduce the concept, tell people a huge show is coming to London and do they want to hold one of these pieces? You take a photo of them holding the banana and then you make them feel as if they were really lucky to get a chance to do that. Then you put it on the website. What stage is your website at?

I tap my head. 'It's in here...'

'WHAT?'

She grabs her head in her hands, her face frozen in a silent scream.

'It's all happened so quickly...'

'You're going to have to do it tonight. I'll help you, but it'll have to be at Farrell's because of your damn cat.'

'Okay, okay...'

She's right. Nothing counts any more unless there's virtual proof. I'm feeling agitated now. I wanted to leave bananas around the city and let people come up with their own conclusion – not shove them into people's hands and tell them what to think. This wasn't the plan. I feel as if my project is in the process of being hijacked.

'So, are you going to do it?' Bibiana says, her Cleopatra eyes challenging me. 'Or are you going to chicken out?'

'I'm not chickening out!'

'Good! I knew you wouldn't!' She slaps her manicured hands on the table and looks excited. 'Now, I was thinking, while Amber introduces her project to London we can go watch a movie?'

'Yes please!' Egbert shouts, and then quieter. 'Do you think you could slip me in somehow without paying?'

'You can't leave me on my own!'

'But this is your moment to shine,' she says, dismissing my panic with a little flick of her hair. 'What about you, Farrell?'

Oh God, I think she actually likes him and that worries me. Bibiana is someone who gets what she wants. The trouble is, I don't think her getting Farrell would necessarily be a good move for him.

There's a moment of indecision. Egbert is waiting with baited breath for the confirmation that he'll soon be alone in a dark room with Bibiana. I'm trying to picture myself walking up to people with my bananas, alone. Can I really do it alone? I already feel embarrassed and I haven't even stepped outside the pub.

'No, I'll go with Amber,' Farrell says, certain this time. 'I think it'll be a laugh.'

'Yeah, I'm sure you guys will have fun,' Egbert says. 'You always like doing weird things together.'

'Do you want us to go with you?' Bibiana says, looking unsure now.

I wave my hand dismissively. 'No, we'll be fine, go watch that film.'

The last thing I want is Bibiana putting me under any more pressure. If I'm going to do something stupid I would rather do it alone with Farrell, rather than in front of a despairing audience.

'We should go with you,' Bibiana says, with an air of finality. 'Don't you agree Egbert?'

'Of course I don't agree,' Egg says. 'It's the worst idea I've ever heard.'

Chapter 20

What better place to have your art exhibited but in the Tate Modern along the River Thames? Well that's not exactly an option for a nobody like me.

Or is it?

Actually, it seems it is. According to Bibiana it's just a matter of looking purposeful and wearing a t-shirt with Tate Modern across the front – available in the shop.

'It's an investment,' Bibiana says, pressing a purple one into my hand and pushing me towards the queue to pay

Afterwards Egg and Farrell hang about in the shop while I head to the loo with Bibiana. There she supplies me with an official-looking identity badge from the last job she worked at. I point out that not only is it for an outdoor concert but it also has her face on it instead of mine.

'Just flash it quickly if there's a problem,' she says.

I practise a smile in the mirror and in my head I say words I hope I won't have to use: *You don't recognise me because I'm new; it's my first week!*

'Is that your phone?' Bibi says.

I dig it out from my pocket. It's my mum calling and I feel a stab of guilt. I keep promising to ring her back but never do.

'Hi, Mum.'

Bibi's eyes widen as if to say, *Really? Now?*

'Amber! How are you?'

Well, Mum, I'm about to plant an alien exhibit in one of the most famous galleries in Europe and my stomach is churning.

'I'm good, fine, yeah...'

I can sense her getting comfortable on the sofa. 'How's everything going? We haven't spoken for ages.'

'I know, sorry. I'm out at the moment. Can I call you back later?'

'Where are you?'

'The Tate.'

'The Tate? If you'd given me a bit more warning I could have met you there. We could have had a coffee... oh why didn't you tell me?'

The bathroom is getting overcrowded and I'm blocking a sink.

'I'm sorry, Mum. We can do it again.'

'Alright,' she says, disappointed. 'Well let me know if there's anything worth seeing, won't you?'

Is a guerrilla banana worth seeing?

I say goodbye and head outside to the foyer, where I find Farrell has had a change of heart.

'It's too risky. What if she gets arrested? Shouldn't we just stick to leaving them around London?'

'She has to do something big and the exhibition upstairs is perfect for her work!' Bibiana argues.

Not for the first time I wonder why they are here, encouraging me. Shouldn't they be persuading me to go home and rethink my whole life?

'Oh God, this is all getting a bit serious,' I mumble.

She grips my arms. 'Amber, this could be a turning point in your life. This could be it, babe. You said you didn't want a boring, predictable life, well having an exciting life means you've got to take some risks! You've got to have faith and jump!'

She's right. I've got to do this. If I don't do this nothing will ever change. I'll be on the hamster wheel of temping life, forever moving but never going anywhere. What's the worst that can happen anyway? They arrest me? They fine me? They ban me from coming to the Tate? I'm hardly risking my life, only my pride if I get caught, and what's to be proud of if I never take any risks?

'You said the exhibition upstairs is perfect,' Farrell says. 'Why?'

'Because the exhibition upstairs is full of penises!' Bibiana cries, tossing her hair over her shoulder with a defiant shake of the head.

I stare at her. 'What do you mean?'

'How can I explain it to you better? Shapes that look like penises; penis-shaped objects. It's a perfect exhibition to incorporate your bananas into. Just get up there and when no one is looking put the bananas down on the carpet of 3-D penises, take a photo and leave. Got it?'

Farrell is nodding his head as if it all makes complete sense now. 'Bibi's right. You have to do this, Amber.'

Shit. I've *got* to do this.

'I'm not Head of Marketing for nothing,' she says. 'Now come on, Farrell, we'll go outside and start on the public.'

'What about Egg?'

We look over at the shop. Through the glass walls, we spot Egg engaged in a very serious game of chess. His opponent is a young boy dressed in chainmail and dragging a sword.

'Let's leave him be,' Bibiana says. 'He looks like he's having too much fun.'

I leave them behind and take the escalators to the next floor. I should be feeling anxious as I queue up for the gallery behind a group of college students, but instead I'm feeling sorry for Egg. It's obvious his feelings for the temperamental Argentinean are not reciprocated and I'm wondering if I should break the news to him so he doesn't bankrupt himself trying to keep up with her. He must have spent his weekly budget five times over today.

It's only when I'm inside the gallery space that my thoughts begin to clear and my eyes settle on the strange white installation in front of me. It looks like a shag-pile carpet that has developed

149

huge elongated tumours. Each growth looks swollen and as if it's reaching out to escape the carpet it's growing out of.

As I stand there staring at it, two things occur to me. One is that, yes, they do look a lot like unpainted penises made of sandbags, and two, I've managed to walk into the gallery without showing a ticket and I was so deep in thought I didn't even realise it.

My chest feels tight as I continue to stare at the mutant shag-pile carpet in the middle of the large room. There are only about five other visitors, which is quite modest for a Saturday afternoon, but that's still five visitors too many. They walk around the installation, their shoes squeaking on the polished floor and they examine the penises with great curiosity.

I can't do it. I can't just boldly walk up and deliver my bananas into the clutches of all that monstrous genitalia. It's not that I've grown protective of my art, it's simply that I'm chickening out. I've frozen. I can't do it.

And yet I *must* do it. Overcoming fear is what separates the 'somebodies' from the 'nobodies'.

'Do you work here?'

The voice gives me such a fright my hand flies up to my chest, slapping my fake identity badge. I keep it there, covering Bibiana's face. The owner of the voice, a thin man in suit trousers and a long, beige gabardine, stares at me with impatient brown eyes. He doesn't apologise for scaring me. He just waits for me to compose myself.

Just say no, I think.

'Yes,' I say.

He waves his hand at the white tumours. 'And what do you make of this?'

I try to gather my wits together. For once, I'm a complete blank.

'What do *you* make of it?'

'I asked you first.'

I can't seem to summon my imagination.

'I don't know.'

'Well if *you* don't know and you're supposed to have some

150

knowledge of the subject, then how the hell are the rest of us supposed to know?' he says, enunciating each word as if he were biting them with his teeth. 'I'm sick and tired of not knowing what I'm looking at.'

'I think, uh, everyone's, uh, supposed to see it differently...'

He looks at me with a mixture of despair and loathing. 'But I don't see anything but white bulges!'

'Really?'

He doesn't see the penises? So it's *me* projecting penises?

'I don't get it. I just don't get it,' he says over and over.

'Do you need to get it?'

'Yes! I'm meeting a beautiful lady in ten minutes downstairs in the coffee shop and if I fail to formulate some sort of opinion yet *again* she's going to think I'm an uncultured moron.'

'Can't you say you don't feel anything?'

'No, then she'll think I'm unfeeling!'

'Well, in this case, you are.'

'No, I feel a lot of things. I feel frustrated and angry and I just wish these bloody artists would get off the drugs they're all so obviously on... I'm sorry, I know it's not your fault... I'm just so... so...' he presses his fingers into the corners of his eyes and takes a deep breath, '...so tired.'

In the silence I realise we are now the only people left in the room.

'Yes, keep your eyes closed,' I say softly and I reach into my bag.

'Why?' he groans, but he does as he's told.

'You've got to forget all your anxieties, all your pre-conceived ideas... just empty your mind...'

My heart is pounding. I'm going to do it. The bananas are in my hand. There's a squeak as I step as lightly as I can towards the installation. Any moment now and someone could walk in and catch me.

I hold my breath as I reach out over the tops of the bloated white shapes as far as I can go and then I let them drop. The bananas

151

land at a jaunty angle on one of the biggest tumours. They could be an exotic bird perched on an unusual tropical plant. They could be anything. I hear the sound of approaching footsteps. I stand up and look behind me. The man in the gabardine has still got his eyes closed. What will he think when he opens them? A part of me doesn't want to stay around to find out.

'Now open your eyes and whatever your first thought is... it's the right one.'

This time it's my voice that startles him. His eyes dart to the installation and his eyebrows fly up into his forehead.

'What the... that's incredible!'

He walks forward and stares at the bananas with his mouth open.

'I can't believe I missed them!'

Other visitors walk into the room and are drawn towards the installation. There are no big reactions, no outrage.

'So it's an environmental piece,' he murmurs.

He suddenly looks infinitely happier. 'Thank you. I see it now.'

'Take a photo for your friend,' I say. 'You never know, she might have missed them too!"

I take a few snaps with my phone before leaving the room on an adrenalin high. Not many artists can boast having their work displayed in the Tate Modern. I can't believe I've done it. This is big! This is newsworthy! It's not quite swapping the Mona Lisa for a birthday card, but it's not far off, either!

With my heart still beating fast, I head out of the front of the building. I'm buzzing and can't wait to tell the others what I've done, just as soon as I find them. Where are they? They were supposed to be introducing the lime-green bananas to prospective Tate visitors and passersby.

There's a queue at the ice-cream van and a man selling pipes that trill like birdsong. I stand there for a while, breathing it all in. Then I turn on my heels, take a few steps one way and then stop. Perhaps they've gone back inside.

I start to walk towards the entrance and that's when I see the man in the beige gabardine walking alongside a very agitated security guard. For a moment we catch each other's eyes.

'There!' he cries. 'That's her! That's the banana woman!'

The next thing I know the security man has started running towards me. I bolt back outside and up the ramp leading to the Millennium Bridge. The wind sweeps through my hair and the sun dazzles my eyes as I run across it as fast as I can. Shit! I can't believe this is happening! I'm a rebel running from the law!

I don't stop until I'm nearly at the end of the bridge and then the sharp, stabbing pain of a stitch makes me falter. I glance back and find the lazy security guard didn't even make it up the ramp. It was all just a show for skinny-gabardine-man, who has plenty to tell his lady friend now. I bend over, my hands on my knees and take a moment to catch my breath. My heart is pounding.

People are walking towards me and I move to the side of the bridge and look into the murky water of the Thames. The current is so strong that apparently you wouldn't survive long if you fell in. I feel a pretty strong current surging through me as I stand there. *People will buy into anything if you can make enough noise about it,* Matt had said. I can't help wanting to find out what would happen if I put everything into this project. It's not just an experiment, either. I want it. I want to become the artist I'm playing. I *am* the artist.

Chapter 21

After I send Matt Costa the photo of the blue bananas sitting on the award-winning penis- shaped tumours I expect my phone to start ringing straight away. When it doesn't I keep checking whether I've put it on silent or if the signal is bad.

Farrell nudges me with his elbow. 'Adrenalin worn off?'

'Yeah, I think so...'

We're in a pub along the river, surrounded by tense football fans who are watching a match on the flat screen above our heads. A few of Farrell's friends are there. They've looked at the pictures on my phone, had a laugh, made a few rude comments, and now they're glued to the screen again. Dee has popped in, but as usual, she won't be staying because she's got a guitar lesson to give.

'You've got so much to tell me,' she says, tapping my knee excitedly. 'I've been following your status updates. So, are you going to see him again?'

She's talking about Elliot. Everyone knows about him now. I probably shouldn't have been so open about it on Facebook. What if it doesn't work out?

'Yeah, definitely. He asked me out today but I was busy.'

He rang *me*, to ask *me* out. Of course it's going to work out.

'You're not busy now,' she says, with a wink. 'Tell him to come so we can meet him!'

'I thought you had to go soon.'

She looks at her watch and her face falls. 'Shit. How can that be the time already?'

'It's alright. I wasn't going to ring him. I've got too much to do.'

The truth is I'm feeling a little agitated because I want to be at home working on my website. It was the others who wanted to celebrate pulling off the stunt. We've ordered the cheapest bottle of fizz on the menu; it costs the equivalent of two cans of spray paint. That would never have occurred to me before.

The football fans whoop when the cork pops and someone runs out of the toilets with his belt undone and shouts, 'Who scored?' He gives us a dirty look when he realises his mistake and heads back into the toilet.

'So does Elliot know you're a crazy banana lady?' Dee asks, grinning.

'Not yet.'

'Do you think he'd approve?'

I think of Montague's exhibition and frown. 'Yes, I think he'd take it quite seriously.'

Farrell leans in at that moment, 'who would take what seriously?'

'Oh nothing.' I don't want to get into it now.

Dee checks her watch again, 'I've got to go, but let me know the goss...'

'Is this about Sir Elliot?' Farrell asks. 'What's the goss?'

'You're up to speed,' I say. 'You were there when he rang.'

'You turned him down, didn't you?'

I roll my eyes, 'you make it sound like he proposed.'

Dee laughs, 'imagine! What would you have said?'

'Oh shut up, don't be ridiculous.'

We hug goodbye, then she hoists her guitar onto her back and squeezes through everyone to get out. I catch Bibiana's eye and she raises her glass of Prosecco to me with a big smile. Farrell's friends are all in love with her, but Egg is not moving from the spot beside her, even though his bladder is famously weak.

'To Amber!' she says.

I laugh, pretend I'm having the time of my life, but the truth is I'm worried that what I thought was an exciting move might actually be insignificant. Has it been done before? Are people forever sneaking their bits of art into galleries, hoping to get lucky, hoping for the masses to go wild about it and declare it the next Big Thing? Is that why Matt isn't ringing me?

Bibiana has tweeted my photos. She says they've been retweeted a couple of times. What concerns me is that the bananas weren't there long enough. I mean, they couldn't have lasted much more than five minutes, ten max, on the exhibit. Some clever-clogs with a programme must have queried why the bananas weren't included in the picture in the booklet.

I check my phone again. Nothing. Perhaps Matt takes weekends seriously. People do that. They work like dogs all week and then they withdraw into their luxury pads, paid for with their sweat and blood during the week, and they shut themselves off to the world.

Soon Farrell is pouring out another glass of fizzy. Egg is flushed. He claims he used to make moonshine at university, but if that's true, surely he should be more resistant to the decent stuff.

'To Bibiana!' Egg cries.

She throws her head back and the pub is filled with her deep laughter. Farrell's friends are momentarily hypnotised by her and half of them miss the goal that follows. There's a collective roar and anyone sitting down leaps up and punches the air, including Egg, who has never watched a football match from beginning to end in his entire life. Farrell grabs hold of me and gives me this massive bear hug. I don't even know who's playing, but the feeling in the pub is contagious. I squeeze him back, but when I try to pull away he keeps on holding me. I pat his back, laughing and he responds by giving me a clumsy kiss on my shoulder.

'You're amazing, you know,' he says in my ear. 'You're so fucking amazing, Amber.'

He lets me go and I don't know what's got into him, but he's looking at me with such affection that he must be on his way to getting seriously drunk. Some people get aggressive when they drink; Farrell gets sentimental.

'Tequila for the lady!' a man shouts, pushing through the crowd with two shot glasses in his hand. He is red-faced and has a manic look in his eye. In fact, he looks as if he might well have been breastfed on tequila.

Egg looks as if he's been insulted as the stranger sets a little shot glass down in front of Bibiana. I bat a twinge of jealousy away. It would have been nice if he'd got us one each. Now I feel like the ugly girl in the group.

'Come on 'ave a shot with me love! I reckon you got us that goal!'

She's not fazed by the attention and plucks the slice of lemon off the rim and holds up the shot glass with her free hand.

'Cheers!' she says, and downs it. In the ensuing raucous applause, Farrell leans towards me.

'You've inspired me, you know,' he says.

'Are you taking the piss?'

'No, seriously, I would've had to get pretty drunk before I did what you did.'

'We did have three pints.'

'It's made me think, I don't want to be scared any more, you know. You're right, I've got to put myself out there more...'

He's talking about his book. He holds my gaze and looks all soulful.

'Good. You should. I think you're brilliant.'

'It means a lot you saying it Amber.'

'Are you drunk Mr Kennedy?'

I stroke his stubble and his cheeks colour up.

'No, I'm serious. Don't stroke my beard like I'm a little kid and do that baby face.'

'Kids don't have beards.'

He intercepts my hand before I can tickle his beard again and holds onto it. Beyond him I see Egg is blabbering on to Bibiana,

157

but she is focused on us. I smile at her and she gives a little head-shake as if I've caught her in a daydream.

'Amber,' Farrell says, searching my eyes.

'Yes, Farrell, what is it?'

But as he opens his mouth someone scores another goal and the pub bursts into noise. One of his friends, his breath laced with beer, grabs us by the shoulders and shouts a song of celebration in our ear. When it dies down again, the conversation has moved on to Egg's memoirs and Farrell says he's forgotten whatever it was he wanted to say.

Chapter 22

Maybe Matt just hasn't cottoned on to what the picture is. Maybe he doesn't recognise the installation. I should have explained it, added the location, but I thought for an expert like him it would be obvious. I send him a new message telling him where it is and 'does anything look out of place to you?' I add a winky face. I don't think a winky face would stand up in court as evidence if I ever get arrested for vandalism.

I use Rupert as an excuse to go home. I say he's too little to be left all alone for such a long time and I never get to see him much in the week. Farrell protests at first, but then two of his friends make their excuses and go, leaving five of us, and then Bibiana says she's hungry and why don't we all go back for supper.

When we get back, the others hover around our front door for a while, but because of her allergy Bibiana can't come in. Egg is torn between seeing Rupert and eating Bibiana's supper. In the end he chooses his furry friend.

'Are you coming over after?' Farrell says, searching my face for confirmation that I will.

'Maybe,' I say.

Rupert is playing with a piece of dried pasta in the kitchen. He stops when we come in and hurries over to Egg, miaowing. Either he's pleased to see us or he's very hungry. He stands up on his back legs and rests his little paws on Egg's shin.

'You'll have to choose,' I say, as I fill the kettle from the tap. 'Bibiana or Rupert?'

Egg's happy smile fades and he looks depressed. 'It's like a Greek tragedy, isn't it?'

'Not really.'

'It is,' he says, picking Rupert up and stroking his head tenderly. 'If I choose my goddess I will lose all I love.'

'So don't choose the goddess,' I say. 'Tea?'

'Tea won't fill the hole in my heart.'

'Of course it will. Every British person knows that tea is the solution to all mankind's problems.'

I take my mug into the living room and switch on the telly. It provides the background noise as I start my internet search for blue bananas. I find children's books, clothing companies, tattooists, models in blue lipstick, but not one banana. Not even a standard yellow banana. I look for *Bananas in the Tate* and an actress pops up in a wedding dress. Researchers must know all the tricks for tracking information online. My own skills are bearing very little fruit.

I update my Facebook banner with a picture of the blue bananas and add 'Guerrilla bananas!' underneath. It gets three likes within the first minute. I realise that unless people know about the artist they'll assume the bananas are supposed to be there.

I look for bananas on Twitter and find that my rivals @ LondonBananas have photographed a new banana skin poking out of a rubbish skip. Well, I think, it's safe to say my photograph is a lot more exciting.

@lookabanana Spotted at the Tate! Blue Bananas pop out of nowhere! #bananaalert #guerillabananas

My rivals respond seconds later.

@LookaBanana Nice photoshop but we prefer the real thing. #keepitreal

@lookabanana #itisreal

@LookaBanana If it's real then tweet a picture of you eating them. #thoughtnot.

Cheeky bastards! I consider drawing over my mouth with a blue felt-tip and tweeting a selfie looking as if I've eaten my bananas. Well, I don't just consider it, I spend fifteen minutes looking for a felt-tip in the right blue, but all I've got is a permanent marker and a skinny-nibbed biro. I reluctantly give up on the idea and tear myself away from Twitter.

Matt Costa doesn't reply. I scroll down my contacts list for lack of a better plan. I pause at Farrell's name and think about them all drinking together up the road and whether I should join them. Bibiana is supposed to be my guest, after all. But the truth is I've probably had enough of her loud voice for one day. I know who I'd like to see, though. My finger is on Elliot's name. One gentle tap and my phone will ring him. I feel suddenly nervous.

If you've got the guts to plant an alien exhibit in the Tate then you can ring a bloody man! But the adrenalin rush has long gone and it may as well have been a dream. I feel an overwhelming sense of dissatisfaction now. I'm afraid that I'll never amount to anything. I'm just going to be another office drone aspiring to get through the day, motivated by the thought of a glass of wine at the end of it all. What did I really expect to happen? All I've done is contributed to the nonsense already out there.

The negativity keeps on coming.

You're a fake! You don't know what you're doing! Those elephants were painted by real artists, not wannabes hoping for the best! You've had no formal training. It's not going to work!

To make it worse, the news is on, which never fails to depress me.

I automatically turn the volume up. I'm waiting for the day I watch it and the politics suddenly all makes complete sense. I suspect it might happen on my thirtieth birthday. I envy those well-informed people at parties who are quick to give their opinion and can hold their own in a debate. They know why they vote for the people they do, or disagree with the people they don't. I, on the other hand, never know what to think. It's not for lack of trying. I always make myself read the dense part of newspapers, but the way some of these journalists write, it's as if they want to lose you. It's probably best if I don't become famous because I'll be rubbish in an interview. All my answers will just be 'I don't know' and 'Maybe?'

On and on it goes. All the worst of humanity compiled in one seamless report.

Economic Disaster. *Check!*

Government Corruption Scandal. *Check!*

Civilians killed in cross-fire. *Check!*

Teenager stabbed by gang member. *Check!*

The white-haired male presenter shuffles his papers after the last piece of demoralising news and smiles at the camera.

'And finally, has London gone bananas?'

I sit up, my ears peeled, my heart suddenly thumping.

'Today visitors to the Tate Modern might have been surprised by an unusual addition to Yayoi Kusama's retrospective.'

No way, no way! I'm not hearing this!

'Concerns were raised when an avid fan of Kusama's work spotted a bunch of blue bananas nestled in the midst of a sculpture featuring phallic symbolism. CCTV footage has yet to be revealed, but the bananas are thought to have been left by a young woman posing as a Tate staff member.'

My mouth drops open. CCTV footage? Shit! But before it has sunk in the presenter drops another bombshell.

'It appears the banana incident is not one of a kind, either.

There have also been sightings of brightly coloured bananas outside the British Museum as well as several pubs.'

Several pubs? What pubs?

'The twittersphere is talking and everyone is asking: Who is this banana woman? And what does it all mean?'

His co-presenter, a mature woman in a bright-pink jacket, responds with a hearty laugh.

'It sounds like we should be keeping our bananas locked up, Michael!'

'It does, Jillian, doesn't it? The question is, are these bananas to be washed away in a torrential storm or is this sunshine set to continue?'

'Well, Michael, it looks like we'll be enjoying some more sunny spells over the next week.'

'Fantastic news. The bananas will be thrilled.'

Another laugh from Jillian, but this time a little more forced. She launches into a full weather report and I just stare at the map of British Isles, too stunned to move. Then I grab the remote, forgetting that we can't rewind on our television, that it's Farrell's television that does that. I should ring him. I should also ring my mum to see if she's watched it. My heart is beating so fast. I want to scream and dance around the room. But mostly I want to see it again, to make sure I wasn't hallucinating. Will they show it on the later news or was that it? Was that my ten seconds of fame? I stand there buzzing with excitement and frozen with indecision about what my next step should be. A moment later my phone starts ringing.

Chapter 23

'Was that you? Did you have something to do with those bananas?' Elliot cries down the phone.

'Yes! You saw the News?!'

I can't believe it! He saw the News! He knows about my bananas!

'Christ! When you said bananas, I didn't know what to think.'

The excitement in his voice fills me with energy. I can't believe how miserable I was a moment ago. Now, I'm on top of the world.

'So what next?' he says.

Of course! It's all about WHAT HAPPENS NEXT?! I've got to get more bananas out there this instant! People who've seen the News will be looking for them, expecting them. I've just been given massive, previously unthinkable publicity and the last thing I'm going to do is sit back and waste it.

'Oh, my God, I've got to get the other bananas in position tonight! What time does the tube stop running? Midnight?'

'The tube?' he says, as if it were the craziest idea he'd ever heard. 'You can't go on the tube. It'll take you hours.'

'Well how else am I going to get across London?'

The public will only retain this news in their heads until the next Premiership footballer cheats on his wife. There's not much time.

'Well, I could drive you,' Elliot says.

I perch on the edge of the sofa, my heart racing.

'Really? You'd do that?'

'Yes. I'll take you wherever you need to go.'

'Wow, that's so amazing of you... are you sure?'

That's quite an offer. This is getting serious. Isn't this what a boyfriend would do?

'Yes, of course. This must be so stressful for you.'

If I wasn't stressed before, I am now. My excitement has turned into alarm. I need a plan of action!

'Give me your address. I'll come right away.'

I do as I'm told and he jots it down, holding the phone under his chin and repeating it back to me.

'Amber, one other thing...'

'What?'

'How many bananas are we talking about? There's a limit to how many Isabella can carry.'

My enthusiasm withers and dies. I don't know who this Isabella is, but I already have an irrational dislike of her.

'I'm sure we can manage with just the two of us.'

'Yes, of course we can. Isabella is my car, silly!'

Relief floods through me, followed by a trickle of indignation. *I'm* silly? He's the one naming his car.

'They'll fit, no problem,' I say.

There are seven bunches outside on the patio waiting for their cue.

'Great! I'm on my way!'

I ring Farrell after that to tell him the news of the famous bananas. I hear him rushing to switch on the television.

'It's too late now!' I laugh.

'I can't believe it! Maybe they'll show it again!'

'They're not going to show it again.'

'Why don't you come over?' he says. 'We're having a little party.'

'No, I can't. I've got loads to do. I've got to sort out the website or Miss Chief of Marketing will yell at me.'

I just don't feel quite comfortable mentioning that I'm heading out for a second banana run with another man. I'm probably being paranoid, but after the day's camaraderie I have this feeling that Farrell might be offended by the idea. Anyway, I will do the website later. Definitely.

'Alright, fine,' he says. 'I'll leave the telly on, in case they're mentioned again.'

It doesn't get better than this: Driving through London in a classic convertible beside a gorgeous man who's not only picked me up from the opposite side of the city but has also come equipped with a box of chocolates. Elliot looks handsome in a white v-neck t-shirt that picks up his tan. He knows it, too. He keeps catching me staring at him and cocking his eyebrows, a knowing smile on his lips.

It's not cold and the warm evening air caresses my cheeks as we head towards the glistening lights of central London. This trip is supposed to be about my bananas, but the tingling chemistry between us is making it hard to concentrate.

Our first stop is the Tower of London, one of the oldest buildings in the city. Once so imposing the medieval stone building is now dwarfed by glass skyscrapers. Elliot grows agitated as we join a sluggish line of traffic. Ahead of us Tower Bridge is outlined in lights like a Christmas decoration. We don't want to cross it and neither is there anywhere to park.

'You'll have to jump out and I'll come back around for you,' he says. 'At the next traffic lights...'

I'd much rather he came with me. The courage of this morning seems so distant. It's finally sunk in that I was caught on CCTV and could be in trouble. I'm half-expecting Policeman Perkins to appear with handcuffs and arrest me. Frankly he should be coming to me for advice. At least I achieved *my* goal with my bananas.

'Now,' Elliot says.

I jump out of the car with a bunch of red bananas and head up the road as fast as I can.

Beyond the black railings that mark out the pedestrian walkway, an expanse of green grass stretches out where once a moat would have been. The Tower is a fortress designed for self-defence. It has two outer walls of stone, complete with turrets and narrow slits where marksmen would have taken aim with their bows and arrows. These days a simple ticket would get me inside. Even if I could afford to dig any deeper into my overdraft, it's already too late in the day to buy one.

I hold my bananas low at my side as I walk frantically around the outer wall. Gaggles of tourist are taking photographs and examining souvenirs. Elliot won't be long and I have to move fast. But where should I leave them? If I were James Bond I would do a running jump over the moat, sneak soundlessly into the restricted areas and... Correction. If I was James Bond's stunt man I'd leap across the moat, somersault over a guard's head, plucking his keys out of his pocket as I do so, and then back-flip into the treasury. Unfortunately the only stunt I've got is a cartwheel-come bunny flop that wouldn't get me over a curb let alone a moat. *Focus, Amber!*

As I'm standing there, considering my options, my eyes settle on a grey-haired man wearing the distinctive red and navy uniform of the famous Beefeaters. It's less of a uniform and more of a costume from the Tudor ages, with a stiff hat of navy material pleated into a red band, a cloak with gold buttons and a tunic with ER embroidered in huge letters across the chest. The Beefeaters are as emblematic of London as a double-decker bus or a red telephone box, and consequently the ideal people to model my bananas.

The guard in question is a portly gentleman, who, after waving a tourist on her way, starts to head away from the main drawbridge. I follow him, feeling exhilarated at the prospect of successfully accomplishing my mission.

'Excuse me!'

He must be a little deaf because he doesn't look up until I tap his arm. He looks even older up close, with his watery blue eyes and his skin covered in tiny red veins.

'I was just wondering...'

'Do I look like an A-Z?'

I'm surprised at his tone. I always assumed Beefeaters were as friendly as the characters walking around at Disneyland. 'I don't need directions! I was just wondering if I could have a photo with you holding my bananas?'

'I beg your pardon!'

I hold up the bunch, but he seems to look through them.

'You might find my uniform titillating and you might have heard rumours, but I don't do that sort of thing.'

'What sort of thing?'

He starts walking briskly, his bloodless hands clenched at his side.

'I didn't mean to offend you!' I say, following after him. 'I'm an artist doing a big project in London. I just thought that you, being such an important symbol of this city, would really give it some gravitas!'

He stops and sniffs thoughtfully. 'I'm proud of this uniform. If I had my way, the tabloids would be tried for treason, chained to the dungeon gates and left to the mercy of the tide like in the good old days.'

He might be old, but I'm sure he wasn't around in the fifteenth century to verify that it really was a great time to be alive.

'I do not use this uniform to attract perverted ladies with unsavoury fantasies,' he continues. 'I'm not interested in playing the Queen and her secret Beefeater lover.'

Wow. I appear to have opened a can of worms. I would never have imagined that the second-biggest request of Beefeaters, after directions to the nearest station, could be sexual role play.

'Do I really look like that sort of woman?'

I'm wearing a red off-the-shoulder top, reminiscent of medieval bar maids, so maybe I should retract the question.

The Beefeater flares his nostrils. 'I am a servant of the Queen. I will not be led astray whilst wearing this uniform. Do you hear?'

'Of course! My project is completely legitimate and it's set to be as big... as big as... Damian Hurst's calf... but more animal-friendly, of course.'

He takes a deep breath and at last his focus settles on my bananas.

'My late wife Mildred was rather partial to bananas,' he says.

He's having a change of heart! I can't believe my luck. But then his gaze hardens again.

'Are you certain Her Majesty won't mind me doing this?

'Not at all! My work has already appeared on the BBC.'

'Very well, then.'

'Brilliant! For Mildred, then!'

I dig out my phone and adjust the settings on the camera while he tries out a range of expressions and settles on a proud pose with his chin up and his lips pursed beneath his thick grey moustache. My bananas look exceptionally regal beneath the Queen's insignia and it gives me a thrill to see them in such distinguished hands.

'I give you my permission to airbrush,' he says, when I'm done.

'You don't need it! You look great!'

When I finally reappear beside the road Elliot is there waiting, his lights blinking. He has probably driven past ten times already. I jump back in and spontaneously lean over and kiss his cheek. He arches one eyebrow.

'Done?'

'Done!'

'Where's your camera?'

'I used my phone.'

'Christ, you need better equipment.'

'I'm an artist not a photographer.'

I pull his poncho over me and his musky fragrance floods my senses. I want to lose myself in it. I want him to kiss me with the same passion of that first date. I'd reach for him now and takes his handsome face in my hands and exchange that peck on the cheek for a kiss fit for the screen. Except that we'd probably crash

169

and I'm not romantic enough to die for one kiss.

Elliot is so close and yet so inaccessible in that driver's seat. We need to get out of this car. We need to find somewhere private where we can discover each other. The adrenalin is pumping through me again and I don't want to keep still.

'So where to next?' he says.

'Your place?'

I laugh as if it were a joke, but his smile emboldens me.

'Unless, of course, the building works are going to be a problem.'

His smile dips and I think he's going to slap a hand across his forehead and say that he'd completely forgotten that his house was a building site. But then the doubt vanishes and he's grinning again.

'No problem at all, the job was much smaller than I'd anticipated,' he says, and he holds my eye long enough for the butterflies in my stomach to take flight.

I stare out at the view of the river as we speed by, excited at the prospect of finally being alone with Elliot. I know Egg will be wondering where I am and when I check my phone I'll find missed calls from Farrell, but sometimes it feels good to fall of the radar for a while.

'Notting Hill is quite the tourist attraction,' he says. 'It might be good to put some bananas around there.'

So that's where he lives. No wonder he invited me there. Beautiful Notting Hill, with its influx of tourist wanting to see the famous blue door where Julia Roberts once stood.

'Well, that's why I suggested your place, of course,' I say. 'Why else?'

We stop at the traffic lights and he leans over, his hand reaches for my thigh and he kisses me as if we were all alone. I try to forget that there's a whole line of traffic watching us, because the roof is down and we're totally exposed. Feeling self-conscious I try to pull back, but his free hand goes up to my face and holds me there a little longer.

The traffic lights must have changed by now and any moment

someone is going to honk their horn and startle the hell out of me. Because I'm worrying about the traffic, it's not the sexy moment it could have been.

'Why else indeed,' he whispers in my ear.

And all I can say back is, 'Green light!'

Chapter 24

Elliot's home turns out to be a beautiful Victorian townhouse with a pillared porch and a smart black door. It's on a street full of similar well-kept buildings. I look up at the polished brass lantern hanging from the centre of the cross-arched porch ceiling as he fiddles with the key in the lock. My eyes flit to the equally polished brass door knocker and lastly to the side of the door where you would expect to find an intercom with at least three flat numbers. But there are none because Elliot owns the entire house.

He opens the door and I follow him into a fragrant hallway. The wonderful smell comes from a bunch of white lilies, which are bursting out of a huge crystal vase. They seem doubly magnificent since they are reflected in a gorgeous bevelled mirror that spans half the wall. Rainbows from the crystal chandeliers above us glimmer across the rich white walls and along the dark wooden floorboards that continue into an equally elegant living room.

'Oh my God, this is beautiful!'

I expected a minimalist bachelor flat with uncomfortable, low-backed leather sofas and glass furniture with cold chrome motifs. Instead I find two cream fabric sofas with freshly plumped cushions in a blend of burgundy and gold. I sink into the nearest sofa and I feel every muscle let out a sigh of delirious pleasure. It's the sort of sofa that could swallow you up whole on a Friday night and hold you hostage for the entire weekend.

'Glass of wine?'

'Yes please.'

He goes off into the kitchen and I consider kicking off my red patent pumps and curling my feet up under me. What stops me is the fact that the sofa is spotless and I've a sneaking suspicion that there are rules protecting it. I suddenly worry that my jeans will leak blue as they did in the last wash, where they dyed half my wardrobe.

Elliot comes back with two big glasses. They are glasses an experienced wine taster could happily plunge his discerning nostrils into. The wine of choice is red.

'This feels dangerous!' I say.

There's a wicked glint in his eye as he stretches out on the sofa beside me.

'Does it?'

He's mistook my meaning and for some stupid reason I feel I have to clarify myself.

'I meant drinking wine on a cream sofa.'

'Oh.'

I feel his eyes on me as I look around the room.

'I can't believe this is all yours...it's stunning...'

There are elegant glass candlesticks on the window sill and moody landscape paintings on the wall. The space is so grown up and it makes me feel young and inadequate. I'm nowhere near getting something like this. It's luck we're living in the damp house that we do. The day the landlord realises how much he could be charging, I'll be back at my parent's house scouring the internet for a single bedroom miles outside London in a house-share of eight – and counting.

'Don't you live with anyone?'

He shudders. 'God no, I'm over the whole sharing thing.'

I drink in the huge bookshelf that reaches the ceiling filled with neat rows of hard-backed novels. Under the coffee table there are books on architecture and gardening.

'So you did this all by yourself?'

He smirks. 'Well, I didn't build the house.'

'I meant the décor, obviously. Did you choose everything?'

'Two words. Interior and designer.'

'But you must have given them an idea, right?'

'Stop asking me questions and just accept I'm very rich and very attractive and you're very lucky to be with me!'

I recoil inwardly at the arrogance in his voice.

'I was joking,' he says quickly.

He places his glass on the floor by his side, which seems significant.

'Come here,' he says.

I feel the onset of panic because it's been so long since I've been alone with a man and now I feel unsure. I'm over-thinking. I'm reading too much into every word, ever expression. *Look at him, he's gorgeous!*

It's normal to be nervous. It's normal to doubt.

I rest my glass on the coffee table and turn to face him, unsure of how to arrange myself. He reaches out for my hands and I let out a nervous giggle as he pulls me on top of him. It's not very comfortable and I feel as if I'm squashing him. I think we were better off sitting up. Now I don't know where to rest my elbows. He presses his lips against mine and pushes my hair off my face. I kiss him back, wanting to melt into the moment, but unable to because his belt buckle is jabbing into my skin. I could say something, but instead I try to shift position. He's ahead of me. I can feel him hardening against me.

His hands sink lower, past my waist. This is what I wanted, but now I'm here it all feels as if it's happening so quickly. I barely know him. I want to drink a little more and take another moment to absorb this room, which says so much about him. I want to make sure I've got him right.

I pull back. 'Wait.'

'What's wrong?'

'Nothing, I just...'

I struggle to sit up on my knees and my shoes fall off onto the floor.

'One second, that's all.'

I need a moment. I need to just stop.

He sits up on his elbow and watches me as I reach for my glass. I'm very aware of the bulge in his trousers and stopping proceedings so abruptly makes me feel like a tease. After all, I'm the one who suggested coming here in the first place.

'Do you need to get drunk to sleep with me, Amber?'

I'm shocked. 'Of course not!'

'I mean if you don't like me...'

His face has fallen and he looks hurt. Where's the smugness now? He's not smug. I'm being judgemental because of his posh voice, his beautiful house... he didn't choose to be privileged.

'I just thought we had a connection...' he says.

I can't put my glass down quick enough. Yes, we did. We still do!

My lips are on his before he can say any more. It was that arrogance in his come-hither smile that had given me cold feet, but now I see he's just like anyone else, with insecurities and fears. I feel reassured.

This time our kiss has slightly better connection and I welcome the touch of his hands as they move down my back. He cups my buttocks and pulls me tighter against him. With a sense of urgency I start unbuttoning his shirt, but before I've finished he tears it off over his head. He has a smooth, toned chest with fine hairs bleached by the sun.

'Let's go upstairs,' he whispers.

I make to get up, but he pulls me back. I wrap my legs around his waist and he lifts me up with his strong arms. It's not all that comfortable, but it's the sexiest things that's ever happened to me. But just when I think it couldn't be hotter, we pass the coffee table and my toes catch the rim of my glass.

'Aah!'

'Shit!' Elliot cries, as it smashes onto the wood floor, sending shards of glass and wine exploding around his feet.

He puts me swiftly back down and I stand on the sofa and look with dismay at the disaster I've caused.

'I'm so sorry!'

Elliot steps gingerly over the mess and I notice his navy loafers have splash stains across the fronts.

'If we don't clean it up now it will stain,' he says, looking anxious.

For the next half an hour the sensual mood is promptly scrubbed out and sucked up with detergent and a posh Dyson vacuum cleaner. It's a tedious interruption and a part of me doesn't believe it's possible to pick up where we left off. However, once the cleaning products have been put away, Elliot comes back over to the sofa, puts his arms back around my waist and lifts me up. We're heading up to the bedroom, which leaves me in no doubt that we're going to finish what we began.

It's sweaty and hot and we both make the right noises, but I'd be lying if I said it's the best sex I've ever had. The problem is half-way through I start thinking about the bananas I've left in his car and how I should have taken advantage and stopped off at more places instead of succumbing to my desire to be alone with Elliot.

'Banana' is the worst word to have in your head while you're trying to focus on working your way towards an orgasm. It's hard enough to get one as it is without such a silly-sounding fruit popping into your head. It doesn't make it better that it has the most phallic shape of all fruit; if anything it makes it worse. Suddenly the very organ working so hard to give me pleasure is rendered comical and silly. I close my eyes and try to connect with the sensuality of his touch, his breath, his lips on my neck. And as the memory of desire starts to rear its head, he starts to groan. A moment later he flops against his feather pillow, completely spent.

It'll be better next time.

He puts his arm around me and I rest my head on his beating

176

chest. Despite the film of sweat on his skin, it feels nice, intimate. It's just a pity that sex requires mental stamina as well as physical because I'm so easily distracted. While he was nibbling my nipple, I was noticing the wrought-iron bed frame and considering the feminine touch of his floral Laura Ashley-esque table lamps. Of course, next time I'll be able to focus better because I'll have already seen his bedroom.

It's a lovely big room with a beautiful bay window, which looks over a garden. From the bed I can just about make out the dark shadow of a mature tree branch reaching up into the night sky. The room has little clutter in it. There's an immaculate desk with a slither-thin white laptop and one silver ball-point pen lying by a pad of white post-its.

It must be getting late. The thought of having to take the tube home at some point is an awful one, made worse when I remember that I'll be carrying most of the bananas back with me, too. I'm secretly hoping Elliot will beg me to stay over, so we can enjoy a Sunday together. I'm thinking a full English breakfast followed by a wander around Portobello market. It was pretty much his suggestion earlier on. The downside of that plan is that I don't have make-up with me or fresh knickers.

'I could stay in this bed all week,' I say.

Too subtle? If he takes the hint, great, and if not, well at least it'll mean fresh knickers tomorrow.

'It could be arranged. We could get the maid to give us room service.'

'You have a maid?'

'Have you seen the size of this house?'

'So get a cleaner.'

'What's the difference?'

'A cleaner doesn't make you sound like...'

'Like what?'

'I don't know. Colonial. You know, *Maid! Bring me my slippers!*'

'I wouldn't mind my slippers, actually.'

'Well get them, then. It's very rewarding doing things for yourself.'

He cocks his eyebrows up at me. 'Like distributing your art around the city yourself.'

I laugh, but he doesn't laugh with me.

'Thank you for driving me around the city,' I say, worrying I've come across ungrateful. 'I do really appreciate it.'

'We didn't get very far.'

'No we didn't. Oops.'

I like the way he says 'we', like he's in my team. Now I think about it, didn't Farrell say 'we' too? There's something about this silly project that attracts a team spirit. And it *is* about the bananas. I mean, Elliot can't have known we'd end up in bed together when he offered to collect me. It might have crossed his mind, as it did mine, but there can't have been great expectations.

'We should be in front of Buckingham Palace slipping bananas under the railings,' I say.

I'm glad we're not.

'You can't do that. You might alarm Her Majesty.'

I laugh. Once again he doesn't laugh with me.

'You're not serious, Elliot?'

'You could be arrested for treason.'

'And then hung, drawn and quartered, I suppose.'

To my relief he breaks into a smile.

'I like you, Amber,' he says, staring at me with misty eyes.

He moves in to kiss me and I offer my lips up for a peck, but he's going for a film kiss, which I wasn't expecting. I just want to stop for a second, to have the post-sex cuddle and get to know him a little better.

His hand slides down my back and he pulls me closer.

Are we going to do it again? I don't think I can manage another round. I'm too tired.

Elliot moans into my ear, which is a bit odd considering I'm not doing anything remotely exciting with my hands. I stroke his back, but now my mind is thinking about the non-existent building works. The place is immaculate. What could he possibly have had done to it?

He stops kissing me and pulls back.

'Are you okay?'

'Yes! Sorry, I'm just thinking about...'

'What is it?'

'I never checked the tube times...'

'Stay over,' he says, kissing me.

'Really?'

'I'm meeting Will for a run at eight, but you can let yourself out.'

'Oh... right...'

That's not the idyllic Sunday I had in mind.

'Unless you don't mind having an early breakfast together?'

'No, that'd be nice.'

He leans forward and kisses me again. But I'm still trying to scoop the pieces of me up off the floor. For a moment then I thought I'd made a horrible mistake.

'Are you sure you're alright?' he says.

'Yeah... yeah, I'm fine.'

'I hope you're more than fine,' he whispers in my ear.

'Oh, I am,' I reply, as seductively I can.

But the truth is, I think I'd be happier polishing off that glass of wine downstairs and finishing off with a cuddle in front of some rubbish television show. It's not that I don't fancy him, I just feel I need to get to know him a lot more and, ironically, I can't do that while he's stark naked and panting heavily in my ear.

Chapter 25

I'm late for work and in the hands of a learner bus driver. A man with a clipboard from London Transport is taking notes at the front of the bus. I'm guessing that if I leant over his shoulder I'd read, *'Driver doesn't know where the hell he's going'* and *'expecting passenger mutiny any second.'*

It's a repeat of that horrible Friday morning, the only difference is this time I know why there's a police car parked outside the catering office. I take some comfort from the fact that I've remembered the camera. It's the reason I'm late. I had to run back to get it after I'd already left the house.

I push open the office door and step across the threshold into what feels like enemy lines.

'Oh good, you decided to show up, then,' Jan says. She's standing behind Vicky's desk shifting through some papers.

Policeman Perkins looks relieved to see me. 'I thought you'd done a runner.'

'My income doesn't stretch to a flight to Mexico.'

'It won't even pay for a Megabus to Wales in a minute,' Jan mutters under her breath.

That's a terrible threat, since a ticket on the Megabus to Wales can cost as little as one pound if you book early.

'Hand it over, then,' Perkins says.

I pass the camera to him and he examines it closely as if looking for scratches. I feel a swell of indignation at the thought that he might hold me responsible for any damage.

'I'll need you to sign a few papers to say you didn't manipulate the footage,' he says.

I sit at my desk and tick endless boxes, then sign my name under a thick paragraph of text I can't be bothered to read. I wonder if either of them saw the news about the blue bananas in the Tate. I'd love to tell them I was behind it. It might change their minds about me. Right now I can see on their faces that they think I'm just some unreliable temp who will never amount to much. Well, actually, I'm a guerrilla artist, the new girl on the scene. I'm going to be big news one day.

Perkins goes and I'm left in the office with just Jan. There's no sign of Vicky.

'She's at the doctor's,' Jan says, reading my thoughts.

'Is she alright?'

'Yes, she's fine, she's just gone to read the free magazines in the waiting room.'

I know full well she's being sarcastic and I struggle to think of something to say that might lighten the mood. Currently, it feels as if Jan is treading on the mood with her huge walking boots. She probably sleeps in those boots.

'Amber, I've spoken with your agency,' she says, spreading her palms across the desk.

Her tone sets my heart racing. The temping agency is my lifeline and if she's blacklisted me I may as well drag my sleeping bag to a street corner and start asking for spare change.

'This isn't working out,' she says.

No. This is not happening. I *need* this job.

'I promise I won't be late again,' I say, feeling desperate. 'I'm really sorry about the last two days, but I've been early all the other days, you can ask Vicky.'

'I told your agency that we won't be needing a temp after today,'

181

she says. 'This is your last day.'

'But I was only late twice!'

I've never been fired from a job before. It's embarrassing and I feel humiliated.

'I'm aware of that. I have spoken to Vicky. But the truth is we simply don't need you working here any more.'

'So, you're not firing me? You just don't need me?'

I feel tears welling up and I blink them away. It's the shock, I suppose. I'm not crying for some stupid job. It's not as if I ever dreamed about working in catering. I'll miss the buffet lunches, but that's all.

'If that makes you feel better,' Jan says.

So I *am* fired?

Jan looks pointedly at her watch. 'Well, you'd better be getting on with your To Do list.'

'I'm really sorry I was late...'

She doesn't reply. I turn to the computer and open the label file. I have a list of canapés in front of me on the desk to write labels for. At first I can barely read them because my eyes are watering so much. After three pages of copying and pasting, though, I start to feel a little better. The truth is, I could be doing so much more with my life.

After seven more pages I'm thinking that Farrell was right. Not many people would have had the guts to walk into the Tate and plant their work there. Okay, so for some people it wouldn't have been a matter of guts and perhaps more of a question of ethics, but whatever, people can be over-precious about these things and it's not as if I broke the installation.

The catering business no longer wants my services! I guess I'll be focusing fully on my bananas! Eeek!

I write the text message before knowing who it's for. I send it to Elliot first and then when he doesn't respond immediately, I send it to Farrell. I'm feeling a bit on edge. I suppose I want someone to tell me it's all going to be alright. I've emailed Daisy, my contact at the agency to ask her about any upcoming jobs, but all I've got back is an Out of Office reply and the news she won't be back for another week.

My phone vibrates and I feel tense. I don't know what sort of response to expect.

It's Elliot.

Excellent news! Call me if you need me to deliver your bananas across the city. I like the way our little outing ended yesterday ;)

The message makes me smile, but I can't help feeling a twinge of regret. I left his house on Saturday morning feeling a bit...

Used is too strong a word. It was my idea to go to his; I can't pretend it wasn't. But it was all so rushed. We woke up to the sound of a horrible alarm clock. There was no sleepy rediscovery of each other, no kisses, no tenderness. He jumped out of bed like a man on a mission, pulled on his running gear and then suggested I grab a coffee from a coffee shop as his espresso machine was broken and he'd run out of milk. He apologised. He said the right words, but they didn't seem to hold any meaning.

I checked the fridge while he was in the bathroom and, to his credit, there was no milk. It made me feel a little better, but it didn't completely wipe away that uneasy feeling that stayed with me for the rest of Sunday.

Back at home again after my last day at work, the evening stretches out ahead of me. I check my stock of bananas and find the few remaining bunches are starting to turn brown and speckled. They're also starting to smell like ripe bananas, so I give them a squirt of bleach. There's a tinkle of bells and then a red, fluffy object goes flying across the kitchen floor, closely followed by Rupert. He bounds after it and pounces on it, pinning it down with his claws.

'What've you got Rupert?'

'A kittybird,' says Egg. He's standing at the entrance of the kitchen, scratching his beard thoughtfully. 'I think he likes it, don't you?'

Rupert freezes, with one paw resting on the ball. I see now that it's a ball-shaped ladybird with black spots. It must have a bell sown inside it.

'It makes a change from a mouse,' I say.

'I think I'll write that.'

'What are you writing?'

'Oh just a review... nothing important...'

I take his word for it and launch into my own news about my prematurely terminated contract.

'It's not like I work for them, so I'm not fired exactly... it just feels like it.'

'Are you going to become a vegan, then?'

'No.'

'But you'll be broke.'

'I'm sure I'll get another temp job next week,' I say. If only I knew what exactly Jan had said to my agency then I'd know how worried I should be. 'For now, I've got a lot of work to do on my bananas.'

'You should get the clip from the news,' Egg says. 'Farrell's been looking for it on YouTube, but I don't know if he's found it yet.'

'Oh, cool... When did you speak to Farrell?'

'Saturday night, when he came over.'

'He came over? Where did you say I was?'

'I said a man had come to collect you.'

'"A man"? You make it sounds so mysterious.'

'I couldn't remember his name.'

'He's called Elliot.'

'Oh, that's what Farrell said his name would be.'

I feel a bit awkward about this revelation and I stand there for a moment wondering what Farrell must have thought. I hadn't lied to him exactly. But I had suggested I was going to be in all night working on my website, which I did do, eventually, on the Sunday.

'Okay, well, good... I'm going to be in my room working.'

'Do you think Bibiana will invite us around for supper?'

'Egg, you can't expect her to cook for us every other day.'

'I know, she's a queen; she shouldn't be cooking at all.'

Alone in my room, I tape sheets of A4 paper together until I have one huge sheet and then I lay it on my bedroom floor and start doodling how I want my website to look. I need to visualise it. I'm not very technical and I'm not looking forward to watching step-by-step tutorials, but at least time is on my side. I've got all night if I want. It's not as if I've got a job to get up for.

My body tenses when I hear the doorbell ring. If it's Bibiana inviting us over for supper, I'm going to have to say no. I hear Egg walk along the hall and then the sound of the latch. I realise my shoulders are hunched up to my neck and I let them go. The door opens and shuts. It must have been a mistake. Or maybe just the neighbour dropping a package left by the postman while we were out. Egg has been getting a lot of post recently. But then I hear footsteps on the stairs and a moment later there's a tentative knock on my door.

'Yep?'

It's Farrell. He looks as if he's just stepped out of the shower. There's water glistening in his hair and he's shaved off his beard. I catch myself thinking how gorgeous he looks.

'Hey, what are you up to?' he says.

He sounds a little hyper.

'Working on my website.'

'I thought websites were supposed to be online?'

His cheeky smile is contagious, but I'm reluctant to laugh. I don't want to make light of my project today.

He sits down on my bed and I notice he's got a sheet of paper folded in his hands. I hope it's not his book because I just don't have time.

'So I got your cryptic message about your job,' he says. 'I'm sorry.'

'Don't be. I'll get something else. Jan is a cow anyway. I was only ten minutes late.'

'Why was that?'

185

I roll my eyes. 'I had a learner bus driver, who thought he had to stop at every single bus stop in London.'

'Oh... so you went from home? ...The usual way? ...I mean, you got the same bus?'

'Same bus, crap driver.'

He frowns and there's something awkward in his manner as his eyes dart around my room and his fingers play with the corner of his paper.

'So how was your weekend?'

It sounds like a pointed question. His cheeks redden slightly. 'I mean, how was Sunday?'

'Sunday I was here brainstorming and a fat lot of good it did, too...'

'Oh, I thought you were with Elliot.'

The memory of him carrying me up the stairs with my legs straddled around his waist provokes a wave of heat across my cheeks. Farrell has come over for the details, but I feel a bit embarrassed now.

'No... we just saw each other on Saturday, it was unplanned, really... he rung me up last minute...'

His big green eyes are fixed on me, his paper forgotten. 'So you like him?'

I shrug, 'Yeah, I think so...'

I don't feel like talking about it.

'But you'll see him again?'

'Maybe... yes... I don't know yet...' I pick up Rupert's fluffy mouse that's lying on the floor and throw it at him. 'Farrell, I *really* need to do some work! Can you interrogate me tomorrow instead?'

He catches it with his free hand and rests it on the bed. 'Can I help?'

'I don't know. What do you think I should call the website? I'm having doubts now...'

'Can't you just use your Twitter name? 'Lookabanana'?'

Of course. Branding. That's exactly what I should do. I'll start with a small site and then build it up. I need to include a request for people's photos. Collaboration. That's what it's all about. People can collaborate not only with their pictures but with their theories about the concept. I will need an official concept, too. The longer I go without one, the more nervous I feel.

'Farrell, you're a genius.'

I move aside my huge patchwork paper and sit at my desk. My laptop whirs into action and I'm off.

Farrell coughs and I turn around in my swivel chair.

'I'll just leave you to it, then, shall I?' he says.

'Probably for the best...I'm going to be up all night at the rate I'm going.'

He gets up and I notice the piece of paper again. I point at it.

'Did you to want to show me something?'

He looks slightly alarmed and his hand curls around it, causing it to crumple.

'No, no, nothing.'

'Yes, you did. What is it?'

'Nothing, honestly.'

I don't believe him. He's just frozen there, wanting to show me, but pretending he doesn't. I'm not letting him chicken out now. I get up and make a grab for it and he pulls his arm back quickly, banging his hand against the back of the door.

'Give it to me!'

'It's nothing!' he says, with a breathless little laugh.

'If it's nothing, then you can show it to me!'

I make another attempt to grab it but he switches it to his other hand behind his back. I try to reach around him to get it, but he's too quick and holds it above his head, too high for me. I'm facing him, on tip toes, trying to get at it. We're both laughing now, which isn't helping either of us. He's shaking and I can't compose myself long enough to leap.

When his arm starts to droop a little I take my chance and make a jump for it. I miss completely and stagger forwards, falling into his arms, which instinctively go to catch me. He stops laughing abruptly and looks at me closely. My breath catches in my throat. The room feels suddenly electric. Without warning, he leans forwards and kisses me.

For a moment, all I feel is the warm touch of his lips on mine and my own waking up to them and responding. And then, in the next moment, I'm pulling back, shocked by this breach of friendship.

He holds up his palms.

'I'm, I'm sorry,' he stammers. 'I... I thought...'

But he doesn't finish his sentence. He holds my gaze for a brief moment longer, enough for me to detect a glimmer of pain in them that I don't understand, and then he heads out of my bedroom.

'Wait,' I call, too quietly. 'Wait!'

I hear him tear down the staircase, his footsteps drumming against the carpet. The front door opens, then slams, and I sink down onto the end of my bed and stare into space with my head buzzing.

What was he thinking? Was it just an accident? A stupid impulse?

After a moment, I realise I'm touching my lips, where the ghost of his kiss still lingers. I close my eyes and take a deep breath. It was nothing. It was just a mistake.

Yet how can I ignore what I saw in the depth of those green eyes? How can I pretend it was nothing, when it was so obviously everything?

Chapter 26

I force myself to focus on my project and push Farrell's kiss to the bottom of the pile of things I need to deal with. It's not easy. Unresolved situations always provoke such a huge avalanche of thoughts, none of which fully go away.

I keep playing out what we're going to say to each other the next time we meet. Will it be that cliché encounter? He says, 'Can we forget about it?' I say, 'Forget about what?' But if he really wants it to be forgotten, why doesn't he send a text message now and tell me that? I just want him to put a full stop at the end of what just happened. He can't just run away stammering that he's sorry; I need something more.

If he's going to pretend nothing happened, then I need to know that too. I'll play along, of course, so no one feels embarrassed. I need to know or it'll drive me mad. If he doesn't say anything tonight, then I'll go over tomorrow as if nothing has happened and tell him about my new website. The sooner we can clear the air the better. We're good at being friends. We're really good at it. I can't imagine my world without Farrell.

The door creaks open and I turn to find Rupert has come to keep me company. I'm quite moved by his timing. I scoop him up and he incorporates himself onto my lap.

'Silly Farrell,' I whisper, as I tickle Rupert's chin.

Eventually the internet works its magic and sucks me in and I stop checking my phone. I take ages over a banner for my site using the photo from the Tate and after a lot of cropping and resizing it finally fits snugly at the top of my page. Next job is to add a welcome message. I fiddle about for ages, writing and deleting and re-writing the same thing. After a while I switch to uploading photos. But I haven't got enough and without the news footage it all looks a bit thin on the ground. I need something to lend it more credibility.

I pick up my phone and before I can change my mind I call Matt Costa. To my surprise, he picks up straight away.

'Amber, I've been meaning to get in touch! How are you?'

'I'm good, but I need your help!'

'I know. I've been thinking about you. How about an interview?'

'That's just what I had in mind,' I say, smiling.

'I saw your bananas on the news. I totally underestimated you...I've been talking to some editors and I've got a few ideas.'

'Go on...'

'Well, first things first, let's start with your full name?'

Ah. The name thing.

'I was wondering whether I should use an artist's name or whether I should use my real name.'

'What artist name?'

'That's the problem. On the news they called me 'the banana woman', but that makes me think of "Bananaman" from those old comics, the Beano. Do you know who I mean? That clumsy prat with stubby half bananas for ears?'

'Why don't you just give me your full name Banana Woman?'

'Fine. Amber Thompson.'

'Why bananas?'

He sounds suddenly efficient, like he's working on a timer.

'Because I was given a sack of them...'

'From who?'

'A Polish chef... they were part of a police operation that went

190

wrong.'

Matt lets out a delighted laugh. 'Wait! I'm going to get comfortable.' I imagine him leaning back in his leather recliner and swinging his legs up onto his desk. 'So you're basically mocking the police with your bananas?'

'No, not at all.'

'But your project could be interpreted as that, couldn't it?'

'No, that's not what I was going for. Are you writing this down?'

'I'm recording it.'

'Aren't you supposed to tell me that first?'

'Do you want some publicity or not?'

'Yes, but it has to be positive.'

'You've got to take whatever you can get.'

Doubts rush in, then, and I bat them away. He's just being pragmatic.

'Give me the concept, then,' he says.

'Well... I thought the city needed brightening up.'

'Brightening up? ... With rotting fruit?' I can hear the scepticism in his voice. 'I preferred the police angle.'

'Actually, scrap that. It's about highlighting something ordinary so people see it for the first time.'

That's the best I could come up with after an entire Sunday brainstorming.

Silence.

I bite the corner of my lip. I'm getting the same feeling I did when Jan told me things weren't working out. Is he going to change his mind about doing the interview?

He sniffs and I hear him shifting position.

'Okay, we'll get back to that... How does your love life influence your art?'

I let out an unattractive snort. A Farrell snort. Typical that he has to come into my head now and remind me of the whole unresolved situation. I quickly glance at the screen of my phone to see if a text message has arrived while I've been talking. Nothing.

'That's easy. It doesn't.'

'Oh come on, Amber. Give me something to work with, will you?'

'I'm not just going to make stuff up.'

'Isn't this whole stunt about make-believe? Is it not a two fingers up at the stupidity of our society? If you shout loud enough then people will think you're important? Because that's what you said originally.'

'I know but...'

I feel cornered. Knowing that I'm being recorded has made me feel self-conscious. I suddenly don't feel confident enough to be controversial.

'I do like my bananas,' I finish weakly.

Matt inhales and I realise he's smoking.

'Alright, Amber. What about Elliot Frinton-Smith? Have you slept together yet?'

'That's none of your business!'

'That's a big fat yes then. Is he interested in your art?'

'Wait, don't write that!'

'Your art, Amber, is he interested in it?'

'Well, yes, I think so. He drove me to the Tower of London so I could leave some bananas there.'

'Great! When are you seeing him next?'

'Wait, you can't write that we slept together.'

'Are you going to see him again, though?'

'Maybe, but I don't know when!'

'Well, let me know. It'll be a great photo opp. Do you know he was asked to be on *Made in Chelsea*?'

'You're not serious.'

'His mum wouldn't let him, though.'

'Thank God.'

'Amber, you can't afford to be judgemental at this point. You're also trying to join the celebrity circus.'

'No, I'm not. I'm trying to be an artist.'

'Oh come on! This was supposed to be an experiment, wasn't it?'

'If you publish that people will thinking I'm laughing at them!'

'We'll be lucky if we can get anything published. I mean, the odds are very slim, actually.'

I feel a twinge of disappointment. I can't help it. I do want to be in a magazine.

'Well, what can I do to help its chances?' I say.

'Good! That's the Amber I wanted to hear.'

I'm not letting the fear get the better of me.

'I've got an idea,' he says. 'But you're not going to like it.'

'Go on.'

An hour later I'm in bed struggling to get to sleep. Farrell hasn't texted me and I need to talk to him. The conversation with Matt Costa has left me feeling unsettled. It wasn't a difficult decision. My immediate reaction to his nude photo idea was a loud, resounding no.

I made it clear that I didn't agree with the objectification of women. I was not about to encourage future generations of girls to believe that to be successful, you have to strip off. My decision may have been slightly influenced by the thought of what my parents would say if they saw a naked picture of their daughter in a magazine, not to mention my grandparents. But mainly it had been a simple matter of the Banana Woman revealing her principles rather than her boobs.

I punch my pillow into a new shape and turn on my side.

Why am I still thinking about it, anyway?

The thing is, it wouldn't have been totally nude. Obviously I would have bananas covering my modesty. It wouldn't take many bananas, either, to cover my little bosoms, which must come from my father's side because all the women on my mum's side shop at Bravisso, a shop catering for the bigger breast. I could have worn a little skirt made out of bananas, too. I mean, there's probably some Caribbean tribe who wear banana skirts and no one would think their women were being objectified, would they?

I don't know. Maybe I've got it all wrong. Is doing a nude picture a form of liberation or enslavement?

I turn on my back and stare up at the ceiling. I've been told I have nice legs. I won't have these nice legs forever. Maybe they deserve to be shown off a bit. What was that thing in the Bible about not putting your talents under a bushel but letting them shine?

Shit. Am I really trying to use the Bible to justify a nude photo shoot?

I need a drink.

It strikes me that I could actually have a drink. It's not like I have to get up early for work tomorrow. Instead of making me feel better, though, the thought sends my spirits plummeting. Not only do I not have a job but I've also said no to a huge opportunity for publicity. What is wrong with me? It's fear, isn't it? That's what's made me say no. Not principles, not morality, not my lack of cleavage but pathetic, knee-weakening fear.

My head is aching from all the thinking. I turn over again and my gaze settles on my mobile phone on the side of my bed. I reach out for it and the touch of my fingers makes it light up in the darkness. I stare at the screen and will it to ring.

Is Farrell awake? Is he kicking himself for making things weird between us? I should tell him not to worry. That's what I'll do. I sit up against my slumped pillow and begin the text. I already feel the anticipation of getting his reply. In a moment everything will be okay again between us. And when it is, I can ask him about the nude shoot and he can reassure me that I made the right decision saying no.

Hey Farrell, let's just forget about whatever happened, okay? I know you were just trying to distract me from grabbing your secret paper...

Yes, I'll keep it light.

... Very sneaky of you, by the way. Anyway, no harm done! Speak to you tomorrow, good night!

I send it.

Then I wait.

Damn it. Instead of putting one lot of thoughts to rest, I've created another avalanche of them. Now, I'm wondering how he's going to react to the message. Was it too frivolous?

I think of him standing in my room looking so handsome and fresh-faced. He'd shaved for me. He knows I prefer him clean-shaven because I've told him so. He'd had a shower and he'd stood in front of that mirror with his razor and he'd thought about me.

I was trying to give him a way out with that text message, but what if I'm being insensitive? I can't forget the humiliation in his eyes. But it was just pride and pride heals, doesn't it?

I turn on my bedside light. I can't go on like this. I'm giving myself a headache. In situations like these, it's important to keep busy. I turn my thoughts back to the photo shoot. The key is to treat this in a business-like manner. It should not be an emotional matter.

Will a tasteful nude photo, which won't actually be nude, since I'll be covered with bananas, help create some hype about my art?

But there's no answer on the tip of my tongue. I lie there thinking about it for some time. The problem is a normal nude photo cannot be justified, since it would have nothing to do with the project but... if I was painted...

I grab my phone and call Matt. It's gone midnight, but I get the feeling that Matt is an insomniac who falls asleep in the early hours watching rubbish on TV.

'Amber?'

'I've changed my mind, I'll do the photo!'

'Really?'

'But only if I'm painted head to toe...'

'Painted?'

'Yes, you know, body art, they can do incredible things... they could cover me in bananas or turn me into a banana tree or something... I haven't thought it through yet, but what do you think?'

When he speaks I can hear the smile in his voice.

'Amber, that's brilliant.'

I feel like running downstairs and getting that drink now. And then I have another thought.

'Shit, it's probably expensive, though.'

'Hmm...'

I can hear a clicking. He's already on the internet looking for an answer.

'It's probably hundreds...' I say, my heart sinking. 'We aren't going to be able to do it, are we?'

'Don't worry... I might just have an investor.'

I sit up. 'Really?'

'I think so.'

'Wow. What does that mean? This sounds serious. Do I need a lawyer or something?'

He laughs. 'No, nothing like that, just someone who would love the idea and I'm sure would be willing to help. Don't worry about it now. I'll sort everything out.'

'Who is it?'

'An art fanatic; you don't know them. Are you free the day after tomorrow?'

'Uh, yes...'

'Good. I'll text you the studio address when it's all confirmed.'

After that I can't get back to sleep. My head is buzzing. I lie there staring up at the ceiling and instead of an ugly, beige lampshade, I'm imagining photo shoots and brightly coloured magazine spreads and a faceless investor inviting me onto a private jet. I'm seeing glittery gallery openings with my name on them and me, with a glass of champagne in my hand, my outfits changing with every sip. And then, unbidden, an image of Farrell slips into the foreground of my mind, and when I close my eyes, it doesn't go away.

Chapter 27

The studio is above an Indian restaurant in Brick Lane. The smell of spicy curry wafts in through the huge window and makes me feel nauseous. I was too nervous to eat breakfast this morning and the second coffee has made me feel light-headed and jittery. Matt is running late and I'm in the hands of the photographer, Alessandro, who hasn't got off the phone since I arrived. He's yelling at someone in Italian and waving his arm about as if he's trying to swat flies.

I haven't got my clothes off and I already feel naked. The studio is open-plan with a long desk running down one side and no obvious dressing area. I wish there was a friendly female face instead of this fiery, macho Mediterranean, who sounds as though he's used to getting his own way. I've brought a backpack full of painted bananas, but I don't know what we're going to do with them. Are we going to attach them to me somehow, or am I just going to pose with them?

The angry phone call ends unexpectedly in hysterics and I wonder if I've mistaken rage for affection. He whips around and shoots me a wide-eyed smile, which makes him look a little crazed.

'*Donna delle banane!*'

'Hello...'

He puts a hand under his chin and examines me from head

to toe.

'Okay, we begin, yes?'

'How? Where's the body artist?'

He stares at me blankly. 'What?'

'I've got to be painted first.'

A twitch of confusion.

'You don't understand what I'm saying, do you?'

He looks indignant. 'Yes, of course! You *nuda con le banane*, very sexy...'

I feel the panic rising fast. 'No, not sexy, it's got to be artistic!'

He waves his hand dismissively at me. 'You trust me, yes?'

'No.'

He laughs. 'Everything is okay!'

No, nothing is okay. Where is Matt? He was the one who organised it, who assured me everything would be professional and done in good taste. Have I been tricked? What if he hasn't booked the body artist? Has he assumed I'd just do the nude photo anyway?

Alessandro hums to himself as he adjusts the legs of the tripod, where his camera is fixed and takes off the lens cover.

'Look, I'm not doing a nude photo!'

My voice has crept up a few octaves and my pulse is racing. I should grab my things and get out of here, but something is holding me back.

'This is an art project. Matt said it would be tasteful and artistic. I'm not stripping off naked! I'm not some glamour girl!'

I unzip my rucksack and grab a bunch of lime-green bananas. I hold them out to him.

'Look, if I can't be painted, then at least I've got to be covered in these!'

He takes the bananas off me, frowning and smiling.

'*Io non ti capisco pazza...*' he replies, unhelpfully. The he holds up a finger. 'One moment.'

He gets on the phone and I feel a surge of hope. The person on the other end of it is bound to know what to do. The conversation is animated, but Alessandro does more listening than speaking this time, which I feel is promising. I blink away the threat of tears and redo my ponytail. I would have made more effort with my hair and make-up if I'd known the photo shoot was going to be so understaffed.

Finally, Alessandro gets off the phone.

'Okay, she coming.'

'Who is coming?' I ask.

He runs his hands over his arm and chest as if he were lathering himself up with imaginary soap.

'Body artist,' he says. 'To paint bananas on skin... very sexy, yes?'

A trickle of relief runs through me. 'Okay, good...'

*Not sexy, artistic...*I suppose I'll have to take responsibility for that with my poses. I won't be pushing my boobs together and pouting at the camera. This is not about sex. It's about stopping in your tracks and seeing something for the first time.

Alessandro points at the stylish coffee machine at the end of his desk. 'Espresso?'

If I drink any more coffee I might start hovering. 'Yes please.'

He fiddles with the little white china cups and I perch on a stool in the corner, wondering what I've got myself into.

The body artist arrives twenty minutes later. She's called Monica and has peroxide-blonde hair and a lip-liner tattoo, which wouldn't look so bad if she was wearing lipstick between the greeny lines. Her name is the only thing I can get out of her. She's from Romania and doesn't speak English or Italian, so both Alessandro and I are forced to communicate in hand signals.

I get some paper from Alessandro and sketch my idea. Like the bananas, I want every part of me covered. She watches, her brow knitted, her lips scrunched together. Every so often she leans in and adds a suggestion in pencil. Her controlled strokes inspire confidence. She seems to be understanding me.

When my phone rings, I assume it's Matt with an excuse. But it's not, it's Elliot and the question of whether I should tell him what I'm doing, or not, rushes through my head.

'Let me guess,' he says. 'Matt Costa hasn't shown up yet.'

My breath catches in my throat. 'How did you know?'

'He hasn't told you, has he?'

'Told me what? What's going on?'

'Who do you think is paying for the body artist and for Alessandro?'

An investor! Not someone I'd had sex with! Not someone I was still trying to work out what I felt for!

'No, wait, no, no, no...You're not paying for these pictures, Elliot. I won't let you.'

Monica hands me what looks like a rolled-up ball of tights, which turns out to be a pair of nude knickers. She tugs at my top, signalling for me to start undressing.

'Amber, darling, I want to do this,' he says. 'I love what you're doing and so does Matt.'

'No he doesn't! He thinks it's a big joke!'

'That's not true. He's gone to a lot of trouble to organise today.'

'I'm not letting you pay for this!'

'Well, you've got no choice. I've already paid for it.'

I can't believe it. And yet Monica is the proof, pulling at my t-shirt and tapping her watch.

'Matt is a penniless bugger with a lot of contacts,' Elliot says. 'After today, we'll sort ourselves out without him. Alright?'

'No, I'm not alright!'

'I wouldn't let the money issue bother you, Amber. Artists have always had their patrons.'

'I don't need a patron,' I say, feeling defensive. 'I'm going to kill Matt when he turns up.'

'I don't think that would be wise, especially with a photographer on hand!'

He's laughing as if this is funny.

'I don't understand why he's got you involved.'

'Didn't Saturday night mean anything to you?'

'Of course, but...'

The air suddenly seems so close. I tug at the neck of my t-shirt and fan my face uselessly with my hand. This is too intense. I'm not ready for this.

'I'll come over after, if you like,' he says.

'I don't know what I'd like.'

I'm a romantic. The day I saw him I daydreamed about our wedding in a beautiful period house. But that's what I do. If daydreaming was a profession I would be in the top spot. I'd be the CEO of daydreaming. I'd give consultations for a grand a minute.

'Amber?'

'What?'

'You know I've got your best interests at heart, don't you? A lot of people would love to be in your skin but can't because they are too frightened of their own brilliance.'

Brilliance? Is that what we're calling this? Because right now I feel like a fool.

'Now don't forget to hold your bananas for the shoot so people recognise who you are.'

I get off the phone and Monica manoeuvers me over to her painting trolley. She nods at my t-shirt and I look pointedly over at Alessandro. She laughs and shakes her head.

'He gay, I think,' she says, smiling.

Monica helps me pull my t-shirt over my head and unhooks my bra. I try to clear my mind as she tests out colours on a piece of card, but the feeling of uneasiness is difficult to shake off. By being excluded from Matt and Elliot's discussion, I feel as if I've lost control.

But I could stop this now if I wanted... So why don't I?

The touch of the paint is cool on my skin. Monica begins with my shoulder and works her way down the side of my body, making huge sweeping strokes with spray paint. When she fills in the first glossy green banana leaf the excitement comes bubbling up. Perhaps I can cope with this situation after all. She's covering

201

my skin inch by inch and turning me into something exotic and beautiful.

But then I think of Elliot's words and the disquiet descends on me again. *Artists have always had their patrons.* By accepting his offer, I've tied myself to him. I owe him. A fresh burst of anger flares up within me directed at Matt. It's his fault! He lied about the investor!

I'll have to pay Elliot back and how am I going to do that when I'm still waiting to hear about my next job? I don't want to be tied to anyone by a debt, especially someone I'm seeing on a romantic level. That's what we were doing, although now nothing feels quite right. I don't want to sleep with my 'patron', I just want a boyfriend I can trust to tell me when I'm being an idiot. Does he really have my best interests at heart or is this just business?

I find myself wondering what Farrell would think of me now. I wish I could rewind time but I don't know how far back I'd go. A part of me wishes I'd never taken the bloody bananas from Andrzej, but there's still that other part egging me on, telling me that this is the test to see whether I have the character to be successful or not.

Monica is now using a brush to carefully paint bananas across my breasts. I feel my cheeks hotting up. It tickles so much, but I manage to keep still. My nipple is painted dark brown and is disguised as the top of the banana skin. I close my eyes because I feel so self-conscious I think I might die. This is real art, I think miserably. I'm just using Monica's talents to promote my lack of talent. It's not right. I should be painting bananas all over *her*, not the other way around. Is painting a naked body really that different from painting a skirting board? Because I did the one in my bedroom and it wasn't too bad. I could always make a stencil. Could I? Do I even have the talent for that?

Oh lighten up, Amber! The force of my inner voice surprises me. *This was your vision! You set this in motion! Stop beating yourself up and be proud of it!*

I open my eyes and give Monica a tentative smile.

'You relax now?' she cries, stepping back and clapping with the heels of her hands.

'A little bit.'

'You relax now,' she repeats firmly.

Hours pass, with few breaks. If Monica could speak better English I'm sure she'd praise me for my patience. I, in turn, would ask her how long there was left to go. Every so often she lets me perch on a stool and sip from a cup of water. Alessandro is glued to his laptop and ignores us both. It's tedious, but at least I grow comfortable in my new skin. In fact I'm quite sad that I'm going to have to wash it off at some point. Monica has done a beautiful job. A blend of orange, yellow and green makes up the tree trunk that begins at my ankles and covers my legs. Luxurious green banana leaves reach across my stomach and curve around my waist, while intricate bunches of brightly coloured bananas adorn my body like jewels.

She finishes off by touching up my mascara and eye-liner, and dabbing my lips with dark-red lipstick. When she holds up a mirror, I stare, amazed at the pattern of foliage winding across one side of my face. The right cheek is left untouched. I look like a forest goddess from a child's fairy tale. My fears of looking cheap dissolve. This is perfect.

'No touch,' Monica says.

There's a knock on the door and Alessandro opens up.

'Matteo!'

'Alessandro, *come stai?*'

'*Bene! Bene!*'

Matt's expression is sheepish as he walks in, but it's swiftly transformed into awe as he surveys me. I remember my nakedness is thinly veiled with paint and I hold my hands up to my chest without touching skin to skin. Lucky for him the result has exceeded my expectations.

'No move!' Monica cries.

'Wow!' he says. 'That's incredible.'

'What were you thinking, asking Elliot for money?' I say, through gritted teeth.

'No talk!'

It seems that under pressure Monica can pull out all the words she needs.

'Elliot has more money than sense, he doesn't mind.'

'But I've been seeing him!'

'Exactly. I knew that if he was capable of investing in Montague's car crash of an exhibition then he would be happy to part with a bit of cash on someone he was shagging.'

My urge to slap him returns with force. Matt has such a way with words.

'Not just that, but someone who managed to sneak her art into the Tate and get it on the news.' His smile is full of admiration. 'Congratulations on that, by the way. I wouldn't have had the balls.'

'It wasn't just me. I had a little cheerleading squad behind me. My friend Bibi can be pretty persuasive.'

Alessandro is tapping his foot.

'We begin now?' he says, with forced jollity.

'Yes of course, *scusa* Alessandro!' Matt gushes. 'Where do you want her?'

Alessandro holds his palm up to me. Evidently I'm to stay where I am. It's everyone else that needs to move. He walks around me, rubbing his chin thoughtfully and then he starts moving the floodlights into position. Matt hands me one of the bunches of bananas, which Monica has touched up with glossy red paint.

'Hold it out, as if your arm was a tree,' he says.

'Don't talk to me!' I growl. 'I'm very annoyed!'

A draft creeps in through the window, making me shiver.

'You'll be warm in a minute with these lights on.'

Alessandro peers through the camera. There's a shock of white light as the flash goes off followed by a profound silence. It's a silence that's promptly broken by the ringing of my mobile. I've left it out on the counter.

'It's mine,' I say.

'No talk! No move!' Monica snaps.

I look back at Alessandro, who is leaning into his camera.

The ringing stops abruptly. Matt answers. 'Hello, Amber's phone.'

'Leave it!' I hiss.

Isn't there a rule against answering other people's phones?

'She's in the middle of a photo shoot at the moment. Can I take a message?'

Why couldn't he just say I'm busy?

'Farrell…Will she know who you are?'

'He's my best friend!'

'No talk!'

'Farrell Kennedy, alright then, I'll let her know. Thank you.'

There's another blast of white light as Alessandro takes another photo. I hear Matt return my phone to the counter.

'Farrell Kennedy called,' he says. 'He wants to ask you something.'

I stand there as if nothing has changed, but inside it's as if fireworks have been set off. Can they sense my nerves? I feel as if my whole body is fizzing with anticipation. I just want to call him back as quickly as possible. But Alessandro looks as though he's going to be taking pictures all day. What does Farrell want to ask me? It's agony to stand still. I need to know now. Damn these unresolved situations!

There's a knock on the door and I feel a wave of dread. For God's sake! No more people! I hold my bunch of bananas across my chest. They might see patterns and beautiful bananas, but when I look down I still see two naked breasts!

Matt opens the door ajar.

'Come back in half an hour,' he says to whoever it is beyond the door.

I recognise Elliot's voice at once. 'Don't be a complete cock, Matt. Don't forget who's paying for this.'

The way he says it makes me feel dirty and I feel a sudden revulsion for both of them.

Alessandro sighs loudly and launches his complaint at the window, '*Non posso lavorare in queste condizioni...*'

'Oh wow,' Elliot murmurs.

I soften a little at the amazement in his voice. I suppose he didn't mean any harm and I do look pretty stunning painted like this.

'Amber, you look incredible.'

'No move!'

I feel Elliot's eyes sinking into me. I don't know which part of me, but I'm guessing it'll be at my nipple-topped banana.

'Stop staring,' I say, through the corner of my mouth.

'I can't help it, darling, you look fabulous.'

Alessandro claps his hands suddenly, making us all jump.

'We continue, yes?'

Elliot and Matt both reply at once, 'Yes, yes, please, carry on.'

They don't move. They stay where they are, gazing at me. I feel a strange mixture of powerfulness and helplessness, which I can't begin to interpret. I stare at the camera defiantly and remind myself this was my own doing. They simply helped the process along, but I am the artist that made it all happen.

You are Amber, the banana woman, the superhero waking up the city to the extraordinary. You have nothing to be ashamed of!

Another flash of light. Another picture closer to fame and fortune.

You are beautiful, you are exotic, you are not afraid to stand out!

My confidence begins to soar.

'You should wear that more often, Amber,' Elliot says in a low voice. 'You look absolutely ravishing."

And just like that, my glorious bubble is burst. Once again I'm reminded of how exposed I am and that in exposing myself I have tied myself to this man. This man who I barely know and am beginning to regret sleeping with.

Chapter 28

After the shoot, all I want to do is lie in a hot bath, close my eyes and let the paint wash off by itself. Of course I'm being unrealistic and I'm not surprised when Matt tells me there isn't a bath in the building. When he confesses there isn't a shower either I'm dismayed. I'm stuck in the middle of London looking as if I've just stepped out of Avatar. How am I supposed to get home on the tube like this?

'Half of Camden looks like that,' Matt scoffs. 'Stop moaning and come with us to the pub. We need to make plans.'

I think of Farrell and feel frustrated. I want to be alone when I call him and preferably dressed like a civilian, not a walking mural.

Somehow Elliot and Matt persuade me to get into my clothes fully painted and join them in the pub for a debrief. I have leaves across my face, bananas twisted around my arms and neck, and my bare legs look reptilian. Every head in the pub turns to look at me when I walk in. Elliot and Matt are too busy arguing to notice that my entrance has had an effect.

'She should definitely do something at Buckingham Palace,' Matt says, pushing his way through to the front of the bar. 'Think of all the tourists waving their phones about. It will go global in minutes.'

'I don't know, it's kind of mocking the monarchy, isn't it?'

'Oh fuck off, Elliot,' Matt laughs, ' wait... you're not serious, are you?'

These are *my* ideas they are bouncing around. Farrell and I wrote them all down on a serviette. Elliot looks at me to gauge my feeling on the matter of mixing monarchy with bananas, but I don't say anything. I've got this sick feeling in the pit of my stomach.

'Anyway... what's wrong with mocking the monarchy?' Matt says. 'They're just a dysfunctional family that's been given ridiculous privileges because once upon a time people believed kings were chosen by God. We know that's a pile of nonsense.'

'Call yourself an Englishman, do you?'

'You can be English and republican, you idiot.'

'Now I remember why I hate working with you.'

'Why? Because you're prejudiced?'

'Oh shut up!' I explode.

'Hang on,' Matt says, as the bar man finally appears to take our order.

I seethe in silence until we're standing at a bar table with our drinks. I can't sit down because if I do I'll smear paint all over the place. The bar man has already given me a warning look.

'What's going on?' I say. 'I mean, *really*. I feel... I feel like you might be using me...'

Yes, that's it. That's what I feel. Confused, used and very much out of the loop.

Matt starts to protest, but Elliot shuts him up with an authoritative raised palm and fixes me with a pained stare.

'Using you? How can you even think that? I don't know about Matt bu...'

'What the fuck?' Matt cries. 'This is me being philanthropic!'

'Philanthropic? You don't even know what that means,' Elliot smirks.

'Yes I fucking well do! I did a journalism degree, you know. I know a lot of fucking long words actually! You don't have to go to Cambridge, you arrogant...'

'Oh shut up!' I cry, clutching my head and remembering too late that my hands are covered in paint. 'Will you stop arguing please? I thought this was supposed to be about my art!'

'Of course it is,' Elliot says, resting one hand gently on my shoulder. 'Of course it is. I believe in your project, that's why I'm here. I care about your art. If you don't want my help, I understand.'

'Well, it's a bit late to say I don't want your help now. You've already paid for this,' I say, waving a hand at my legs. It's a fact that I'm having difficulties stomaching. 'And you've driven me and my bananas across the city...'

'I'm doing it for the love of art and my love of...' Elliot looks at me pointedly. *No! Don't say 'you' for God's sake!'*...your energy,' he finishes, without taking his eyes off me.

'I'm hoping to get paid a decent sum for the article about you,' Matt says, with a shrug. 'But you get the publicity. We're both helping each other out, aren't we?'

I suppose it makes sense. It's all legitimate. Normal. Elliot is an art fanatic with too much money and Matt is a journalist. All completely fine. I raise my beer to my lips and take a deep drink. It cools my parched throat and goes straight to my head. It's gone three o'clock in the afternoon and I haven't eaten a thing.

'So no one is using anyone, are they?' Matt continues.

Well, when he puts it like that... I just got cold feet, that's all.

Matt raises his eyebrows. 'Are they, Amber?'

'I suppose not.'

'Thank you. I don't like to be accused of being the baddy. It wasn't easy setting up that shoot, okay.'

'Thank you, Matt.'

'That's all I wanted.'

'Onwards and upwards?' Elliot says, squeezing my shoulder and rubbing the paint deeper into my favourite white t-shirt.

'Just don't do anything behind my back, okay?'

Matt does some scout's honour thing with his hands.

Elliot kisses me right on the lips and my reaction is to dodge

209

it. He looks surprised.

'Paint!'

'It's already rubbed off your lips, silly,' he says, putting his arm around me.

Matt raises his eyebrows. I worry he's taking notes of these affectionate gestures to fuel his article. I would have liked to keep things private until I'd sorted a few things out in my head. Maybe it's because I'm hungry, or tired, or maybe it's because it's been a stressful morning... but right now I don't feel like being around Elliot. Right now, I'm finding him very annoying.

I clap my hands over my pocket as my phone starts to vibrate.

'You didn't ring your friend back,' Matt says.

His name comes up on my screen.

'What friend?' Elliot asks, and his tone irritates me.

I turn away as I answer; my heart in my throat. 'Hi.'

'Hello,' Farrell replies softly. 'Are you free to talk?'

I swallow. 'No.'

'Where are you going?' Elliot calls.

I hold my hand over the receiver and point outside. Elliot looks disgruntled and I feel a flash of anger. I've spent half the day standing still, being painted! I deserve a little fresh air and five minutes to myself! What's his problem?

Passers-by gawp at me when I walk into the sunshine, but I don't care. I feel daring in my new skin.

'Amber?'

'Sorry, I had to get out of the pub...'

'I can call back if you're with someone.'

He must have heard Elliot's voice in the background and for some reason I feel compelled to deny that he's there.

'I was just with some friends...'

For a moment no one says anything. It's so quiet I can hear his intake of breath. I'm not great with silences and I want to get rid of this horrible feeling in my stomach.

'Look,' I say.

'Amber, don't...'

'What?'

'Don't try to make it better. You don't need to make excuses. I'm fine.'

'I wasn't going to...'

'You were. You were going to say that I slipped, or that I was hungry and mistook your mouth for a strawberry, I know how your head works.'

A laugh escapes me. He's right of course.

'Alright, no excuses,' I say, smiling. 'But everything's okay between us, yeah?'

In the moment before he speaks, I feel a tap on my shoulder. It's Elliot. I frown at him and he points at Matt, who's lighting up a cigarette. Farrell says something but I miss it.

'What did you say?'

My skin is prickling with heat and I'm annoyed my privacy has been snatched from me.

'Will you come to the bookshop?' he says. 'This evening.'

I'm confused. 'Why? Is it late-night shopping?'

'No, Amber, we're running our first poetry evening ever and I'm going to read something... something short and...'

'Of course I'll come!'

Why didn't I let him finish? What was he going to say?

'Sorry, I interrupted you... were you going to say anything else?'

He lets out a weak laugh. 'No, I'll say the rest tonight. It starts at eight.'

'Great! See you tonight, then.'

All sorted! All is well. I slide my phone back into the pocket of my skirt and turn to face Matt and Elliot. I feel so much better for talking to Farrell. Now I know things can be alright between us. I regret missing his last reading, but this time I'll be there and will prove that I'm a good friend. That's what we are. Good friends. So, why do I feel so bloody excited all of sudden?

'So we thought we'd make the most of your look,' Matt says,

211

'and head over to the South Bank. I'm thinking London Eye, Westminster, Houses of Parliament... there's so much in that area. Buckingham Palace is best to do at the changing of the guards.'

I check my phone. I'm going to have to leave lots of time to scrub this paint off before I head down to the bookshop.

'What's the matter?' Elliot asks.

'Just working out the time. I can't miss my friend's reading again.'

'The poet?'

I roll my eyes. 'He's called Farrell.'

'Yes, I know. He rings you up every time we meet.'

'Not every time.'

'Every time,' Elliot says, firmly.

Matt lets out a low whistle. 'Someone jealous?'

'Yes, *he* is evidently,' Elliot says.

'We're good friends,' I say, but I feel a little bit guilty now. I haven't taken a moment to look at things from Elliot's point of view. How would I like it if every time I was on a date, some girlfriend rang him up?

'Well, if you're just friends, then you won't mind me coming to the reading will you?'

I look at him, surprised. His eyebrows are raised in challenge. There's no excuse in my head. But I don't want him to come. I *really* don't want him to come.

'Well...uh...'

I don't know what to say.

'I knew it,' Elliot says. His jaw clenches as he pushes a hand through his hair.

Matt is smirking at me. Elliot's face is clouding up, withdrawing into that hurt expression that makes me feel under pressure to make everything better.

'No, yes, of course you can come,' I hear myself say. 'I just thought it might be too far.'

'We'll get a taxi,' he says, beginning to smile.

'Yes, of course.'

What could be better proof that our friendship is intact than bringing a date?

But I feel so disappointed.

Matt grinds his cigarette butt under his heel. 'Right, let's get you to the South Bank before that paint rubs off.'

'Yep,' I say, trying to muster some enthusiasm. 'Let's do this.'

Elliot kisses me and this time I make a conscious effort not to pull away. I close my eyes and try to enjoy the feel of his anxious tongue parting my lips, but the truth is, all I can think about is how I'm going to dissuade him from coming to Farrell's reading.

Chapter 29

This is the last photograph and then I'm out of here. The clock is ticking towards six o'clock and I need to get home fast and wash off this paint before Farrell's reading at eight.

Behind me the London Eye rises up into a sky of gathering clouds like a giant's bicycle wheel. Tourists watch from the glass pods as the wheels spins on its axle and an increasingly impressive view of the city spreads out before them. Down below, I'm the attraction of the moment. I stand with one hand supporting a bunch of orange bananas on my head, the other resting on my hip. All around me people watch and take sly snaps with their camera phones, not wholly certain if I'm somebody, but not wanting to make the mistake of not getting a shot in case I am.

'Please!' Matt begs.

But I won't do it. I won't take my top off in front of all these people. I don't know how well the paint work is doing underneath my t-shirt, but I imagine that after all the walking and posing, I must be looking more like mashed bananas than banana tree.

Elliot is on the phone again. He's been trying to get in touch with a gallery owner called Aurelia, who he knew very well at university. Apparently she's going to want to gobble me and my bananas up as soon as she hears about the project. That or she owes him a favour. I'm not sure how my bananas are supposed to capture people's interest in a gallery. At the moment I think they're only stimulating because of the iconic backdrops they're set against.

'That's it,' I say. 'I'm done.'

'But we're virtually on top of the Houses of Parliament!' Matt moans. 'It'll only be another half an hour and then we've covered the lot!'

It's been a long day and I'm tired and anxious to get cleaned up. I don't want to be late for Farrell's reading. I wish I was at the bookshop already, helping my friend with preparations, with plenty of time to relax with a glass of wine. But instead I'm going to be rushing like mad, and with Elliot tagging along too, unless I can stop him.

'I'm sorry, I can't. I've really got to make a move.'

Matt lowers his camera, 'Fine, but I'm disappointed.'

'We can't do everything in one day.'

'But *you* said, to have an impact we needed to blitz London with bananas,' he says. 'Now all this effort is probably going to be for nothing.'

'I can't let my best friend down again.'

'Yes you can! And anyway, if you pull this off everyone's going to want to be your best friend, so it's a win-win situation.'

But my mind is made up and nothing will make me stay.

'Smashing!' Elliot says to the person on the phone. 'Well, I look forward to hearing from her.'

He lowers his phone and launches into an excited rant about how close we are to reaching Aurelia. I find my temperature soaring and it takes all my powers of self-restraint to stop myself crying out *Not now!* My stomach is in a fist. I'm worrying the paint won't come off in time, or that there'll be a delay on the tube. There hasn't been a signal failure for at least two weeks, so one must be imminent.

'I've really got to go,' I say. 'You don't have to come if you don't want to. It's been a really long day and it's miles away from your house.'

We're in central London; it's easy for Elliot to get home from here. All he needs to do is jump on the Jubilee Line up to Bond Street and then it's a couple of stops to Notting Hill Gate on the Central Line. Maybe if I point this out he'll change his mind about coming?

'Of course I want to come. If you're so worried about being late, let's just jump in a cab.'

I'm a temp waiting to hear about my next job. Jumping into an expensive cab is only going to add to my worries. But he wouldn't understand that. In fact there's probably a lot he takes for granted.

'The tube is fine,' I say. 'Come on, let's go quickly.'

'Are you sure you want to go on public transport looking like *that*?' he says, one eyebrow cocked.

'What does it matter now? I've spent the whole day looking like this, haven't I?'

'Yes but...'

'Two minutes as an artist and you turn into a right prima donna,' Matt says. 'I suppose the experiment worked too well.'

I don't have time to point out to Matt that a prima donna would be far more likely to snap about not getting a cab than getting one.

'Fine! Let's get a cab!'

'Great!' Elliot says, beaming.

'Have a great night, guys. Don't think about me working late to get this project off the ground!' Matt calls after us.

I want to remind him who started 'this' project, but I swallow my pride and give him a thumbs-up as I walk away. He's on my side, after all.

After being stuck in traffic and the taxi driver taking us the scenic route, we finally pull up outside my house and I empty the contents of my wallet into the driver's hand because I don't want Elliot to pay for another thing for me.

Elliot doesn't walk up the garden path; he saunters, taking time to examine the overgrown grass and the thorny rose bush that has seen better days. I unlock the front door and look back at him, willing him to hurry up.

'Okay, we're here,' I say pointedly.

He walks up the steps so slowly he might as well be going backwards.

'You don't like gardening, then?' he says. 'You know, you could really do something wonderful with this...'

'I know, it's a mess. Can't do anything about it now, though.'

'No, summer's not the greatest time for planting, I suppose.'

'Right, are you coming in, then? I've got to get in the shower.'

He follows me into the corridor and I quickly shut the door. He digs his hands into his pocket and taps his foot against the tiles. I wish he wouldn't as some of the slabs are loose.

'Original tiles,' he says. 'Very nice. Victorian?'

'Yes, I think so.' I haven't got a clue. 'So, I'm going upstairs... do you want to just chill in the living room?'

'A glass of wine would be lovely.'

'Right...'

'If it's not too much trouble.'

'No, no, I'm just hoping this paint comes off...'

I hurry into the kitchen with Elliot following at a leisurely pace behind me. Rupert lets out a high-pitched miao from under the table. I look underneath and find he's curled up in a brand-new fleecy bed. Egg must be digging into his savings. I don't know how else he could have bought such a luxurious-looking item.

Elliot lights up when he sees him. 'Oh he's adorable, what's his name?'

'Rupert, like Rupert Bear.'

'But he's a cat.'

I ignore this acute observation and open the drinks cabinet, where I find a huge bag of cat biscuits. The location of it doesn't surprise me as much as the size of the package. Beside it are sets of tins wrapped in luxurious gold wrapping boasting the tastiest experience known to cat. I don't know what's got into Egg, buying

217

all this stuff.

'Red, please,' Elliot says.

I snap out of my reverie. My investigation into Egg's purchases can wait until tomorrow. I retrieve a bottle of wine from the back of the cupboard. It's a small miracle I've got one stashed away and that it's the correct colour. I discreetly scrape off the price label before plonking it on the counter.

'Oh God, not Blossom Hill,' he says, rolling his eyes. 'It's like being a student all over again.'

'Don't be such a snob.'

He laughs and I feel myself momentarily softening towards him. It's not his fault we're late. Why am I being so irritable with him, anyway? All he's done since I met him is try to help me.

I look into the cupboard and find the only clean glass is a pint glass that Farrell once accidentally brought home after a drunken night out. He'd forgotten his keys and not wanting to wake Danny, he'd slept on our sofa.

As I'm standing there with my back turned, Elliot puts his hands on my waist.

'Come here, my gorgeous little avatar,' he says, his wet lips on my neck.

'No, I've got to get this paint off me!'

I wriggle out of his grasp and reach up for the pint glass. He looks at it with disdain.

'I think I'd rather drink out of the bottle.'

'Suit yourself,' I say, placing it on the table. 'Make yourself at home. I won't be long!'

I leave him to it and head upstairs. He's a grown man and can entertain himself for fifteen minutes. That's all the time I've got if I don't want to get to the bookshop by the skin of my teeth.

In the bathroom, I strip off and rediscover the body art painted expertly over my skin. I look at myself in the mirror and feel a lump in my throat. It's so beautiful. This, my own body, familiar and yet so unfamiliar. Isn't this what I wanted it to be about?

Seeing something ordinary in a different light?

Now that it's all over, I can't believe I've done it. But I have, and those pictures are in someone else's hands now. Matt's hands. Am I a fool?

I close my eyes for a moment as the hot water rushes over me and an image of Farrell forms in my head. He is as he was the day he came to see me, dressed in that shirt that brings out his eyes, sleeves rolled up. Relaxed but with an effort behind it. Handsome jaw twitching with the uncertainty of the moment. Lips like I've never kissed before. His green eyes look deeply into mine and they hold a question.

I play it out again as I have so many times these last few days. My feet stumble and he catches me. He has strong arms. I hadn't noticed them before. He leans forwards and kisses me. And in my head, I don't pull back.

There's a knock on the door. I instinctively hold up my hands to cover my breasts.

'How's it going?' Elliot calls. 'Is it coming off?'

I look down at my arms and find my pale skin appearing from under the tropical colours.

'Yes, it's coming off fine,' I call back. I grab the shower gel and pour it generously into my hands and lather it into my skin.

'I told you it would!'

I listen out, but he doesn't say any more. My heart is beating fast. I can't pretend I don't feel anything. How can I when the thought of seeing him makes me feel as if I'm bursting with excitement and nerves?

But it's too late. I'm here with Elliot.

I abruptly turn off the shower and stand there dripping wet.
Focus.

It's a weakness of mine to flit from one thing to the next. That's why I've failed to make anything of myself. Perhaps that's why I'm so full of doubt; about my bananas, about Elliot, because for once, I'm sticking to something.

219

So stick to it.

I've got to try to make this work.

I'm relieved to find Elliot's not in my room when I get there. I rush to put my underwear on and then I hover in front of my open wardrobe, hurriedly scanning my clothes rack, feeling as if at any moment I might be caught doing something I shouldn't. I want to look good. Not good. I want to look amazing.

I think of the past outfits Farrell has seen me in and it makes me cringe. Those granny jumpers and old tights will have to go. I never want him to see me looking like that again.

'There you are,' Elliot says softly, stepping into my room. 'Nearly ready?'

I slip behind my wardrobe doors. 'Nearly.'

'I'm really looking forward to meeting this poet of yours,' he says. 'I know he's important to you...'

I feel a stab of guilt. If Elliot only knew how much he wouldn't be smiling like that.

'Yes, he's one of my best friends.'

The words don't feel right in my mouth. He's more than that. The question is, when am I going to stop pretending he isn't? And what on earth am I going to do about it?

Chapter 30

The door of the bookshop is closed when we get there, but the lights are all switched on. Beyond the window display I make out the backs of heads of people seated in clusters. In front of them is a standing microphone. Just seeing it makes me nervous; as if I'm the one who's going to perform.

Elliot is talking too loudly about a book in the window as we walk in and I feel self-conscious. If the audience is already in its place then the reading must be about to start. I relax a little when I hear the low murmur of conversation of people only beginning to settle down.

The first person I spot is Bibiana, who is sitting in the far corner beside an empty chair. She sees me and waves.

'Wine?' Elliot says.

'Yes, I'll grab us a seat.'

There's a table with glasses already filled, but I'm so anxious to get to my seat, I leave him to it. I cross the room. My eyes are darting all over the place, so I don't see Farrell until he's standing in front of me.

'Amber!'

His eyes are lit up as if he can't believe I'm there. He looks so happy to see me and I feel this confusing mix of joy and pain because in that moment I know his kiss was not a mistake. He meant to kiss me. And I'm about to hurt him a second time.

'I'm so glad you're here,' he says, and then lets out a nervous laugh. 'And slightly terrified now, too.'

'Farrell, I... I...' the words come crashing out. 'I'm not alone.'

He doesn't understand.

'I'm sorry I didn't know how to say "no"...' I blunder on.

Elliot appears at my side, tall and confident. He can't offer his hand because he's holding our wine, but in a voice that seems to reverberate around the room he introduces himself.

'Elliot Frinton-Smith. How do you do?'

'Oh...' Farrell says, his face falling for one horrible second. 'I'm Farrell...'

'I'm very much looking forward to your reading,' Elliot says, his voice sounding even more alarmingly posh than usual.

Farrell opens his mouth, but nothing comes out. He looks so uncomfortable. His eyes flit from Elliot to me. I want to spill out everything I'm feeling, but the only thing I can do is look at him with apologetic eyes. *Say something!* I think, as Elliot's smile turns to a frown and Farrell begins to seem rude.

'Thanks,' he says, at last. 'Um... I'd better get ready.'

Farrell squeezes past us and I turn to see him heading for the table of wine.

'Well, he was very friendly,' Elliot says, looking amused.

My cheeks are on fire. 'He's nervous, I think.'

Bibiana beams at us and pats the seat beside her, inviting me to sit down. Elliot rests the wine on the floor and turns to get a third chair, giving her the chance to wink at me meaningfully, and mouth, 'He's hot!'

I wish I could shoot her back a genuine smile, but my heart is on the floor.

'Hello,' Elliot booms, thrusting his hand out to Bibiana. 'Elliot Frinton-Smith.'

She flashes him a radiant smile. 'It's lovely to meet you. Bibiana Fuentes.'

'Spanish?'

'Argentinean.'

'Well I'll try not to hold that against you.'

Her smile dips. 'And I'll try not to hold your Englishness against you.'

'So what have you been up to?' I jump in, sensing the mood turning sour.

She grabs my arm, suddenly excited. 'I had a job interview today. It's for a role at this small advertising company in West London... I don't know,' she shrugs and takes a sip of wine. 'I mean, they've probably interviewed about two hundred people.'

'When will you find out?'

'In a couple of days they'll tell me if I've got a second interview,' she says, crossing her fingers. 'Let's not talk about it, I'll get too nervous!'

She nods towards the microphone. 'This is exciting isn't it? I've been reading Farrell's book, it's really good.'

I feel a stab of jealousy. I try to dismiss it but it lingers. It's uncalled for and mean-spirited. I could have read his book too if I'd pressed him, but I didn't, so I've only got myself to blame.

Bibiana is looking particularly gorgeous this evening with her big lashes and glossy black hair arranged in a beehive ponytail. She's wearing a low-cut top and my eyes slips to the curves of her sexy cleavage.

'I thought Egg might have come,' I say.

She laughs. 'He came over specifically to tell me he wouldn't be making it because he's very busy. I was like o-kay...'

There's a cough from the front of the stage. It's Phil, the owner of the bookshop, standing slightly hunched in front of the microphone. The lights are lowered, too much, and then not enough. There are a few laughs and then the room falls quiet.

'I want to welcome you to our first poetry reading of the year. We hope it will become a regular thing, so please buy a book or two to keep us going! We have some great talents in our midst and without further ado, it gives me great pleasure to introduce our first writer, Farrell Kennedy...'

My heart is racing. *Come on, Farrell!* I'm nervous for him because I want so much for him to blow us away. Oh how I wish I'd spent time with him practising his poem out loud so I could know he's going to be alright.

His head is bowed as he makes his way to the front and he doesn't look happy. He stands in front of the microphone and he briefly glances up, his forehead knitted and his teeth biting furiously at the corner of his lip.

'Hi, everyone,' he says.

'Oh please don't let him be a mumbler,' Elliot whispers.

I bat away a bolt of anger. It's only because it's Farrell up there. I can't stand mumblers either and last week I bet I would have squeezed Elliot's hand and mouthed 'I know!' rather than wished him a million miles away.

Farrell pulls out a piece of paper from his back pocket. It's folded into a small square, which he unravels carefully. It's just like Farrell to have a scrappy piece of paper. I would have got him to print out a fresh copy if I'd known. *Come on Farrell!*

'He should really know it by heart,' Elliot says, a little too loudly.

'Shss.'

'Well he should.'

Farrell stares at his paper and then up at the audience. His eyes roll over each person and briefly settle on me. He swallows and then is completely still. When he speaks, his voice is low and his Irish lilt lends his words a soothing melody.

'*Alone was not intense before we met*
My words – old friends – abandon me to this:
Beyond a friendship, and yet...'

He looks up, finds me and I realise I've been holding my breath.

'Fuck,' he splutters. 'Sorry.'

A ripple of surprise runs through the room as it dawns on everyone that a swear word and an apology isn't part of the poem.

'I'm so sorry, everyone,' he says again, his free hand anxiously rubbing his chin. 'I've only gone and brought the wrong draft with me.'

My mouth drops open. There's a titter of nervous laughter from the audience. I know he's not telling the truth. I know that he's got the right draft in his hand. But it's about me. It's about me and that's why he can't read it. Tears prick my eyes. I want to run over there and beg him to keep reading to me, just to me.

'He can't be serious,' Elliot murmurs.

'So, now that I've set the bar so very, very high,' Farrell says, attempting a jovial smile, 'does anyone fancy taking over?'

'We have to do something!' Bibiana gasps, looking frantically around the room.

Before I know what's happening, Elliot has stood up. He holds up his arm.

'I'm happy to stand in.'

Farrell flinches at the sound of his voice. The rest of the room, however, seems to breathe a collective sigh of relief. They recognise the confidence in Elliot's voice and they feel safe in his hands. He won't mumble, they think, he won't fluff his lines.

Farrell moves aside and Elliot takes centre stage. My eyes are on my darling friend as he passes by Phil, who squeezes his arm and whispers something in his ear. Then he heads to the back of the shop, and leans heavily against a bookshelf, his arms crossed, waiting for Elliot to begin.

'Good evening, I'm afraid I'm going to borrow some lines from a little-known playwright. He's someone I always return to when I get stuck with my own poetry.'

Elliot goes through the motions his drama teacher must have instructed him in. Head up, shoulders back, feet firmly on the floor; he was trained for this moment. He was trained not to fail.

'*All the world's a stage,*' he begins.

He can't be serious! Shakespeare? This is not a school concert! You've got to read your own work at an event like this or nothing at all! I feel my cheeks reddening with embarrassment. It's not as if it's me up there and yet the fact I came with him makes me feel responsible.

> '*And all the men and women merely players;*
> *They have their exits and their entrances,*
> *And one man in his time plays many parts,*'

I zone out. I think of the part I'm playing now, of big, stupid idiot. I've been a fool, but I can still fix this. I look over at Farrell and attempt to get his attention with the power of my mind. He continues to look ahead.

Was that poem really about me? Already the words are slipping from my head.

I don't need to be a rocket scientist to know what I have to do. I need to break it off with Elliot.

I take a sip of wine and pretend to be listening intently, but inside my head the decision has caused a huge stir. I'm thinking about the photo shoot Elliot's just paid for. I'm thinking of him driving me around in his car. I'm thinking of this gallery-owner, Aurelia, he's been trying to get in touch with for me. I hate the thought that I've strung him along. That I've used him.

It's not your fault! He chose to get involved!

But it doesn't make a difference. There's no point trying to rationalise it. Elliot is handsome, rich and well-connected – but so what when I love Farrell?

I love him. It hits me in the pit of my stomach how much. A warm glow spreads over me. It feels like something old, something that was dormant, waking up and breathing new life. I don't know how long I've felt like this, but I know I never want it to go away.

There's applause. Elliot is taking a bow.

'I'm going to cheer up, Farrell,' Bibiana says.

'Wait! I'll come!'

But the reading isn't over and there's someone else now bracing himself in front of the microphone, beads of sweat forming at his greying temples. The man reads out his first line before the audience has barely finished congratulating Elliot and I feel compelled by my British fear of offending to remain in my seat.

Bibiana doesn't have the same weakness. I watch her boldly cross the room and loop her arm through Farrell's. His look of surprise is followed by a sheepish smile, and then the next moment they are heading outside the bookshop.

Elliot sits down heavily beside me.

'And *that* is how you recite poetry.'

'It was a sonnet...' I say, before I can stop myself.

'I just saved the evening and that's all you can say? Thank you very much.'

'Sorry...' I put my finger on my lips and nod my head at the speaker at the front. 'Well done.'

'And for your information, a sonnet is a type of poem, so it's still poetry.'

'Okay.'

I really have more pressing matters on my mind.

'I didn't think much of Farrell's beginning, probably best he stopped...' Elliot whispers.

I glare at him and he shrugs. The room is too quiet to hold a conversation, much less an argument. The poet drones on and on. His words fall like rocks on the room; his voice a monotone wasteland. It's unbearable to sit here. I glance behind me to see if I can make out Farrell and Bibiana beyond the shop window, but it has grown dark already.

'It was about you, I bet...' he says.

I shoot him a dismissive frown and pray that I don't look as red as I feel. He's jealous and I can hardly tell him he's being stupid.

227

He should be feeling jealous. I'm in love with another man.

The poem comes to such a random, abrupt end that there's a hesitation before the applause. I sneak a look behind me. Farrell has come back inside with Bibiana. He catches my eye, but looks away at once. I sense something has changed in his demeanour, as though he's grown hard. But then Bibiana says something and he softens again, and then she's embracing him. I try to catch his expression as he rests his chin briefly on her shoulder. I see him close his eyes and I feel a wave of panic.

'We're going to have a very short break now,' Phil says, 'then we'll be back with two more poems.'

I stand up at once.

'I'm going to check Farrell's okay.'

'Alright. I'll get us another glass of vinegar.'

As well as Bibiana there's now another man from the audience who has come up to talk to him and Farrell is laughing quietly at something that's been said. I catch the end of the man's sentence '...not as embarrassing as Mr Shakespeare' and then they notice me and open up their circle.

I reach out and touch Farrell's arm. 'You okay?'

'Oh, just great,' he says, not meeting my eye. He glances to my side where Elliot has appeared and he directs his apology at him. 'I'm sorry I got you both to come so far for such a poor show.'

'Don't worry, we were in central London; it wasn't too far,' Elliot says.

I want to sink through the floor. I don't know how to make it better. Should I make a scene? Declare my undying love for all to hear? No. I can't do it. I can't do it to Elliot. I'm not a bitch. That's not me. Just a coward.

'Will you...?' my voice falters.

'What?' Farrell says.

'Will you let me read it another time?'

Everyone in our small group turns to look at him, curious to hear his answer.

He looks at me, but it's as if he's not really seeing me. I feel the tears well up inside me.

'No, I don't think so...' he says. 'I don't think I'm feeling it any more.'

I feel as though I've been winded. I start to speak, but the words don't come out properly and then Elliot has to butt in all mouthy and posh.

'I think you're making the right decision. It sounded as if it needed a bit more work.'

There's a ripple of surprise. The friendly man who has been talking to Farrell looks disgusted. In that moment everyone's opinion is set and two things become clear. Elliot is a prick and I'm the one going out with him.

Bibiana glares at him frostily. 'Well, at least it came from the heart.'

Farrell lets out a strangled laugh and rubs his hand over his mouth.

'You know, I think I need some air...' he says.

'So do I,' I say.

For a fleeting moment I see in his eyes the same man who came to my home that day, the same emotion, the same longing. But then he looks down at his feet and the connection is lost again.

Don't give up on me! I love you!

'Actually, Amber, I just need to have a moment by myself if that's alright...'

Rejected, in front of everyone.

'Of course,' I say, forcing a smile.

Chapter 31

We're back in our seats and I'm nursing a second glass of wine. It's not much of a solution, but what else can I do? Everyone has to stay where they are until the man at the front finishes serenading some imaginary chicken stew.

> *'Oh chicken stew so meaty and true,*
> *The dish I would have married*
> *If I hadn't met Sue...'*

At my side, Bibiana sighs audibly and crosses her legs. She glances behind her and I find myself following her look right back to Farrell. He's had his moment outside and now he's leaning by the bookshelf again, his face in shadow. I want him so much. The desire rises like a storm. I want everyone to melt away and leave us alone, so I can tell him how I feel.

But we aren't alone and I'm very conscious of Elliot shifting beside me. I look at Bibiana and she smiles and then rolls her eyes towards the poet. I smile back, but it feels false. I find myself wondering how it's been working out for her staying at Farrell's. It dawns on me that she must still be sleeping in his bed. Farrell wouldn't let her sleep on the sofa. Before I would have said it was because he was a walkover, but the truth is it's because he's kind and chivalrous.

Does he cook for her? I know *she's* been cooking for him. I've seen the evidence on Facebook. What have they talked about over those meals when wine has loosened their tongues? They seem to have become quite close. She hugged him with the confidence of an old friend.

Now I'm picturing them in domestic bliss, him frying eggs, her laying the table. I blink the image away. It smarts like a cut.

At the front, the poet turns his page over and a few shoulders sink in resignation.

> *'Poor Sue, she has her uses,*
> *But oh chicken stew, if I could only bathe*
> *in your seasoned juices...'*

'The rhythm's off,' Elliot mutters.

I feel my eyes widen involuntarily. 'Is that your only issue with it?'

'You can't beat a great chicken stew... unless of course there's beef bourguignon.'

He smiles, but I don't find him funny. I watch him sniff at his wine, as if he doesn't trust it and then take a sip. He seems ridiculous in here, out of place.

'Vinegar...'

'It's free!'

'Well if it wasn't, I'd have to go back for a refund.'

Bibiana touches my knee. The lightest touch, but I'm so wound up it makes me jump. She leans in so close I can almost taste the coconut sweetness of her perfume.

'Did you and Farrell ever date?'

I answer so quickly it must sound like I'm horrified by the idea. 'No!'

She lets out a little laugh. 'Sorry, I just wondered.'

Is it the poem? Has Farrell said something? The questions are on the tip of my tongue, but the room is so quiet and I don't trust myself to speak. I open my mouth, but she beats me to it.

'I thought you had history, that's all,' she whispers. Then she leans forward on her crossed legs and smiles to herself.

'and so chicken stew, I wish you adieu...'

Suddenly the room is clapping with relief because it's over. Everyone springs out of their seats almost at once and then hover out of politeness, waiting for Phil to round up the evening, which he does with a note of apology in his voice. A few people head straight outside while others circle the wine table, hoping for refills.

Elliot stands up, interlaces his fingers behind his back and stretches. I feel conscious of trying to look nonchalant as I survey the back of the room.

'Shall we be sociable?' Bibiana suggests brightly, and we follow her lead.

My heart is thudding as we approach Farrell. He has been joined by a circle of people, most of them quite elderly and he's listening politely. I recognise the half-hearted smile on his lips that tell of wanting to be far away.

'I'm sorry, we're actually closing in ten minutes,' I overhear Phil say, to someone asking for more wine.

I feel a surge of panic. Time is running out for me to get a message to Farrell. I need to tell him that I'm going to end it with Elliot as soon as I can. But as we mingle with the circle, Elliot puts a protective arm around my waist and I feel trapped.

Farrell sweeps an eye over us and smiles tensely at Elliot.

'So do you write too or do you prefer to leave it the experts?'

It's not like Farrell to be unfriendly, but his hollow laugh does nothing to defuse the challenge in his voice. Elliot is unfazed. I can feel him standing straighter, puffing out his chest.

'I've had a number of my poems highly commended in competitions, actually... but I don't like to boast.'

232

Some cast Elliot a look of mild irritation, but others are impressed. The elderly lady who was talking to Farrell earlier showers Elliot with an adoring smile.

'You have a fabulous voice,' she says. 'You should be on the radio.'

'Thank you very much. I hope you're not saying I've got the face for it.'

She laughs. 'Oh no dear, if I were ten years younger...'

Raised eyebrows from everyone as we all think that fifty years younger would be more accurate.

'And what do you do?' a man besides me asks. I'd barely noticed him before and now he's looking at me with interest, along with everybody else. I'm aware of Farrell's eyes on me and my breath sticking in my throat. I swallow.

'Me?'

It's so hot in here. I need a drink.

'She's an artist,' Elliot says.

'Oh how wonderful,' the man replies.

'Well...' I say, feeling denial bubble up.

'I meant to ask you how that was going?' Farrell says.

He's staring at me and I feel my cheeks burning.

'Well, you know...'

'Not really. I feel as if I haven't seen you for ages.'

'Oh you know each other, then?' the man beside me asks.

'We used to,' Farrell says.

I feel as though I've been knocked down with a battering ram. I stand there with my guts strewn across the floor. My voice, when it comes out, sounds unfamiliar.

'What's that supposed to mean?'

'Nothing... I just meant I don't know what you've been up to lately.'

'She's been very busy with her new project,' Elliot says.

Please don't talk for me!

He looks around at everyone else. 'You might have heard of the bananas that have been popping up around London?'

Blank faces, except for mine, which is coloured a deep burgundy. Then a gasp from a middle-aged lady.

'Yes, the coloured bananas!' she says.

It's like a Mexican wave, the way people announce one after each other that they have heard of them after all.

'So what's it all about?' the first lady asks, her eyes brightening, as if she's going to be let into a secret.

I'm still reeling from Farrell's words and too slow to get my answer out.

'What do you think it's about?' Elliot says.

Farrell glances at me, one eyebrow raised.

'Global warming?' suggests a man wearing glasses as a big as windscreens. 'About it being deceptive. On the one hand we think it's good because it will mean bananas can grow in the UK, but it's bad because it's not natural, which is why they aren't painted the right colour, am I right?'

I open my mouth. Blink. Close it. Why can't he be right? Why does there have to be one concept?

'It's a homage to the banana-growers of the Philippines who lost a quarter of their crop in a typhoon,' another woman says, with total confidence. She looks at me solemnly. 'Isn't that right?'

'Well a typhoon is global warming-related isn't it?' says the man with the glasses.

An older man with a sophisticated grey beard chooses that moment to give his opinion. 'They are clearly a warning to society! That if we don't stop rushing around we're all going to go bananas.'

Elliot lets out a deep laugh, enjoying it all, while my brain goes berserk trying to register and record what they're saying. I want it on the site; every concept, every idea. But unlike me, everyone else wants one correct answer. They are all looking at me, waiting for it.

'I think Amber wants to keep it a secret a little longer,' Farrell says.

I flash him a grateful smile. 'We're having a proper launch soon...'

'Is that what you were doing today?' Farrell asks. 'Whoever answered your phone earlier said something about a photo shoot. What were you photographing?'

Oh crap! Please don't say anything, Elliot!

'No nothing much, just some bananas, you know,' I say, waving my hand dismissively.

Farrell can't know about the pictures! Not like this! He won't understand!

'It wasn't nothing. You were exquisite, darling,' Elliot says, kissing my cheek.

Farrell looks away, his brow twitching, his mouth tense.

'They weren't nude photos by any chance?' the elderly lady chuckles.

'How did you guess?' Elliot says.

That gets everyone's attention. A couple of the women look horrified.

'No, of course not,' I say quickly.

Elliot frowns at me. 'Yes they were. I mean I know you were covered in paint, but they were most definitely nude. You looked fantastic.'

'Wow,' Bibiana murmurs, her eyes huge. 'Amber, is that true? I can't believe you didn't tell me!'

'How do you mean "covered in paint"?' the man besides me asks. His eyes roll up to the ceiling, as if he's trying to picture it.

'No, it wasn't like that,' I stammer.

'You were either naked or you weren't,' Farrell says brusquely. 'Which was it, Amber?'

The tension is palpable. The sizzle of excitement about the bananas has been replaced with an awful awkwardness. I can't bear to look at him.

'It's not like that,' I say.

'You can't deny it, can you? You got your kit off for this... this joke...'

'It's not like that,' I say again, sharper now. 'It's not a joke!'

Why can't he just wait for me to explain? I feel humiliated enough as it is.

'What, then?'

I'm aware of people murmuring excuses and slinking away. It feels as if we are the only people left in the room. In his eyes there is confusion and anger.

Listen to me! You don't understand!

'What's your problem, mate?' Elliot says. And the 'mate' sounds silly in his voice. 'Who are you to judge?'

'He's not judging,' Bibiana says, coming to his defence. 'He's looking out for her. They're best friends.'

'Oh come on! Of course he's bloody judging!' Elliot says, looking aghast.

'It's okay... leave it,' I say.

On another occasion I might have been grateful to be defended like this, but tonight everything feels as if it's balancing on a hair.

'No, it's not okay,' Elliot continues. 'I mean, honestly, who are you to stand there and judge?'

'Shall we all calm down?' someone suggests quietly.

'A lousy excuse for a poet, that's what you are!'

'Yeah, you're right,' Farrell says icily. He reaches into his back pocket and pulls out his poem. Then to my horror he shreds it to pieces.

I watch the papers float to the floor. My heart falls with them.

'And you know what else I am?' he says, looking from Elliot back to me, 'A fucking bad judge of character.'

With that, he turns and walks out of the bookshop, leaving a horrible silence in his wake. Bibiana immediately follows after him. I hate her for it.

'That was a bit uncalled-for,' someone says.

'I think the lad's having a bad day,' says another.

Elliot wraps his arms around me and kisses my forehead. Before I can stop them, hot tears are running down my cheeks. I have nowhere to run. I'm trapped in his embrace, his arms the only place to shield me. But they aren't the arms I want to be in. I want Farrell. I want him so badly.

'Shall we go home?' Elliot says.

'I want to be alone,' I say, quietly.

He backs off, shocked. 'What's that supposed to mean?'

'I need to think.'

'Think about what? I just stood up for you and now you're going to push me away?'

I brush away tears, but they keep on coming.

'It's been a long day. I'm tired. I just want some space.'

'Well, that's really nice... really nice... really lovely timing, too...'

He's disgusted with me and I don't blame him.

'I'm sorry,' I say, burying my face in my hands. 'I'm so sorry.'

I feel so wretched. So useless. I need to get home, safe. I can feel something desperate and destructive wanting to be unleashed.

'Alright,' he says, his voice gentler now. 'Let's get you home. We can talk about this in the morning.'

I nod, grateful to be let off for now. I'm simultaneously dreading and desperate for the morning to come. I need to explain myself to Farrell, I need him to know how I feel. Perhaps everything will be alright if I just tell him how I feel?

Chapter 32

I can hear the tap of fingers on a keyboard as I make my way upstairs. It's Egg, busy at work. I wonder if he's writing a new book. I wonder if he's going to mind being interrupted like this. But there's no way I'm going to be able to sleep with all these thoughts running through my head. I just have to talk to someone.

I rap on the door. 'Egg... Egg...'

The tapping stops.

I take that as an invitation and open the door into his dimly lit bedroom. An articulated desk lamp is arched over his laptop, illuminating the most cluttered desk I've ever seen. He swings around on his seat and looks at me with a bemused expression.

'Egg, I'm in love with Farrell!'

He frowns and scratches his beard. 'Why are you going out with that other man, then?'

'Because I'm an idiot!'

I flop onto his bed with a groan, landing on something hard, which produces a sharp squeak.

'Ouch!'

I pull out from underneath me a bright-yellow plastic kitten curled up in a plastic 'wicker' basket. The tiny hole in the base tells me it's a bath toy.

'Ah, yes, the alternative to the classic duck,' Egg says. 'I'm not rating it too highly because on the whole cats aren't fond of water. There are exceptions, however. There's a breed called the Turkish Van...'

My eyes have adjusted to the dull light and now I can see that I'm surrounded by cat-related paraphernalia. There are toys all over the floor, in plastic packages and brightly coloured cardboard boxes. His desk is not covered with the usual mess of books and papers but with tins of cat food, packs of biscuits, felt balls, cat collars and what look like doll's clothes but must be cat costumes. My great revelation is relegated to second place as I try to get my head around what I'm seeing.

'Where the hell did you get all this stuff from?'

Egg looks disappointed. 'You don't want to know about the Turkish Van cat?'

'No, I want to know what's going on!'

'Yes, right, yes...' he say, slapping his hands together. 'It's just I've added a whole section on the Turkish Van in my new e-book and...'

'Egg!'

'Alright, well...' He looks suddenly sheepish. 'Let's talk about you first... you and Farrell... so, you, it's fair to say, are an atheist and he, I believe, is an Irish Catholic. Is that going to be a problem?'

'Egg! Where does all this stuff come from?'

'Alright,' he says, wincing. 'I may have borrowed your little idea about filming Rupert, and I may have posted a few films online, and they may have generated millions of hits, led to a few advertisers getting in touch and erm, lots of freebies... but, don't be mad, because I'm doing it for us!'

My mouth drops open. 'If you're doing it for us, then why did you keep it a secret?!'

'Not for "us" as in you and me,' Egg says, looking surprised. 'I meant for Bibiana and me. For our future.'

'Are you completely nuts?'

'I'm calling it the Cat Empire.'

'Isn't that an Australian band?'

'Yes, it's wonderful, anyone who looks for them will end up on our site.'

'*Our* site? Seriously, are you crazy? Have you even told Bibiana what you feel?'

'Have you told Farrell how you feel?' he shoots back.

Touché. I look down at my hands and pick at my nails. 'Not yet. I want to, but I don't know if it's too late. I brought Elliot to Farrell's poetry reading and it was a total disaster.'

'That's a strange tactic.'

'It wasn't a tactic, it was a mistake.'

'I thought girls were supposed to be good at this kind of thing.'

I cover my face with my hands. 'I love him, Egg, and I don't know what to do.'

His desk chair squeaks as he turns from side to side. 'Well, what if...'

I look up, my heart so full of hope. Just maybe my eccentric red-bearded housemate holds the answer.

'... What if you bought a puppy and started the Dog Empire?'

The tears come gushing out.

'You don't have to!' he says hurriedly. 'It was just an idea!'

The fact that Egg is at a loss to know how to console me makes me feel sorry for him and cry even harder.

He joins me on the bed and prods at my knee.

'Just tell him,' he says.

I wipe my eyes and try to control my hiccups.

'You know he loves you,' Egg says, with a shrug. 'So just tell him.'

Chapter 33

It's seven o'clock in the morning, but I can't wait any longer. I've spent the night daydreaming about the outcome. At one point I almost convinced myself to stand outside his window at two in the morning and throw pebbles. But then I realized the only windows looking onto the street belonged to Danny and the toilet, so unless I was lucky enough to catch Farrell having a tinkle in the night, my plan was going to fail.

At four o'clock I had another urge to get out of bed and rush to his house, but I managed to stop myself. Logic dictates that you are more likely to be loved back by someone if you haven't woken them up at some ungodly hour.

Five o'clock came and went. At six o'clock I straightened my hair and dabbed concealer over the grey beneath my eyes. I explored my make-up bag slowly and with an interest I'd never felt before, until finally there really was no way I could delay any longer.

It's still too early really, but I can't stop myself now. I'm walking up the street towards Farrell's house and there's a huge lump in my throat. I'm nervous, but I'm excited, too. In fact I can almost taste the relief of letting out those words. *I love you.*

I know I have some explaining to do. I know he'll want to know why I brought Elliot to the poetry reading if I love him. But if I speak from the heart he'll know that I never meant to hurt him.

He knows me. He'll understand.

I'm walking down the pathway to Farrell's house when the door opens and out steps Danny. He does a double-take when he sees me and freezes with his hand on the door knob.

'You're up early. I'm pretty sure Farrell's asleep.'

'I know, it's important... can you let me in?'

He looks uncertain. 'Why don't you come back in an hour?'

'Please.'

'But they're asleep.'

'Oh come on, Danny, Farrell's used to my ways... please...'

He shakes his head, still not entirely happy, but resigned to let me have my way. 'Go ahead, then, but I'm telling you everyone's asleep.'

The door closes behind me. For a brief moment I stand, listening out for any signs of life, but there are none. My gladiator sandals barely make a sound against the wooden floorboards of the corridor as I head for the living room.

What I'm going to do is sit beside him on the sofa and stroke his head until he wakes up. It will be a gentle awakening, then. I'll tell him about the photos properly. He'll realise he was over-reacting. I don't think he'll still be angry. After all, he did kiss me. And he wrote about me. Surely those feelings can't be extinguished from one day to the next?

I take a deep breath, my heart beating with excitement and I step into the living room. My eyes land on the sofa and at once my stomach clenches. It's empty. I hurry towards it, lean down, start patting it as if I'm looking for something. I am. I'm looking to feel his warmth locked in the material. But the sofa is cold.

Danny's room! He must have moved in with him because the sofa was killing his back. With a mounting panic I retrace my steps down the corridor and head up the staircase. On one side of the passage is Danny's room, which is open ajar, and on the other side Farrell's, which is shut tight.

I visualise Farrell on a foam mat on Danny's bedroom floor,

curled up like a prawn in his orange sleeping bag. I push open the door, tentatively at first, and then fully. The duvet is pulled back on the bed and the curtains are open. But there's no one there.

My heart is pounding as I turn to face Farrell's door. I must leave and yet I'm rooted to the spot. My excitement has all gone, replaced by a clawing anxiety. Beyond that room is something I don't want to imagine, but my mind wanders there anyway, makes a scene.

I blink it away. My mind is a traitor. I can't know for sure.

There's movement from inside the room. My whole body stiffens. *Move, Amber!* But I can't. There are light footsteps and then the handle is pulled down. It's too late to hide. Farrell sees me and slams his hand against his chest.

'Jesus Christ! You scared the shit out of me!' he gasps, before quickly closing the door.

He's wearing nothing but a pair of navy boxer shorts. Suddenly the reality of the situation comes crashing down on me.

'I'm sorry, I should have called... Danny let me in...'

He hugs his arms around himself and shivers. 'No, it's fine, it's early, but it's fine.'

She's not in there, I think. She stayed with a friend. He wouldn't say it was fine if she was in there with him. The tightness in my chest fades a little.

'I'm sorry about last night,' I say.

'You came over to tell me that? At seven in the morning?'

'I wanted to come earlier. I couldn't sleep. I just couldn't stop thinking about you.'

He looks pained. 'Amber, wait...'

But it comes tumbling out. 'I know I've been an idiot. It was horrible being there with Elliot last night when all I wanted was to be with you, and I see that now and I just need you to know...'

'Amber...'

'Farrell, I love you.'

I'm breathing fast, waiting for the words to sink in. He's in

243

shock, his eyebrows skyrocketing into his forehead beneath his messy hair.

'Oh, Amber,' he says softly.

I can feel my lips braving a smile, because I think he's about to take me into his arms and tell me that he loves me, too.

But he doesn't move. And then I hear the sound of bedsprings as, inside his room, someone climbs out of the bed. *His* bed. The smile is wiped off my face and I feel physically sick.

'Wait, Amber, wait,' he says, raising his palms, as if he were trying to calm an animal.

My cry is muffled in my hand. 'Oh, shit, no I can't face her...'

I hold his gaze for one hopeless second and then I bolt down the passage.

Bibiana's husky morning voice follows me down the stairs.

'Who are you talking to, babe?'

And then Farrell starts calling my name.

'Amber! Wait!'

I thunder down the staircase, along the corridor and slam the front door behind me. I hear it open a second later and Farrell shouting my name.

'Amber! Stop!'

But I don't stop. What is there to say that can possibly make this any better?

I turn the corner and keep on running. The blood throbs in my ears and my lungs feel as though they're bursting. I don't want to go home, where I can be found, where Egg can ask me what happened. Not because I'm thinking of Egg's disappointment, but because I don't think I can stand to formulate my own. To admit that Farrell slept with Bibiana is too much to bear. I keep seeing it in my head; glimpses of bare skin, his hands, her lips, her glossy hair cascading over her naked back. And the worst thing is, I know it's my own fault... if I hadn't brought Elliot... if I hadn't been so blind... if I had chased after Farrell that day he kissed me...

I slow down to a stop. The image melts. I look around and

find that I've run all the way to the train station. Commuters are trickling in through the entrance, reaching for the free newspaper as they go. I head to the entrance, too, my head suddenly bubbling with ideas of escaping the city. But at the last minute I stall. People mutter their disapproval behind me. I grab a paper, as if that's my excuse for slowing down. Stupid, really, that I care what these strangers think.

I move away from the station, still carrying the paper. I feel as though my inner compass has just been smashed and I no longer know what direction I should be moving in. If I stop for one moment, I'm afraid I'll be hit by an avalanche of despair.

Get a grip, Amber!

I've got to calm down. I can't run away from this. I'm a grown-up. I must deal with this in a grown-up way. But even as I'm thinking this I feel as though I'm being wrenched apart by an ear-splitting scream of agony and regret. Why did I let her think that there was nothing between us? Why did I let her think that Farrell was the last man I'd ever date?

I've lost him. I've lost the love of my life. My feet stop moving, my knees feel weak. I lean against the railings.

'Are you alright?' a gentle voice asks.

I look up and find a familiar face of a woman looking down at me. I recognise her from the poetry reading.

'It must be a shock,' she adds, 'seeing yourself in the newspaper.'

'Sorry?'

She nods at my hand, which is holding the paper. 'Double spread, too. If I wasn't in a rush I'd ask you for your autograph... are you alright?'

She cocks her head, waiting for me to answer.

'Yeah, I'm, I'm fine,' I stammer.

'Good. Take care, then.'

She heads past me and I look down at the paper with fearful anticipation. I'm not sure what's awaiting me on those pages.

Chapter 34

I'm running again, but this time there's a small grin tugging at my lips. The heaviness I felt has lifted like a theatre curtain. Any doubts I had about the part I was playing have been pushed aside. My costume is exquisite. It's as if I'm suddenly standing in the middle of the stage and instead of feeling afraid, I'm excited.

The adrenalin makes me clumsy and I fumble with my keys in the lock. Egg is up. I smell the coffee as soon as I open the door. I head straight for the kitchen and he turns around, a look of expectation on his face, as though he's been waiting for this news.

'What happened?'

'Look!' I gasp, slapping the newspaper down on the table.

From the thin pages of one of the city's most popular newspapers, I look out with a self-assured smile. I am swathed in colour from head to toe, colours so vibrant and so dense it's almost impossible to make out any features of my naked body. I am turned to the side and holding out a bunch of red bananas that reach over the page.

Egg bends down so close, his beard scrapes the paper.

'*The Banana Goddess has Arrived,*' he reads aloud.

I blush with pleasure. 'Ridiculous... but wow, right? Wow-bloody-wow?'

The Beefeater will be happy as he's also made it into the paper.

There's the snap I took of the blue bananas in the Tate gallery. In fact, the pictures dominate the feature, leaving little space for words. I've scanned it quickly, but only now I start to read. Egg is ahead of me.

'The writer mentions where you got the bananas,' he says, looking grim. 'The police will be on to you now.'

He runs his finger under the paragraph and we read together in silence.

The bananas were reportedly part of a police operation to record drug dealers working in the King's Cross area. A sack of bananas was left on the street overnight with a video camera inside. The leader of the operation, an aspiring film maker and DJ...

That stops me in my tracks. 'Really?'

'What?'

'Perkins. He was just trying to be creative at work....' I think about the young policeman and feel a rush of sympathy, 'Aw, I hope he fulfils his ambition. I wouldn't have done any of this without him.'

I turn back to the paper.

The leader of the operation, an aspiring film maker and DJ, didn't stop to consider whether leaving bananas outside a catering company might lead to a mix-up. The following morning the official police bananas were gone and the following evening an artist was born.'

Egg straightens up and goes over to fetch the coffee. He hands me a mug and lets out a little laugh.

'I was so sure you'd gone to talk to Farrell. I was quite excited for you; I couldn't get back to sleep.'

My face falls and I find myself taking a sip of boiling-hot coffee to mask my emotion.

'You should go over and show him,' Egg says, nodding at the paper. 'I'm sure he'd like to know his girlfriend is famous.'

'I'm not his girlfriend, Egg.'

'Not yet.'

An image of Bibiana and Farrell, their naked bodies entwined, bursts into my head like a loud noise. I shudder and push it away.

'I've been thinking that maybe we're better off as friends.'

I turn to look at the newspaper again so I that don't have to look into his eyes, but I can hear the frown in his voice.

'No, I don't think so,' he says.

I feel guilty that my secret would devastate him, too. I won't tell him. Bibiana made him no promises. She didn't lead him on. But Farrell kissed me. And with that kiss he woke me up. Now I wish I could fall back to sleep again, blissful in my ignorance that I can't have him.

'I don't think Farrell would appreciate this picture anyway,' I say, shrugging. 'Yesterday he seemed pretty annoyed that I'd done it.'

I remember his brusque tone, the anger in his brow. He had no right.

'I need someone who can support me without judging...'

'I don't understand,' Egg says. 'He *has* supported you. He was there at the British Museum and at the Tate. You're perfect for each other. Like me and Bibiana are perfect for each other.'

'Oh, Egg! You can't see what's in front of you! Do you really think Bibiana..?'

I clamp my mouth shut.

'Do I really think Bibiana what?'

'...is ever going to like cats?' I cry. The words just fly out of my mouth. 'I mean you're doing all this cat stuff and you're saying it's for her and you're talking about this cat empire you're building but...but the truth is she HATES cats!'

'That's a bit strong.'

'She's allergic to them, Egg! They make her head swell up! If Rupert made your head swell up, would you still like him?'

Egg looks thoughtful. 'If I gave you flu, it wouldn't automatically turn you against all humanity.'

I would argue that it might if I wasn't preoccupied by the sudden vibrations coming from above us.

'Hold that thought!'

It's my phone. Expectations come pouring in, so many bloody expectations. I storm up the stairs with my pulse racing. I've got to reach it before he hangs up! I throw myself across my bed like a goalie trying to save a penalty and swipe my phone from off the floor, where it has fallen between bed and bedside table.

Shit, it *is* him! I can't believe Farrell's calling!

'Hello?'

'Amber!'

Come on, tell me it's all a misunderstanding! Tell me you were sleeping on the floor!

'You can't just run off like that!' he says.

'Why not? *You* did once!'

'I don't understand you. What do you want from me? What was I supposed to think when you brought *him* with you last night?'

'It was a mistake.'

'And then that thing about the nude photos... Christ... I just keep imagining the two of you in a studio... was he naked, too? Fuck I don't even want to know.'

'No, of course he wasn't!'

Indignation soars within me. I could tell him about the newspaper spread, but now I'm angry. If he thinks I'd be involved in pornographic shots, then clearly he doesn't know me at all. This is not the conversation I imagined.

'Look... maybe we just need a little time to get our heads straight?' he says.

'Did you sleep with her?'

He doesn't answer.

I become aware of my heart pounding in my chest.

'Do you *like* her?'

'I'm not answering that.'

I think I'm going to be sick.

'She's my friend,' I say pathetically.

There's an awkward silence that I don't try to fill.

'I can't do this,' Farrell whispers.

Without another word, he hangs up the phone.

Afterwards I run a bath and soak in it until the water turns cold. I think about my new identity. I think about what Matt said about having complexes. *You're going to need a few of those if you're going to be a celebrity. You've got to have something to cry about in the interviews.* A broken heart? Will that do? *Yes, the pain did influence my art*, I'll confess to Vogue, *you'll notice my colours during that period are weaker because I used to dilute the paint with my tears...*

After the bath I paint my nails different colours and curl the ends of my straightened hair. Then I change my mind about the nails and spend ages wiping the polish off and repainting them blood red. At nine o'clock everyone starts phoning.

'I saw it on the tube and I cried out loud!' Dee squeals down the phone. 'I told the woman sitting next to me I knew you, and she just nodded politely and turned back to her Kindle! It was so funny!'

'Do you know how many people have called me up this morning?' My mum cries. 'Apparently I've got a famous daughter! At first I thought they must have mixed you up, but then I looked for myself on the internet!'

'The internet?'

'On the newspaper's website! Keep up, Amber! And there you were!'

Is she angry? I can't tell. I realise I'm furiously biting my bottom lip.

'Stunning!' she cries. 'Absolutely beautiful! I don't know what your grandmother is going to say, but never mind about that.'

'Really? You like it?'

'Yes, but I wish you hadn't kept us in the dark. You don't tell us anything any more.'

'I know, I'm sorry. It all happened so fast.'

'Now when's this exhibition?'

'Exhibition?'

'It was at the bottom in italics, said it was *coming soon*...'

'I don't know.'

'Well, who does?'

'Um, Elliot?'

'Who's Elliot?'

'My... manager?'

'Your manager? You haven't signed anything have you? Because you should've asked your father to look over any papers first.'

'No, I haven't.'

'Good. Well I'm off to get some newspapers! I think thirty copies should be enough, don't you?'

After we've said goodbye, I take a deep breath and phone Elliot. The fact is, I need his help with the exhibition. Rationally, if I keep going out with him, securing his help will be easy. But emotionally, that plan doesn't suit me. I can't be his girlfriend. I just can't force myself to go along with it when my heart isn't in it. So what am I supposed to do?

When he picks up, his voice is bursting with excitement and it seems as if he's forgotten all about last night.

'I've been talking to Aurelia. She loved, loved, loved the feature! Now what we've been thinking is that your exhibition should just appear out of the blue, like your bananas...'

'But if there's no warning, no one will come.'

'Don't worry about that. We've sent out an email to everyone who matters, telling them to be at the ready.'

I feel a stab of irritation. 'Shouldn't I be involved in planning any of this?'

'Yes! Sorry, I know we've rushed ahead, but time is of the essence. We need to get things moving. I was thinking your exhibition should be next week. What do you think?'

'Next week?' I gasp.

I don't even know what I'm supposed to be putting in this exhibition!

'Well, this week would have been better,' he says, with a sigh. 'But next week will have to do.'

'But what are we doing in the exhibition?'

I roll my eyes as I hear the 'we' in my question.

'Ah,' he says, as if he's remembered something important. 'Well, there are a few things we need to discuss. Aurelia isn't keen on you using real bananas.'

'What do you mean?'

'It was fine using the police bananas because they would have been wasted, but if you start buying new ones, it won't look good. Not very eco. I mean, effectively it's a massacre.'

I'm surprised that he cares. And I'm surprised that I agree wholeheartedly that it would be a massacre. Being on the same page is going to make my job of telling him we're through even harder.

'She suggested you made your future bananas out of something else...I don't know what....'

'Papier-mâché?'

'That could work.'

I remember making a lion's head in primary school for our performance of the Wizard of Oz. The teacher did most of the work, while we dipped our hands in the wonderful jelly-like paste.

'Wait, no,' I cry, feeling another wave of panic. 'I can't just bash out a load of papier-mâché bananas!'

'You need to see the gallery space, I understand. Look, I'm coming over to pick you up.'

'No, Elliot, don't!' And then I just come out with it. 'I can't give you what you want.'

'I wouldn't say it's what *I* want particularly,' he says, sounding confused. 'Papier-mâché isn't the only option either. How about throwing in some barbed wire? A touch urban, don't you think?'

'I'm not talking about the bananas Elliot! I'm talking about us!'

Silence. I hear his footsteps pacing. I close my eyes and imagine his beautiful Victorian house.

'I don't think we're right for each other.'

Cowards break up over the phone.

'Is that so? And when did you decide this?'

He sounds angry. I guess that's the end of my exhibition. I don't even know Aurelia's surname.

'I'm sorry, I really appreciate everything you've done and I understand if you no longer want to be involved in...'

'I'm in this for the art,' Elliot interrupts coolly. 'We've got a lot of work to do.'

Relief that I've said it and that it's not all over. Dread that we've got to see each other again.

'I'll collect you in an hour,' he says. 'Please don't read anything into it. It's simply quicker that way.'

I get ready in front of the bathroom mirror. I even practise a smile. Foundation does wonders for a broken heart. At least, it looks that way. Inside I'm aching.

Maybe you can't have it all. Maybe you can. Whatever it is, you've got to give it your best shot. That's what I intend to do. I won't sit around and let despair wash over me. I'm going to get up and get out. If the papers say it, then it must be true: The Bananas Goddess has arrived!

Chapter 35

Even in vertiginous heels, Aurelia is tiny. Her lack of stature does nothing to undermine her sense of authority, which is evident from the moment she greets me.

'Good morning,' she says, giving my hand a firm shake. 'I thought to begin we should have coffee in the meeting room.'

At my side, Elliot seems agitated and I wonder if he, like me, is a little intimidated by Aurelia. Even if he was talking to me, which he doesn't appear to be, he wouldn't admit it. Apart from a grunt about the weather, he hasn't opened his mouth, and I'm starting to wonder if he's come to sabotage my chances of success.

The meeting room is above the gallery space, which I've only had a quick glance at on the way in. My first impression is that it's small; smaller than expected, at least. This is good news since it means fewer bananas to magic out of the ether.

Elliot slides into the furthest chair away from me around the large oval desk.

'Since time is against us I think we should consider the possibility of live art, don't you think?' he says, his attention solely on Aurelia.

'That could be interesting,' she says. 'What do you think, Amber?'

It takes me back to that exhibition Farrell and I went to with the white-faced teenager, texting from up a ladder, the so-called 'space between'.

'No.' The strength of my voice surprises everyone. 'There will be no live art.'

'But it's a brilliant idea!' Elliot cries.

Aurelia purses her lips in a tense smile. 'The exhibition is next week, so if you have some thoughts, Amber, we'd love to hear them.'

'That's the other thing,' I say, shaking my head. 'I can't do it for next week.'

Elliot and Aurelia exchange baffled looks.

'What do you mean you can't, Amber?' Elliot says. 'What on earth has come over you? I don't know what happened that evening but...'

'Nothing happened! I'm just not prepared to put my name to a rubbish exhibition just because you want to do it as quickly as possible.'

'But...'

'No, Elliot. I've not been very vocal about my ideas lately or my feelings,' I say, and I find myself blinking away an image of Farrell.

'I think you've been perfectly vocal about your feelings.'

'My feelings about this project.'

Aurelia looks confused. She leans forwards on her elbows and clasps her long, manicured fingers in front of her. 'Do go on...'

'I might have begun this project a little frivolously, but that doesn't mean I don't care about it. I know I'm not a genius, or even a very good artist, but now that I'm here, whatever "here" means, I want to do the best I can.'

'What are you saying then?' Aurelia asks.

'I'm saying it can't be next week.'

'Then when?'

I know I can't push my luck. 'The week after that?'

Aurelia raises her eyebrows. 'Two weeks from now?'

I nod and she almost bursts out laughing. 'I thought you were going to say six months.'

'Oh, can I do that instead?'

'Absolutely not,' she says. 'Don't take this personally, but in six months I very much doubt anyone will know who you are.'

My ego curls up in a ball and whimpers.

'Moving on to invitations,' Aurelia says briskly.

Elliot straightens up in his seat like an eager schoolboy. 'Yes, I've had some thoughts. I was thinking a touch of Swarovski would be...'

'Too expensive,' Aurelia interrupts. 'Amber?'

'What about if we have some wild card invitations?' I say. While Elliot was giving me the cold shoulder in the car, I'd had lots of time to think. 'What if we leave banana-shaped invites in the places where I left the original bananas? Plasticised, so they don't disintegrate in the rain. I know we'll have to advertise that we're doing this, otherwise no one will know...'

'Yes, let's make the wine scroungers work for it,' Elliot says.

'Talking about wine,' I add. 'I think I know a catering firm that might be able to give us a discount.'

'I thought they fired you.'

'No, they didn't have any more work for me; it's different,' I say blushing.

Aurelia looks as if she's ready to go and it dawns on me that the promised coffees never materialised. It was obviously just a figure of speech and she's far too busy a woman for such niceties.

'I think you should look at the gallery space now, don't you?'

It's a rhetorical question and a moment later the three of us are standing in the dimly lit gallery space, which is currently exhibiting a work of photography called 'Imperfection'. I take a look and find that every photograph has a black blur in the corner, where the photographer's finger has crept over the lens.

'Wonderful, aren't they?' Aurelia says breezily. 'The blur represents the weakness of the photographer to embrace perfection.'

'Fabulous,' Elliot murmurs.

I keep my mouth shut. There's no point upsetting them with my thoughts on the matter.

The room might be small, but the ceiling is vast. I stare up at it, my hands on my hips and I let my imagination fly.

'If only I had some decent space to work in,' I muse.

'Is your studio very small?' Aurelia says.

'Yes, it's so small it's practically non-existent.'

Elliot clears his throat. 'You can borrow my studio for a week, if you like.'

'Why do you have a studio?'

'Because I do. Would you like to use it or not?'

'You know I can't pay for it.'

He throws me a pitying look. 'I don't want your money, Amber.'

I really should be trying to minimise ties with Elliot. The trouble is, he's making it all so easy.

'I'll drive you there so you can have a look,' he says.

The studio turns out to be not far from Elliot's house in Notting Hill. It's a big, airy space on the second floor of a block of studios and must be freezing in winter. At the moment, large windows are letting in the last of the sunshine. There's a small kitchen in one corner, and a wide work table in the centre. Elliot leans against it, his arms folded and watches me as I peer out of the window.

'It's the poet isn't it?' he says.

I turn around, surprised.

'Did you throw yourself at him after I left?'

'No! Nothing happened.'

'But you want something to happen, don't you?'

I let out my breath, fix my eyes on his. 'Look... I'd be lying if I said no.'

His jaw clenches and he looks away. It's the first time I think I've seen him look defeated, but I don't feel any victory. I think we've both said enough. He holds out his hand and the light catches on a set of keys.

'A new tenant is coming in the following week, so I'll need it back by the weekend.'

'Of course. Thank you... and I'm sorry about, well, you know, it not working out...'

He nods. 'I'll leave you to it.'

'Yes...whatever "it" is!'

I take a few steps towards him thinking a kiss on the cheek would be appropriate, but he doesn't move to meet me and I stall. In the end we just nod at each other. Then he turns and shuts the door behind me. The next thing I know I'm alone in a studio with an exhibition date looming and a huge task ahead.

I have no tools and no materials. I haven't got much money, either, but I have got an email from Daisy promising a reception job at a hotel soon. It's for a whole week, overseeing some conferences. It'll fill up the hole in my bank account and stop the worry.

But I'm not going to think about that other life now. Today I'm an artist, a painter, a sculptor. Today I'm going to enjoy what I do.

I stick the kettle on and the empty room fills with its roar. I stare up at the ceiling and in my head I picture the lofty gallery.

What could I do to surprise you? What could I do to make you laugh?

I turn off my phone and feel comforted by the black screen, as though I've fallen into a time warp. While I'm here I can't do anything to sort out any other part of my life, and that's okay.

The kettle abruptly switches off and I pour myself a cup of black tea. I cradle it as I walk around the room. My head is swirling with thoughts. I have one week, one small week. How am I supposed to produce enough work to fill an entire gallery?

I sip my tea and stare into space.

Impact isn't always achieved by quantity. Size plays a part, too, in creating sensation, from portrait miniatures that require a magnifying glass to be seen, to the gigantic frescos in the Sistine Chapel. Would Michelangelo's David be so famous if it was half the size? I don't think so. I've been doing a lot of research on Wikipedia lately. I know of a few artists who have played with size. A woman called Rachel Whiteread made a concrete cast of an entire Victorian house, while Christo and Jeanne-Clause once wrapped a whole coastline in fabric. The point is, it's not about how many bananas I can fit in a room.

As the sun falls behind the clouds and a chill creeps into the air, it dawns on me what I'm going to do. I grab the keys and rush out.

A less-impulsive person would have considered where they were going before they left the building, but not me. I trust that I'll find what I'm looking for. This means I end up walking for miles, probably in circles, and don't come across a hardware shop until I'm at the point of giving up hope.

A buzzer sounds as I walk in, prompting some movement at the back. It's an old-fashioned establishment, packed to the rafters with tools and machinery. A man with a greying mop of hair and a bushy moustache makes his way slowly to the counter.

'You don't look like an electrician,' he barks. 'I've just had four builders, two plumbers, one lost tourist and a gardener, by my calculations I'm due an electrician.'

'Okay...' I say, uncertainly. Perhaps I should pretend to be another lost tourist and get out of here before I make a fool of myself.

'So what can I help you with?'

'Well, I'm sort of building something...'

'If you "sort of" build something I guarantee it'll fall down in a couple of days. Seen it happen many times.'

'It's not a room or anything, it's more of a conceptual piece...'

As soon as I say it I want to stuff the words back in my mouth.

'Okay it's like this,' I say, my cheeks burning. 'I want to build some really big bananas.'

He narrows his eyes like he's working me out, and then his face splits into a big grin.

'Well, why didn't you say so?'

'So you think you can help me?'

He slaps his hand together. 'Course I can. I'm better at pineapples if I'm honest, did a few for the Notting Hill Carnival. Right, grab us that pen for me there and we'll make a list of what you need.'

259

I do as I'm told and he reaches for his half-moon glasses by the till, which instantly turn him into Pinocchio's father.

'I tell you what,' he says, peering up. 'I'm glad you aren't an electrician now.'

As he scribbles down item after item, I start to worry he's thinking a little too big.

'Did I mention I only have one week to make them?'

His only reaction is to sniff and keep scribbling. 'Well, like the saying goes, you either make bananas or die trying.'

'Yes,' I say. 'Very true.'

Chapter 36

I'm leaving the house to head over to the studio when I hear her voice.

'Amber! Wait!'

I turn to look, feeling nervous. Bibiana is hurrying down the street towards me. We haven't spoken since the evening at the bookshop, despite her attempts to contact me. When she came round, I told Egg to tell her I was in bed with flu. Thanks to Rupert, she couldn't come in to check up on me. Last night I watched her name on the screen of my mobile as it rang and rang. I felt bad about not answering, but I just couldn't bring myself to pick up. I didn't have any words.

She reaches my gate, her cheeks flushed. She's wearing a fitted grey suit that cinches in at her slender waist and beautiful black-velvet heels that accentuate her long legs. How can I blame Farrell? She's gorgeous.

'Are you avoiding me?'

'No.'

'We have to sort this out.'

'Can we talk later? I've got to get going.'

'No. You've got to go nowhere. We have to talk now.'

I cringe at the thought of discussing what happened. Her having sex with Farrell. Farrell kissing every inch of her body. I don't want to talk about it, or think about it. I want to forget.

'I've got an exhibition to prepare for,' I say, feeling desperate to escape the awkwardness. 'I'm running out of time.'

I walk down the path, hoping she'll move out of the way and let me go. She reaches out for my arm. Her face is close to mine, her dark eyes frantic.

'Amber, you didn't tell me,' she says. 'You said there was nothing between you. How was I supposed to know?'

My shoulders crumple. I thought I'd cried it all out, but I feel the tears closing in again. She lets me go.

'I would never have... you know I wouldn't have if I'd known...' she searches my face. 'Amber, I'm so sorry...'

'No, it's my fault... it's fine, really...'

I try to smile, but she's looking at me with such concern.

'Amber, I don't want it to be weird between us.'

I flap my hand at her. 'It won't be. I'm just tired, that's all.'

'No you're not, you're upset. I know when you're upset...I'm moving my stuff out tonight. I'm going to stay a few nights with a friend. By then the flat will be ready so I can move in.'

'No you can't do that, that'll be so much hassle for you.'

'I don't want to ruin things for anyone.'

I look down at the floor.

'There was a lot of wine involved...' she says.

Do you like him? The words are on the tip of my tongue. *Does he like you?* But I can't bring myself to say them.

'Where are you going now?' I say instead.

I catch a glimmer of excitement in her eyes. 'I got that second interview.'

'That's great.'

'I think you wish I was back in Argentina.'

'Of course I don't. I'm happy for you.'

I *am* happy for her underneath it all. I just wish things had gone differently. I wish she'd been able to stay at mine so we could have had some proper girly time together. She would have noticed my feelings for Farrell before I had and maybe she would have urged me to do something about them.

'You mustn't be late,' I say.

'I won't, I just had to talk to you. You're okay, aren't you? You don't hate me, do you?'

'Of course I don't hate you. I'm just... gutted, that's all.'

Gutted. It's the only word that seems to fit this hollow feeling tugging at my insides.

She squeezes my arm, 'It's going to be alright, though, trust me. With a bit of time and space... and I don't know... maybe a tequila shot?'

I smile weakly, 'No, I'm not drinking anything until I've got this exhibition sorted.'

'Good,' she says, nodding, 'That's the best way. I can't wait to see what you come up with.'

I can't help laughing at that, 'nor can I...'

We're going to get through this, I think. Our friendship's going to survive.

'Will you answer the phone if I call you later to tell you how it went?'

'Yes... of course... Good luck.'

She smiles as if a weight has lifted off her shoulders and then she grabs me in a tight hug.

'He saw you in the paper,' she says softly. 'He said you looked stunning.'

I close my eyes, my heart racing and breathe in the coconut musk of her coat.

'We're all behind you, Amber, you know that, don't you?'

Chapter 37

At the studio, I write down my plan of action. It looks simple and I'm feeling confident.

Day 1: Mould chicken wire into bananas
Day 2: Papier-mâché bananas
Day 3: Paint bananas

But the chicken wire proves more stubborn than I anticipated and I end up wrestling with it on the floor. I swear at it, punch it, and then thinking it might respond to positive energy, I start talking to it and showering it with compliments.

'Oh what clever chicken wire you are! I bet you know just how to turn yourself into a banana, don't you? I bet you could do it all by yourself, but I'm just going to help you...'

I think I've finally secured it into position and am beginning to smile when it suddenly springs apart, whipping the back of my hand and sending shooting pain through my fingers. I suck in my breath and prance around the studio, shaking my hand as if the throbbing might just fall away.

'Bad chicken wire! Bad chicken wire!'

I continue the struggle until at last I get the material into some sort of shape. Then I step back, only to discover that 'some sort of shape' is all it is.

Who would have thought that the banana form would be so difficult to replicate?

I take a lunch break and turn my phone on to Google papier-mâché tutorials on YouTube. They are really quite enthralling. I sit through the making of a chicken, a Darth Vader helmet and a red M&M. When my battery starts to run low I turn to my sketchpad and spend time drawing my chosen fruit. What I end up with is a page covered in boomerangs.

Re-fuelled after a soggy cheese and tomato sandwich, home-made because I've got to keep costs down somehow, I get back to work. I'm not sure whether my eventual progress is down to me lowering my standard of what I think constitutes a decent banana shape or whether I've accidentally learnt a technique.

I keep at it until I realise my eyes are aching because the sun has nearly set and I'm working in the dark. I leave exhausted but relieved that I have something to come back to. Only once I'm home does my head flood with thoughts of Farrell and I spend the night tossing and turning, and feeling sorry for myself.

What if Farrell's poem wasn't about me? The only phrase I can be sure I heard is *'beyond a friendship'*. Doubt creeps in and teases me. If it meant something, why doesn't he call?

By the time Day 2 comes around I'm grumpy from too much thinking and too little sleep, and my scratched arms are aching from writhing around on the floor in mortal combat with some chicken wire. As I failed to complete my goal of moulding five bananas on my first day, Day 2 turns out to be a repeat of Day 1. My bad mood evaporates as I focus on the job and I'm sorry when my phone rings and breaks the spell. I'd meant to switch it off while I was in the studio. It's Bibiana. Every time I see her name I think of her with Farrell. I guess only time will change that.

'Let me guess,' I say. 'You got the job?'

'Yes! I'm so excited!' she cries. I lower the volume on my phone as she describes the interview, how she'd been sure that it hadn't gone well, how many other people there had been waiting to go in who had looked more experienced, more determined and spoke better English.

'Congratulations, that's brilliant, Bibi.'

'I thought we could all go for a drink to celebrate this evening, what do you think?'

Who does she mean? Me and Farrell? I doubt she's thinking of Egg.

'Unless you'd rather it was just the two of us? Of course! Just me and you?'

'I'm sorry, I can't, I've really got to get on with this project. But we'll go out soon.'

'Promise?'

'Yes, soon...'

I just need a bit more time to get my head sorted. After we say goodbye I turn my phone off so no one else can contact me.

On Day 3 I finally get to mix up my pot of wallpaper paste, glue and water. I've written down the instructions carefully in my sketchbook, but soon I'm doubting myself and pouring everything together, hoping for the best. It's only when I'm squelching the goo between my fingers that I realise I've forgotten to bring newspapers and the only material I've got to papier mâché with is the toilet paper in the communal bathroom.

I know I shouldn't, but I take a roll to test it out.

It's that cheap stuff that feels more like wrapping paper than tissue. Bad for bottoms, but possibly better for bananas. I wrap it around my mesh and spread the transparent jelly over it. The paper instantly thins like a fine membrane and does little to disguise the chicken wire. As I'm accepting the inevitable fact that I must go out and hunt for newspaper there's a loud bang on the studio door.

I freeze. My immediate thought is that I'm being burgled.

'Elliot, I know you're in there! I can see the light is on!' a well-spoken woman's voice shouts from the other side. 'For God's sake, make yourselves decent and open up this minute.'

I snap out of my stunned paralysis at once. It's a voice that demands obedience and I hurry to the door, feeling terrified. Whoever she is, she sounds furious.

I open the door and move aside to avoid being mowed down by a tall woman in a bright- orange dress. She storms into the middle of the room and her eyes widen into huge, fiery cannon balls. I notice the resemblance with Elliot at once and there's suddenly no doubt in my mind that this is his mother.

She holds a hand up and closes her eye and I think she's going to sneeze. But then she snaps them open again and fixes me with a fierce stare.

'Let me guess, you're a poor artist who Elliot has decided to rescue.'

Her words are like a stinging slap across the face.

'No, I didn't need rescuing,' I say, my voice quiet but defensive. 'I just needed some space and he offered me this studio. I didn't realise it wasn't his to offer.'

'It certainly wasn't his to offer!'

I could kill Elliot for putting me in this embarrassing situation. My eyes dart down to my chicken-wire creation, now part-bandaged with dripping toilet roll. How the hell am I going to get it home? Because it's quite clear that I'm being chucked out.

'I'm so sorry,' I say, holding up my hands in surrender. 'I'll just get packed up at once and I'll be gone.'

She lets out an exasperated sigh. 'There's no need to be so dramatic. What's your name?'

'Amber.'

'You'll have to excuse me, Amber, but I've just got off a mammoth flight from New York, only to come back and find I'm locked out of my own house. That Elliot didn't pick me up is bad enough, but not to be at home when he knew I didn't have the keys is completely unacceptable!'

I feel like I'm being told off and struggle to arrange my face into an expression of sympathy. 'That's terrible. Do you live far?'

She narrows her eyes for the briefest second. 'No, Notting Hill. I'm surprised he hasn't taken you there.'

My cheeks are on fire. The lying bastard! Of course that beautiful house wasn't his. That sophisticated, elegant house with its female touch evident throughout. Deep down I must have known it.

'I wonder where he is,' I say, weakly.

'Call him for me, will you?' she says, striding over to the kettle. 'My phone has run out of battery.'

'Of course.'

'I haven't had a decent cup of tea since I've been away,' she says. 'I don't know why other countries find it so bloody difficult.'

The atmosphere is tense and I'm dreading spending time with her.

'I hope for his sake that the house is in a better state than he left it last time,' she mutters under her breath. 'That boy thinks he's some sort of celebrity who can wander around doing what he pleases. It's not for lack of education, I can tell you that.'

I've dialed his number and it's ringing. I feel nervous and twiddle my hair into knots as I wait.

'Hello darling! Are you missing me already?'

Elliot sounds jubilant and possibly drunk.

'*I'm* not, but your uh...'

I haven't actually had confirmation that this woman is his mother.

'Give me that,' she says, holding out her hand.

I pass her my phone. If she asked for it, I'd hand over my wallet too. Her voice is as persuasive as a knife.

'Elliot Frinton-Smith. This is your mother speaking. I'm in my studio with a young lady friend of yours called Amber. Would you care to explain what is going on?'

How many other wannabe artists has he brought here? Not just here, but to his parents' house. I bet that fancy car isn't his either. I'm so angry with him, so angry with myself for being drawn in by the act.

'Are you drunk?' she snaps suddenly.

Oh God. I feel like an endless night is stretching ahead.

'I don't care what contacts are at the party! In a minute you'll be too pissed to remember them anyway!' she shrieks. 'Get a taxi this minute and pick me up. If you're not here in less than half an hour I'm cutting off your allowance.'

A surprised laugh escapes me, which one look from Mrs Frinton-Smith turns into a cough and a splutter.

She hangs up the phone and the studio is plunged into silence. I look longingly at the door.

'Tea?' she says sharply.

If she wasn't holding up a cup I'd think she was asking me to make it.

'I think I better go. I feel really bad intruding. If I'd known...'

'You're not going to leave me in my hour of need,' she interrupts. 'Now how much time did Elliot say you had to finish your... whatever it is you're doing?'

'He said a tenant was coming in next week.'

'What an idiot.'

'Yep.'

'Careful, that's my son you're talking about.'

There's an awkward silence.

'I did originally book to be away for longer,' she says, softening a little. 'I suppose you can stay for a little while.'

'No, I couldn't.'

'There's no point letting your pride stand in the way now, Amber,' she says. 'We both know you won't be able to transport that *thing* anywhere fast.'

She narrows her eyes at my chicken-wire creation. 'Three days. Let's not argue.'

'Thank you.'

'Now, did you want a tea or not?'

'Please,' I say, feeling defeated.

'Oh well, that's something,' she says. 'The last girl would only drink diet coke. It was intolerable.'

I need to clear this up once and for all. 'We're not together.'

She looks at me with interest. 'I'm sorry?'

'Elliot and I. We're not going out.'

'Oh, I know,' she says, rolling her eyes. 'You'd have me to contend with if you were.'

It's late by the time Elliot rocks up in a taxi. He calls my phone, his voice stiff, and asks me to tell his mother to go downstairs. She asks if I'd like to share the cab, and I want to tell her I'd rather die, but instead smile politely and say I'm going in a different direction.

I end up running for the last tube home, which stops for half an hour in a tunnel, giving me plenty of time to replay the encounter with his mother and to get worked up over what a false, pompous prat he is. Exhausted and still feeling the sting of humiliation, I finally burst into my living room, with every intention of crashing onto the sofa and burying my head in its cushions, possibly forever.

But Egg has beaten me to it.

He's sitting in the middle of the couch with his legs up, enveloped in a poncho. He's got a tub of ice cream perched between the mounds of his knees, a spoon in one hand, a pint of beer in the other. Even more surprising, perhaps, is the fact that he's watching Bridget Jones.

'Egg, what's the matter?'

At the sound of my voice Rupert pokes his head out from underneath one side of the poncho and miaos forlornly.

'The general consensus online is that to get over a heartbreak you either need alcohol or ice cream,' Egg says. 'I'm being clever and having both.'

I nudge him over and sit down. 'Pass them over, then, let's see if it works.'

Egg hands me his glass and I take a gulp. Rupert climbs onto my lap and I tickle his chin.

Next he serves me up a spoon of ice cream. The combination is horrible.

On the television, Bridget Jones and her friends are eating blue soup. Lucky for her, a happy ending is around the corner.

'So what happened exactly?' I ask.

'I told Bibiana it would never work between us.'

'How did she take it?'

'She said she didn't understand.'

'I bet.'

It must be a shock to have someone break up with you when you didn't even realise you were going out with them.

'I told her cats are my life now and I couldn't sacrifice everything to be with her.'

Egg eats another scoop of ice cream and stares ahead at the television. I hold onto the warm beer and wonder about the conversation Bibiana and Farrell must have had in the aftermath of Egg's break-up with someone who never was his girlfriend. Did they go out for a celebratory drink without me? Every decision I make seems to throw them closer together. I take another gulp of beer. The thought is so depressing and yet I've got no one to blame but myself.

'You'll get over it, Egg,' I say.

'Oh yes, the consensus online is it'll take me about three to eight weeks to recover,' he says, still staring ahead. 'I thought I might do some online dating to speed things up. Cat-lovers are always easy to spot. They either put a cat as their profile picture or write "cats" in their hobbies.'

It feels as if Egg and I have moved ahead in our friendship. Beer, ice cream, Bridget Jones and a shared problem. It's all I ever wanted from a housemate. I just wish I didn't miss Farrell so much.

'You'll just have to avoid bumping into her,' I say.

'Oh that'll be easy now she's moved.'

So she did it. She did it for our friendship.

Egg shrugs. 'The commute would have ended our relationship if I hadn't.'

I start to laugh with relief, until Egg gives me a hurt look.

'Oh God, sorry Egg, I always laugh when I'm sad.'

He nods at the television. Bridget Jones is running through the snow after Colin Firth aka Mr Darcy.

'I like this bit,' he says.

I can't believe he's seen it before. I gaze at the television and as Colin and Renee kiss under the snowflakes, I imagine all the things I'd love to say to Farrell and wonder if I'll ever get the chance.

Chapter 38

The song on the radio is coming to an end. My palms start sweating and I try to focus on my breath. It's a local station, with probably only a handful of listeners; there's really nothing to worry about. The radio presenter turns to me, one hand on his huge earphones and blasts me with a high-voltage smile. It's supposed to reassure me. It's easy for him; he does this every morning. I've never been on the radio. It was Matt pulling strings. He went to school with this guy. I suddenly can't remember his name. Was it Gary or Barry?

'And with me this morning is Amber Thompson, the lady who has been brightening up our city with eye-catching and completely bonkers bananas. Your exhibition opens tomorrow, Amber, are you ready?'

I want to say I was born ready, but that would be a lie.

'No, not really.'

Gary or Barry laughs heartily.

'I wish I was joking.'

More laughter.

'Now, Amber, tomorrow is the exclusive private view, am I right?'

He knows he's right. He's reading it off a piece of paper.

'Yes, that's right.'

'With a strict guest list, am I right?'

'Well...'

273

His eyes widen meaningfully. 'Tell me I'm right.'

'You're right.'

I feel like I'm in a pantomime.

'But there's a twist. Can you tell us the twist?'

'Yes, I can, Barry.'

'Gary.'

Damn. I knew it.

'Sorry, Gary, it's all the paint fumes.'

It's not. I haven't even got around to the painting yet.

Gary grimaces. 'Remember kids, don't paint at home, it's dangerous.'

'Well, not that dangerous, you just need to open the windows.'

'Let's get back to these wild card invitations which will be left at iconic London monuments! How will people find them?'

It's a good question and one we haven't properly sorted out yet. Originally Elliot had volunteered to take the car and I was going to jump out at each spot and hand out a couple of invitations to anyone who looked marginally interested. But this morning, Elliot sent me a text message to say his car had a flat tyre, which I interpreted as his mother had reclaimed it.

'They'll need to look out for red envelopes early in the morning, they'll be in Trafalgar Square, around the Tower of London, somewhere on Tower Bridge, the British Museum...'

The invitations are the last thing on my mind right now. I'm sure Aurelia will find a solution. My thoughts are with my papier mâché, which is taking forever to dry. My poor hair dryer can't take much more. Six fuse changes in six hours must be some sort of record.

'Amber, we've got some listeners on the line who'd love to ask you some questions,' Gary says, smiling as if he were in front of a camera.

'Great.'

I shrink a little lower in my seat.

'Good morning to our first caller!'

274

There's a crackle on the line. Gary tries again, 'Hello? Anyone there?'

'Yes, Edith here, my toast just popped so I had to get it,' the voice of an elderly lady breaks through.

Gary glares at the skinny producer in the corner. 'Edith, hello... again.'

'I've got a question for the young lady, Gary. Does she buy her bananas in bulk?'

Gary rolls his eyes at me and mouths 'she rings every day!'

'Actually, I don't use real bananas any more,' I say. 'They're made from paper.'

There's a pause and then, 'And do they taste as good?'

'O-kay thank you Edith! We have another caller on the line. Alfred, what would you like to say to Amber?'

A gruff voice comes on. 'I just want to congratulate Amber on her choice of fruit. I think the banana is such a... such a... such a...'

It's a long and uncomfortable moment waiting for Alfred to find the right word. Thankfully Gary has a few songs up his sleeve to give him more time. Unfortunately the line cuts out before poor Alfred has nailed the adjective. He's the second and last caller and after some breezy chit chat I escape the radio station and hurry back to the studio. Gary may think I was joking, but I'm seriously behind schedule. I honestly don't know how I'm going to pull it off. There's transportation to think of and issues about how I'm going to hang the bananas once I get them to the gallery.

I just wish I knew someone who could help.

'We meet again,' Elliot's mother says, as I burst through the studio door. She's dressed down in cargo trousers and a t-shirt with an orange neon owl on it holding a paintbrush.

She must read the horror in my eyes.

'Oh don't look like that, Amber, you need help don't you, and I've got a Masters in fine art.'

No, I can't work with this woman!

'I promise I won't boss you about. I'll do exactly, and only, what I'm told.'

She smiles and the delight in her eyes looks positively genuine.

'But why do you want to help me?'

'In case you *are* the next big thing... and because it looks rather fun.'

I snort. A real Farrell snort. He'd love this story.

'Are you any good with spray paint?'

'Oh, yes,' she says, looking smug. 'I spent a week volunteering with juvenile offenders once. It was very educational.'

Chapter 39

It's eight o'clock in the evening and I'm standing in the gallery, my stomach in knots. In front of me two men are constructing a scaffolding tower. The horrible realisation that a normal ladder wouldn't be tall enough happened only an hour ago. When I admitted the problem to Aurelia she looked as if she was going to murder me. A second later she was on the phone flirting with someone and telling them they owed her a favour.

Thanks to Mrs Frinton-Smith the bananas did dry in time for me to paint them. She deemed my hair dryers 'too piddly to mess about with' and hired a couple of powerful blow heaters instead. My bananas will be arriving later with the help of a man with a van. Aurelia wants them installed tonight, so there's no stress tomorrow.

Through the frosted glass I make out Elliot heading towards the gallery with a large cardboard box. I haven't seen him since I met his mother and found out about his stupid lies. I'm not in the mood to pull him up on this now. I open the door and he acknowledges me with a grim nod.

'Are they the photographs?' I ask.

He puts the box down and wipes his hands together. 'No, I've bought you a puppy. I thought you might like to spray paint it.'

'That's helpful of you.'

'Yes, they are the photographs.'

Alessandro's mounted photographs are an easy solution for the blank walls and also a way to make some income. It would've been fun to have a video projected on the wall of the bananas around London, but there's no time to sort that out now. Elliot and Aurelia are splitting a seventy percent commission on each picture, which is fair enough considering their investment.

'I didn't think you were going to let us put the nude pictures up,' he says, 'sorry, *body art* pictures.'

'My mum thinks they're beautiful and that's good enough for me.'

He smirks. 'I didn't think it was your mother's opinion you were worried about.'

'Talking of mothers, yours has been very helpful. It was really kind of her letting me use her studio. But you know all about her kindness, no doubt, what with you still living at home.'

Elliot winces and I enjoy the way his cheeks turn pink. 'If you chose to misunderstand, that was your problem.'

'You lied.'

'I didn't lie. I didn't tell the complete truth, that's all.'

'We'll just have to agree to disagree.'

'On what exactly?'

'Everything.'

'Fine.'

We stand there with our arms folded staring up at the scaffold. I don't think either of us is really seeing it. We're both seething. It's ridiculous because there's so much to be done. Someone needs to be the bigger person, and since Elliot's scowl looks as if it's sculpted in stone, that person will have to me.

I unfold my arms and turn to look at him. 'Elliot, I'm sorry I hurt your feelings. Can we forgive and forget... and get on with this project as a team?'

He considers my outstretched hand and then let's out a dramatic sigh. 'Alright, and I'm sorry I gave the wrong impression, although one day that house will be mine, so technically...'

'Elliot!'

'Fine, fine.'

One of the scaffolding men is trying to get our attention. 'Oi mate! This is done up here, did you want to pass something up or are you going to do it yourself?'

Elliot looks at me, his eyebrows raised in question.

'I'm doing it myself,' I call up.

Judging by the expression on his face, the man clearly doesn't think women should be let loose on a scaffold. He mutters something to his colleague and they start to make their way down. It's time to get the bananas and we're going to need all the help we can get. Egg should have arrived at the studio by now. I send him a text message to make sure.

Ready?

He replies with lightning speed. *Ready!*

Then I text Mrs Frinton-Smith: *On our way!*

A reply comes from her phone a few moments later: *Actually it's Egg again, Rosemary can't text very fast.*

First-name terms already, well done Egbert.

Ten minutes later, Elliot and I are heading over to the studio in a van with a driver who has read all about my bananas and is over the moon about being involved.

At over one and a half metres long each, the five bananas make up a colossal bunch, which are joined at the top by hidden wires. Unlike real bananas they don't fit snugly together, but wave about like independent, giant fingers. To get them through the door requires Egg and I pulling them carefully through one at a time. Elliot and Rosemary help us once we're on the other side. We edge along the corridor towards the lift, each one supporting a different banana, and as we get closer, we notice it has acquired a notice that says 'OUT OF ORDER'.

'Not again!' Rosemary cries.

'We're going to have to take the stairs,' Elliot says.

It's only two flights, but the descent is excruciatingly slow and tense. I'm concerned that everyone's rubbing their hands over the barely dry paint and the glossy finish is going to lose its shine. The frame feels a little too malleable and I'm not enjoying its jerky movements as each of us, with our different heights and different speeds, advance down the stairs.

As we turn the corner, the only banana that isn't getting individual attention smacks against the wall.

'Shit! Is it damaged?'

We all hold our position as Egg checks it over. 'Why did the banana go the doctor?' he says.

'We don't have time for jokes, Egg,' I say. I think I'm having heart palpitations.

'Why?' Rosemary asks.

'Because it wasn't peeling well.'

'I don't get it.'

As Egg opens his mouth to explain, Rosemary lets out a delayed howl of laughter that reverberates around the stairwell, and probably around all of London itself.

'Mother!' Elliot says in a disapproving tone.

'Come on, we're running out of time!' I cry. I feel as if I'm racing against a clock that everyone else is oblivious to.

We start to move again. I'm anxious to get outside because I feel at any moment the bananas could rip. They might be hard to the touch, but they're only made of paper.

We're nearly at the second corner when my phone starts to ring.

'Well we all know who that is,' Elliot says.

Farrell!

'Wait. Sorry...'

'Can't you call them back dear?' Rosemary says.

Elliot lets out an exasperated sigh. 'No, she's in love with him, and you know love can't wait.'

'It can when there are giant bananas at stake,' she replies.

I rest my huge orange banana on my shoulder and free up a hand to get out my phone, which is vibrating manically. My heart does a somersault when I see his name on the screen. Everybody is staring at me, waiting.

'Hello?'

'Amber, it's me.'

'Hi, how are you?'

'Yeah, good... good...'

There's an audible sigh from Elliot. Oh God, this is awkward. Egg has closed his eyes and seems to be meditating, Rosemary is shifting from leg to the other and the movement is making the bananas very unstable.

'What have you been up to?' he asks.

'Just, you know, getting ready for the exhibition...'

'Oh yeah, that's soon isn't it?'

'Tomorrow.'

'Oh right...'

Elliot starts to whistle.

'Look, I'm just in the middle of carrying something... big...'

'Do you need help?'

'I'll be fine, I just need my hand back. But I'll call you back.'

'Whenever you're ready.'

'I will.'

'Okay, well... Bye, Amber.'

'Bye.' I hang up the phone and feel an urge to throw it down the stairs. 'Shit! Shit! Shit!'

'Yes, that was poor,' Elliot smirks.

'Do you realise you didn't actually invite him to the exhibition?' Rosemary says.

'I didn't?'

Egg is frowning at me. 'You're very bad at this.'

'Oh God, I didn't did I?'

We start moving again, painfully slowly. I'm so distracted that I don't notice my banana scraping along the wall until Rosemary yells, 'wake up, Amber!'

'I've got to ring him back,' I say.

281

Everyone starts to protest, but I ignore them. I can't go on another second without asking him. What if he thinks I don't want him to come? If I leave any later he might make plans. He might be arranging something with friends as I dial. *Don't be engaged! Don't be engaged!*

The phone is ringing. I hold my breath. The brightly coloured bananas sway in front of me.

'That was quick,' he says, a smile in his voice.

'I forgot to ask you... What are you doing tomorrow evening?'

'Nothing... why?'

'Would you like to come to my show?'

He lets out a little laugh. 'Yes. Of course I would. God, Amber, I thought you'd never ask.'

A big happy smile spreads across my face. I give Egg a thumbs-up and he beams back at me.

'Right,' Rosemary says. 'Can we get on a move on please? These bananas are making me hungry.'

Chapter 40

I shouldn't have worried so much about whether or not people would come. There's already a queue at the door and a woman ticking off names from a guest list. It's exhilarating. Normally I'd be the one stealing glances at the artist, but today it's me people are looking for and smiling at, and wanting to talk to.

So far there are only a few familiar faces. Egg is tucking into a glass of wine and talking to Rosemary, who's wearing a shirt covered in miniature embroidered cats. The last time I glanced over she was pulling it taut over her chest so he could examine them better, the cats I think, not her breasts, which are sufficiently visible as they are.

Egg's reenactment group is here too. They're huddled in a corner arguing over who said they were going for full dress code. Two are wearing white linen togas and rush woven slippers, the third has opted for red chequered trousers and a denim waistcoat. They're all getting approving looks from the fashionista types, most of whom look as if they've also rolled out of a fancy dress box.

A waiter hovers by me with a tray of Prosecco and I gratefully take a glass. I need something in my hands to make me stop looping my fingers through the tassels of my new dress. I panic-bought it this morning from the local high street. It's black with a gold geometric pattern running through it. It's what Cleopatra might have worn if she'd been a flapper. It's a dress to dance in, not for standing around trying to look important. My hands suddenly fly up to my neck, where I expect to feel the price label sticking out. But no, I did cut it off.

Relax, this is your show!

My show. It hasn't sunk in yet. I need to pinch myself a few more times.

'Fabulous,' a young woman says, offering her hand. My eyes flit to her head, where a pink miniature top hat rests at a slant. 'My name's Bethany James, I blog about contemporary art.'

'I love your hat,' I say.

She beams. 'And I love your bananas. I was wondering if you might want to do an interview on the blog. We get about twenty thousand hits a month, so not massive but...'

'Yes, I'd love to.'

I would have said yes if she'd said a hundred hits. I don't want this to be the beginning and the end rolled into one. I want to wrestle with wire, paint until my eyes blur, sketch until my hands are black with pencil lead. It might have started as a joke, but now I'm here, I've know it's what I want to do. I can't let it be a one-off experience. I've got to take every opportunity to keep it going.

Bethany hands me her card. 'I'm sure everyone wants to talk to you tonight, but do let me know when you're free for a drink,' she says.

'I will, definitely.'

Out of the corner of my eye, I notice Elliot has arrived. He's with a waif-thin girl in a dusky-pink dress. I look on as he fetches her a glass of wine and for a moment she stands alone looking slightly lost. I recognise that feeling and I excuse myself from the group of strangers hovering around me and head over to her.

'Hi,' I say, offering my hand. 'I'm Amber.'

She shoots me a grateful smile. 'Lauren.'

Elliot joins us. 'Oh, I see you've met.'

'Oh!' she gasp. 'You're *the* Amber. Oh my God, I love your work.'

284

I feel slightly embarrassed. I'm struggling to call what I've done 'work'.

'Lauren is an artist too,' Elliot says, his eyes not meeting mine.

'Oh what a surprise!' I bite my lip to stop myself laughing. What a relief not to care.

A waitress stops beside us, 'Would you care for a goujon?'

My eyes light up as I look over the array of fancy chicken nuggets. 'Yes, please, are they from Flamingo Catering?'

The woman smiles knowingly. 'Vicky sends her love.'

'Only her love? No sacks of anything?'

She casts her eyes up at the gigantic banana suspension above us shimmering under the spotlights. 'I think you do better making the fruit yourself.'

'Thank you, I appreciate it.'

'So what will you be doing next, Amber?' Lauren asks.

I've just caught sight of my parents in the queue. It's the perfect excuse to dodge the question. The answer is *I don't know*. But I'll think of something. I head over as my mum bursts in, voicing her approval as loudly as she can. My dad stops, hands in pockets and stares up at the bananas.

'I hope that's fixed on properly,' he says. 'It won't look good if someone gets killed on opening night.'

'Or any other night, for that matter,' my mum says, enveloping me in a big hug. 'You look gorgeous Amber.'

'Thanks, Mum. Can I get you drink?'

'I bet it's pricey in here,' my dad says, lowering his voice. 'Everyone's very lah-di-dah, aren't they?'

'It's free.'

My dad looks as though a light has just switched on in his head. 'Oh, so that's why you're always going to gallery openings. I thought you were just being a snob.'

'I saw Dee in the queue,' my mum says, 'and that other friend of yours with the curly hair. And I think I saw... oh what's her name, John?'

'Oh yeah, the one with the nice legs, you know,' my Dad says, nodding at me. 'Foreign.'

'Dark hair,' my mum adds.

'Bibiana?'

'That's it,' she says.

'Yeah, she's moved to London.'

'And where's *whatshisname*?' my mum says, clicking her fingers.

I can guess who she's talking about but I hold myself back from blurting out his name. She'll know if I do. She'll know there's something funny going on between us.

'Oh, you know, the Irish lad you're always hanging out with...'

'The one who usually looks like he needs a shave,' my dad says.

'Blue eyes...' Mum adds.

'Green,' I say, and then blush. 'You mean Farrell.'

'Farrell, that's it!' she says. 'No, I'm quite sure they're blue.'

'No, they're green.'

'When did you see him last? You're still neighbours, aren't you?'

I glance over at the door, wishing he and his green eyes would appear. It's early still. But I'm so used to him being the first to arrive. Perhaps he's caught up at the bookshop. He has to come. He was the only person I was thinking about when I chose this dress.

'About two week ago... we've both been so busy.'

It seems like ages.

'Is he coming?'

I'm looking towards the door again. 'I think so, but I'm not sure,' I answer honestly.

Mum spots a tray of drinks heading the other way and chases after it with my dad following close behind. I'm not alone very long. The drink has made people feel more relaxed about coming up to me.

'I was handed the invitation on Tower Bridge,' one lady gushes. I smile with relief, because Aurelia succeeded in getting it all done in time.

The woman, stylish in a high-waisted brown skirt, white shirt and skyscraper heels, is clearly keen to talk. She asks me about my work, her eyes narrowed to show she's really listening.

'I'm about to open my third fashion boutique,' she says.

I'm suddenly aware that this conversation might be going somewhere. She talks about a glove collection she's working on inspired by coconuts.

'I think "tropical" is going to be the next big trend, don't you?'

'Oh, definitely,' I say. 'Tropical is so much fun.'

'It is, isn't it? I'd love something big and bold like your bananas in our window display,' she says. 'Is that a job you might consider?'

'Absolutely.'

Too eager?

'I mean, I'd have to see the space...'

'Of course. Perhaps next week?'

I think of the hotel job waiting for me in my other life.

'I'm a bit busy the following week, but I certainly could do the one after.'

Aurelia appears at my side and gently touches my arm, 'Sorry, can I just steal you a moment?'

'Take my card,' the woman says. 'Let's put something in the diary soon.'

'Yes, that sounds great,' I gush. 'Thanks for coming.'

That woman is interested in my bananas! This could be my first-ever commission!

'The pleasure is all mine.'

Aurelia's apologetic smile dissolves as she steers me away, 'There are two policeman here to see you.'

My stomach clenches. 'What?'

'I've kept them waiting on the stairs to my office. I didn't want to alarm anyone.'

I follow her, a weak smile struggling to stay on my lips as I squeeze through the groups of people. I haven't got away with it. It's the blue bananas. I've damaged one of Yayoi's penises and she wants compensation. I won't be able to pay the fine so they'll arrest me. They're going to give me ten years' community service picking up litter. That's Karma come back to bite me in the bum for leaving rotten fruit around the capital. Please don't let them arrest me now in front of all these people!

We slip through the side door and almost bump into Constable Perkins himself. He straightens to attention. Behind him, on a step further up is another young policeman holding a tablet. He gets up, his eyes darting from Jamie to me, his raised eyebrows all expectant.

'Hello again,' I say, feeling sick to my stomach. 'Am I in trouble?'

Aurelia folds her arms. 'This is her opening night, can whatever it is not wait?'

'Good evening...' Jamie says.

'Let's just show her...' the other policeman cuts in, handing the tablet to Jamie, who looks uneasy as he takes it.

'We're not here to spoil your evening...' Jamie says. 'We all have our dreams...'

I frown. Where is he going with this?

'...and me and Constable Dhaliwal here, we've always wanted to make music and music videos... and well, we know we shouldn't have but we made a tune to go with your video...'

'My video?'

Spots of pink appear at his cheeks. He swallows. 'You signed that we could use it...'

The memory of signing all those papers comes back to me. I had a raging hangover, I just wanted to get it all over with as quickly as possible and for everyone to disappear. I assumed it would all be bona fide since it was from the police! I didn't know the policeman I was dealing with was a... what had the newspaper said? *An aspiring film maker and DJ.*

'Show us then,' says Aurelia. 'We haven't got all day.'

He holds up the tablet for us. A base guitar beat starts to pound out of the mini speakers. The image is grainy and dark but, even so, I instantly recognise my own kitchen. I can make out the side of the cupboards and the door to the outside patio. My mouth drops open as I watch. The base is joined by a catchy keyboard accompaniment. Then there's a female voice, which sounds as if it's under water.

Don' you worry... Don' you worry... Don' you woo-oOo-ory

Suddenly there's movement. A shadow crosses the camera. Then I see my legs and the hem of my navy Audrey Hepburn dress, the one I wore to Montague's exhibition. I can feel my eyes widening involuntarily as I recall that night. I watch myself bend forwards and then I'm holding a bunch of bananas in my hand and I'm singing to them in the voice of Cher.

Don' you worry... Don' you worry... Don' you woo-oOo-ory

I know what's coming. I remember that night; marching into Rose's shop, my mission flashing like a neon sign in my brain. There's a bottle of wine somewhere that hasn't made it into the frame.

... maleetel ones I weel show you... I weel show you... I weel shoo-oOo-o you to the wo-oOo-orld

'Wow,' I gasp, as the bananas in my hand turn from yellow to pink to blue to red in the video.

'I did that...' Jamie says. I hear the pride in his voice.

I'm speechless.

... maleetel ones I weel show you... I weel show you... I weel shoo-oOo-o you to the wo-oOo-old

The video jolts back and forward like stop motion as I talk to my bananas and tell them I'm going to show them off to the world. I become aware that they're bopping to it. Not just Constable Dhaliwal, who is now sitting on the stairs neck pumping, not just Constable Perkins, who is moving side to side, but Aurelia too. She's nodding her head to the beat. It's a very catchy beat, to be fair.

'How did you do this?'

It almost sounds as if I can sing.

'It's auto-tune...' Aurelia says, before the others can answer. 'It's fabulous.'

'Oh my God...' I murmur, covering my mouth.

Oh yes, there it is. I can make out the bottom of the bottle of that chemical Chardonnay. I feel queasy as I remember what I did next. Any minute now... 1... 2... There! No more dress hem. Thank God I was standing so close to the sack at this point. Not close enough! There's a flash of my thighs and then my pink knickers. *Shit*. And there's a glimpse of a spray can in my hand as I head out the door.

The music is fading out... *Don' you worry... Don' you worry... Don' you woo-oOo-ory*. A circle is narrowing in on the image, which is no longer of my kitchen but of the blue bananas in the Tate and then the red bananas in The Beefeater's and then the circle closes completely leaving the screen black.

'That was YouTube?' I cry.

'Tell her how many views it's got,' says Constable Dhaliwal, sounding as if he's going to burst.

Jamie turns the screen around and reads out the number, '10,732... now 33...'

'It's gone viral,' Aurelia says, 'We've got to set it up next door... project it onto the wall...'

Isn't this what I wanted? Something whacky lit up on the wall?

'But I'm in knickers!'

She looks at me like I'm mad. 'Says the woman who posed naked in the newspaper.'

'It was body art!' I protest.

'Come on, Amber,' Jamie says, 'I've had to put up with so much crap from the boys over that sack of bananas. This going viral will let me off the hook... we've worked so hard on it.'

'Amber, ' Aurelia says, gripping my arm, 'You must show that it's official. That this is you. This could be huge. This will mean you're not forgotten in six months' time.'

'Alright... ' I say, taking a deep breath. 'Let's do this.'

'Excellent! Now get back in there and enjoy yourself!' Aurelia says, shoving me towards the door.

Chapter 41

A waiter passes by and I take another glass of Prosecco. It feels like a dream. I look up at my huge multi-coloured bananas suspended from the ceiling and think of the struggle it was to hoist them into place. More a miracle than a dream, I suppose. We almost dropped them twice.

People in the room must be looking up at them and wondering what they mean. What *do* they mean? That anything is possible if you set your mind to it?

I take a step back and do a double-take when I recognise the couple from Montague's exhibition, Tiger Shirt and Mickey Mouse Girl. They must be on a special mailing list. Mickey Mouse Girl is wearing a green tutu skirt with a polo shirt, and Tiger Shirt is in an orange jumpsuit and looks as though he's just escaped from a high-security prison. Perhaps they are artists, too.

Too? Have I accepted my new identity, then?

We stand together staring up at the glossy bananas and I wait for them to pass judgement. In the corner Aurelia is overseeing the setting up of the projector and I think how they're bound to like the video.

They are silent for some time and I start to panic. If my bananas don't elicit any response, then I'm doomed.

Mickey Mouse Girl is first to speak. 'I love the curves,' she says.

'It's very voluptuous, very mother banana like she's looking over us, ready to give birth to new life...'

Okay. That could work...

But Tiger Shirt doesn't agree, 'No, not at all, I mean you can completely see the influence of Yayoi Kusama,' he says. 'This is about male dominance. They aren't bananas, they are five swollen members...'

I cough politely, possessed perhaps by the spirit of Ghost. They both turn around.

'Hi, I'm Amber, the artist.'

Here to stop you projecting any more penises onto my work!

'Oh hello, what an honour,' Tiger Shirt beams. 'I was just saying how wonderful it must have been to collaborate with such a great artist like Yayoi. Your piece at the Tate was very arresting, I've heard. Is it still on show?'

'Well, no actually, it was a guerilla installation, in and out very quickly.'

'Ah yes,' he says, winking. 'Very symbolic indeed.'

I smile awkwardly and turn to Mickey Mouse Girl, just like Ghost had done to me, with that *and what do you think madam?* look on my face.

'I'm fascinated by your use of colour,' she says, nodding in agreement with herself. 'It must have been quite a challenge getting them just right.'

Blue, yellow, red, green and orange. Not unusual colours by any stretch of the imagination.

'It took me a while choosing the right blue,' I say, not wanting to disappoint her.

'And what a blue colour it is,' a soft Irish voice says, nearby.

It's a voice that makes my heart dance.

Farrell nods up at the bananas, his expression solemn.

'I've never seen anything like it. The juxtaposition of colour is incredibly revealing.'

Tiger Man glances over at Farrell, a flicker of annoyance on his face, and then he looks back up at the bananas again, squinting hard.

'Yes,' he says. 'I see what you mean. Any other arrangement wouldn't have worked.'

My own voice is tremulous with suppressed excitement.

'I didn't think people would notice.'

'Oh you can't help but notice,' Farrell says. 'Even if you can't formulate what it is, emotionally it grabs you.'

He's so handsome. He's never changed, but it's as if I'm seeing him for the first time. I love his face. I love those lips I tasted for too brief a moment. I want to kiss him again.

'I'd like to see it from a different angle,' Tiger Shirt says, and crosses the room with Mickey Mouse Girl trailing.

When I look back at Farrell I find that the funny act is over. All the emotion of these last weeks is written across his face and he gazes at me with so much tenderness it takes my breath away.

'Amber,' he says.

I can almost taste the words I want to hear, but instead he reaches for something in his pocket and pulls out a folded piece of paper.

'This is for you,' he says. 'You don't have to say anything... but will you think about it?'

I take it from him and when I look up I see my parents heading towards us. The noise in that small gallery suddenly seems magnified. I can hear every footstep, every laugh, every clink of glass on glass.

'There you are!' my mum cries. 'Farrell, it *is* you, isn't it? Now let me look at those eyes of yours.'

Just like that, our bubble bursts and my parents are in our midst, larger than life, cheeks rosy from their second glass of wine. I feel mortified as my mum stares into Farrell's face, while he stands still, looking as if he doesn't know whether to laugh or sink through the floor.

'Green,' she concludes. 'Just as I thought. Amber thought they were blue.'

'No, I didn't!' I cry, outraged.

'No, she didn't,' my mum says, with a little laugh, and I realise she was only teasing me, and also that she has a pretty good idea of what's going on.

The folded paper is burning in my hand. I want to look at it so badly. I glance at Farrell. Now it's my dad who has his attention, and his arm, and isn't going to let go soon.

'Any luck with that book yet?' he says.

Like me, my parents always feel compelled to ask.

'Yes...' Farrell says, surprising us all. 'An agent liked my first three chapters and so I've just sent him the rest of it.'

I stare at him, open-mouthed. I can't believe it!

'Nothing confirmed yet, so don't get too excited, Amber.'

'Still! That's brilliant!'

'Well done, love,' my mum says.

'Well it was about time, wasn't it?' My dad says. 'Now you must know a thing or two about books. Last night we were at a pub quiz and there was a question about the Odyssey... do you know it?'

'Don't go anywhere!' I say to Farrell.

I can't wait any longer. Patience isn't one of my virtues.

It's not a classic place to read poetry, but the bathroom is the only place I know I'll be alone. Behind the closed door, I finally read his words, and as I do the little hairs on my arms stand on end.

Alone was not intense before we met
My words – old friends – abandon me to this.
Beyond friendship suddenly, and yet
Enduring to the point I yield. One kiss
Risks all. No kiss: I'd lose all but regret.

How long had he considered it? How long had his mind toyed with that risk? Because now I know he hadn't acted on impulse; it hadn't been a spur-of-the-moment decision. No, it had been something that had been growing within him, until one day he couldn't ignore it any longer. He had always meant to kiss me that day.

My eyes wander over the page and it's then I notice my name written down the side, one letter locked into each line. It's a poem that could only have been for me.

A tear rolls down my cheek, lands on the smile that has crept over my face.

What did he want me to think about? My mind is made up... so what the hell am I still doing in the gallery toilet?

I squeeze through the groups of people in conversation, throwing out apologies like confetti. When I break into the space where Farrell should be, he's not there. Only my parents remain, flushed and happy, talking to a big man I vaguely remember.

'Where did he go?' I ask, as the man throws out his hand to shake mine.

'Amber, it's Thomas,' he booms. 'Thomas Fitzpatrick, art collector. We met...'

'At Montague's! Yes, I'm so glad you could come!' I say, sounding a little hysterical.

'I'm very curious about your bananas...'

'Yes, I'd love to talk, but I've just got to find someone. It's quite important, will you stay for a bit longer?'

'Amber!' my Mum says, with a look that translates roughly as *He might want to buy your bananas!*

'Well, yes, of course...' Fitzpatrick say, looking baffled.

'Mum, did you see Farrell go?'

'He left a minute ago. Why? What's the matter?'

She calls after me, but I don't stop. I leave the show and head outside, where it's busy with people doing last-minute shopping. I feel frantic. I look up and down the street, trying to find him, desperate to know what direction he might have gone in.

And when I think that I'm being a fool, and I should just accept he's gone, I catch a glimpse of his dark-green shirt in the distance and I hurry after him.

But my heels slow me down and I panic, thinking I'll lose sight of him. For a split second I consider the stained paving stones, the low risk of dog crap and the seriousness of the situation, then I whisk off my shoes and start to run.

One minute I've nearly reached him and the next minute he's vanished. I come to an abrupt halt in the middle of the street and look desperately around me. How could he have just disappeared?

'Amber!'

I spin around at the sound of my name. Farrell is standing in a doorway of the shop next to me, a shop that I now notice is a florist. In his hand is a bunch of red roses wrapped in brown paper.

'What are you doing here?' He walks towards me and catches sight of my bare feet. 'What happened to your shoes?'

I hold them up. 'I thought you had left for good!'

'No, of course not, I just felt I wanted to give you something.' He comes closer, looking concerned.

'Farrell...' I say, and then I blurt it out. 'I don't want to be your friend any more.'

He looks surprised 'You don't?'

'No,' I say, shaking my head. 'It's not enough.'

I look at his face, at his big smile.

'That's a relief,' he says, and with the bouquet of flowers still in one hand, he wraps his arms around me and pulls me in close. 'Because I don't want to be your friend either.'

I let my shoes drop to the floor and I throw my arms around him.

'I love you, Amber,' he says. 'Even if you are completely bananas.'

There's no thought in my head as he kisses me, just a warm glow of happiness and the feeling that everything is going to be alright.

He brushes his hand against my cheek and my skin tingles.

'Come on,' he says.

I pick up my shoes and he takes my other hand.

'Where are we going?'

'There's this little gallery opening near by,' he says casually.

'Oh, really?'

'And you know what a gallery opening means, don't you?'

I narrow my eyes at him. 'Free wine?

'No,' he says, suppressing a laugh. 'Great art.'

'One day you'll take me seriously, Farrell Kennedy.'

He stops walking and I turn around, wondering why. One minute he's standing there, looking at me strangely with a mixture of excitement and fear and then the next moment he's taking both of my hands in his. My heart starts pounding.

'I should have told you how I felt. I was an idiot. You know I don't care if you want to cover yourself in paint, or ink, or paper, or fuck it, mashed potatoes, as long as you're happy. I made a big mistake and I'm sorry... and seeing you today in your show, it just...' he swallows, and his eyes are glistening with tears. 'It just made me so upset... because I wanted to have been there to help you, to help you hang up those ridiculously big bananas...'

I let out a nervous laugh, but he hasn't finished.

'Next time I'll be there, and the time after that, and every time, because I love you and I want to spend the rest of my life with you... Now is that serious enough for you?'

I can't get the words out because I'm laughing and crying. My arms are around him and he lifts me up and kisses me as if he never means to stop. And I don't know what passers-by think. They don't start clapping. This is London not Hollywood, after all. The hustle and bustle of market stalls being packed up and rolled off home continues beyond us. From a nearby pub the first notes of live music carry in the warm summer air; a base guitar melody to accompany the setting sun. And we are in the middle of it all, wrapped in our moment, our lips locked, our hearts beating with the excitement and anticipation of our shared adventure ahead. 'Farrell, that's the most serious thing you've ever said to me.'

'I know and it's true,' he says, setting me down and taking my hand. 'Now let's go see what's happening with those bloody bananas!'

Author Note

I've got a Happy Folder on my computer. It contains all the positive comments I got when I originally posted this novel on Wattpad. Back then it was called *Spray Painted Bananas* and the ending was just a scribble on a post it note.

It still surprises me that I chose to write a whole novel online. At the time I'd been struggling with a book for over two years and was acting like one of those tortured writers. I remember my husband saying, 'why do you write it if it doesn't make you happy?'

When a Wattpad community engagement manager emailed me to say that if I wrote a novel for them they'd include it in their popular Featured section, I decided to go for it. To be safe, I wrote a buffer of 10,000 words before I started posting one, then two, chapters online a week. I knew that if I was reading a book and suddenly I had to wait a month for a chapter, I'd be so frustrated, and I didn't want my readers to feel like that.

I've been blogging for six years so I'm used to getting feedback from strangers, but my experience on Wattpad was overwhelming. It was like writing with a band of cheerleaders behind me. Over the course of posting the novel, I'd often wake up to enthusiastic comments of: I LOVE IT! WHAT HAPPENS NEXT? and I'd honestly think: I don't know yet!

I wrote like mad for four months and there wasn't a day I didn't have a giggle at my computer. Wattpad helped me reconnect with my love of romantic comedies and I was finally writing what made me happy; I was writing about life and love and of course, bananas. I'm so grateful to all those thousands of readers who cheered me along the way. Thank you. If you were one of them, I hope you enjoyed this new improved version of the novel!

Acknowledgements

I've day dreamed a lot about writing this acknowledgement page. In my mind I'm at the Oscars and I thank everyone until I've collapsed in a heap sobbing. Luckily I can edit the sobbing out here!

I originally wrote this book chapter by chapter on the online platform Wattpad and called it *Spray Painted Bananas*. Thanks to all the lovely Wattpad readers for voting and commenting on it, without you I might not have got an agent or a publisher.

I want to thank my brother, Oriol, for urging me to take that step and for making me see the bigger picture. Thank you to my Mum, for checking every single chapter before I posted it online. Mum, your generosity and love bowls me over. Thank you to Javier Rosa who made the original cover and refused to let me pay him. I owe you dinner.

I want to thank Isabel Rogers, who is the author of the Farrell's poem. I would still be stuck on Chapter 30 if you hadn't responded to my cry for help on Twitter. Isabel just won the Cardiff International Poetry Prize which makes me feel even more chuffed her poem is in my book!

Thank you Piera Lizzeri for never seeming to tire of telling me to keep on going. And thank you to Ben Blackman, Monal Patel, Rachel Surtees, Euclides Montes for all the encouraging messages.

Thank you to my Dad for instilling a love of writing in me. This is probably all your fault.

Thank you to my agent, Fiona Barrows, for getting me here and guiding me in the right direction...

Thank you to Kim, Marine, Charlotte and everyone at Harper Impulse...

Finally, thank you to my husband, for giving me the space, security and love to further my dream. I couldn't have done this without you.